DREAM GUY

CANDY HALLIDAY

NEW YORK   BOSTON

Cover art and design by Michael Storrings
Book design by Giorgetta Bell McRee

Warner Books

Time Warner Book Group
1271 Avenue of the Americas
New York, NY 10020
Visit our Web site at www.twbookmark.com

Printed in the United States of America

First Paperback Printing: February 2005

10 9 8 7 6 5 4 3 2 1

ISBN 978-0-446-61455-9   ISBN 0-446-61455-6

For Blue—My forever Dream Guy

Acknowledgments

Special thanks to my invincible agent, Jenny Bent, who fights the good fight for me and makes Lara Croft look like a wimp.

Extreme thanks to Karen Kosztolnyik and Beth de Guzman for giving me the incredible opportunity of working with Warner Forever's *Dream* Team.

A heartfelt thanks to all the unsung heroes behind the scenes at Warner who pull everything together — you guys rock.

Thanks to my fellow writer, Emilie Rose, who talks me down from the ledge with every book.

Thanks to Johnny McGee, Tony Garcia, Bill Roane, and Larry Lee Chabot — you boys know why.

And thanks always to my wonderful kids, Shelli, Tracy, Quint, and Caroline — your love and support mean everything to me.

DREAM GUY

Chapter 1

Annie Long could trace her problems with men back to her first high school dance. Billy Ray Smith begged her to put her sweet lips where her sweet lips *didn't* want to go. Annie gagged at the thought, and vomited bright red punch all over the white leather interior of his rich daddy's brand-new Cadillac.

Even for a naïve sixteen-year-old with a weak stomach, that should have been Annie's first clue that more often than not relationships basically do *suck*. But instead of heeding that warning, Annie bravely continued lily pad hopping her way through life, fully convinced she would eventually find a prince among the usual suspects milling around in society's frog-filled pond.

Hop. Hop. Hop.

Zip past successful entrepreneur Ben, who claimed he was a leg man instead of a boob man — Annie's mile-long legs really were her best feature. Dirty liar Ben dumped her at twenty-two for a waitress from Hooters with fake boobs the size of Annie's beloved state of Georgia.

Zoom past independent moviemaker Dan, whom Annie met at the popular Atlanta Film Festival when she was twenty-four. Slightly perverted Dan dumped Annie when she refused to star in his upcoming documentary *Women Making Love to Women.*

And skip past handsome pharmaceutical salesman Ron altogether. Amazingly, idiot Ron somehow got it into his hypochondria-impaired mind that some evasive mineral in Annie's twenty-six-year-old saliva was responsible for his excruciating migraine headaches.

It wasn't until promising young advertising executive Dave came along when she was twenty-nine that Annie thought she'd finally found her Mr. Potential. Dave claimed he *loved* Annie's small perky breasts just as much as he loved her long silky legs. He had no apparent lesbian sex fantasies as far as she could tell. And he didn't even mind swapping saliva on a regular basis.

Dave, in fact, was the reason Annie was humming happily to herself during Thank-God-It's-Friday early-morning rush hour. *Black lace teddy. Candles galore. Dom Perignon and Russian caviar.* She ticked the items off in her mind, ignoring the downtown Atlanta traffic that was a total bitch as usual.

Music? The red light caught her, giving her a minute to ponder. Dave was a huge jazz fan, Annie knew that. But jazz really didn't fit the mood she had in mind. She'd have to give it more thought when she reached her office. Go with something more Motown maybe. Something slow and sexy.

A pushy SUV the size of a tank cut her off, which usually catapulted Annie close to the road-rage edge. She didn't even honk her horn. *Clean sheets. Fresh towels. The new Hilfiger terry cloth robe as a surprise gift for Dave.* She smiled. He would complain she was spoiling him, of course. Tell her she shouldn't spend her hard-earned money on him. But he'd love it. She knew he would.

Finally, she inched her way to the Bank of America Plaza — not as tall as buildings in Chicago and New York City, but a skyscraper nonetheless with fifty-five stories of prime office space. She parked her vintage 1975 Volkswagen convertible in the underground parking garage, unconcerned that her bright purple bug looked like a giant Easter egg sitting between a shiny Lexus and a sporty BMW. Trendy had never been at the top of her to-be list.

Still thinking about the special night she'd carefully planned for Dave, Annie reached the parking garage elevator with a cheerful smile. "Have you ever seen such a glorious June morning?"

She'd made the comment to no one in particular as she and fifteen other people crammed themselves into the elevator. But a heavyset man standing beside her mopped his moist brow with a handkerchief, looked over at her, and said, "It's the Prozac, right? That's the only explanation for anyone calling seventy-two degrees at eight a.m. a *glorious* June morning."

Annie ignored him.

Everyone else laughed.

She hopped off the elevator on the thirty-second floor and entered the offices of Paragon Technology, one of the nation's major interactive software developers and second to none in the video game industry. Today Annie didn't even give in to that crestfallen I'll-never-be-anything-but-the-token-female-of-the-creative-department feeling.

Not today.

After a monthlong business trip to San Francisco, Dave was finally coming home.

Nothing was going to rain on Annie's parade today.

"Wow. Annie. You look wonderful."

Annie smiled appreciatively.

Kathy Welborn, her only true gal-pal at Paragon, was pretty and blonde. A dead ringer for Helen Hunt, most people said, but Annie thought Kathy was prettier. Like most receptionists, Kathy always had the inside scoop on everyone in the company. In other words, a good friend to have.

Annie made an exaggerated curtsy in front of Kathy's desk. "I thank you. The academy thanks you. My mother thanks you."

And yes, she had gone a bit overboard today.

The Anna Sui floral sundress fit her like a second skin. And her sexy Manolo sandals had a price tag that still made her shudder. She'd bought the shoes partly because they matched the periwinkle blue flowers in the dress perfectly. But mainly she'd bought them because she wanted to see what all the Manolo Blahnik hype was about. Sadly, three hundred and fifty dollars poorer she still hadn't figured it out.

She'd even managed to restrain her stringy mop rather neatly in a poofy strawberry blonde swoop on top of her head. And she'd applied a little makeup, which she rarely ever wore. Because today, dammit, called for one of those sundress, Manolos, and makeup kind of moods.

"You really do look great, Annie," Kathy said. "What time did you say you were picking Dave up from the airport this afternoon?"

"Four o'clock sharp," Annie said, beaming.

"And does the poor guy have any idea about the deliciously sinful agenda you have planned for him the entire weekend?"

"Not a clue," Annie said with a wink.

She headed off down the hallway to the large corner office reserved for the creative department, complete with a coveted window and a breathtaking view of the city of Atlanta. For once, she was the first one to arrive.

Annie stopped at her desk, which had *Nerdette* on her nameplate. She had just stuffed her purse into the desk's bottom drawer when Collin Adair rushed into the office, two large paper cups deftly clasped in each manicured hand.

He came to a screeching halt the second he saw her.

And the first words out of Collin's mouth were, "Well, aren't you a sight for my queer eye. You look fabulous, Annie. Absolutely fabulous."

Annie twirled around for inspection, pleased.

Any compliment coming from Mr. Buff-to-the-Cuff (one of Collin's favorite expressions) was one Annie didn't take lightly. The man had a designer-filled closet himself that would make a grown woman weep. The double-box pleat tan Geneva pants, pale yellow Cacella silk shirt, and the Pelagio linen oxford shoes he was wearing today were Collin's idea of "casual" wear.

He tossed his Brad Pittish dirty-blond locks back away from his forehead and looked her up and down again with eyes ten times bluer than any color-enhanced contacts could make them. "If Dave doesn't throw you down and ravish you the second he steps off that plane, the man's a complete buffoon."

Annie laughed. "No, I'm the buffoon. For letting you talk me into blowing an entire week's salary on Dave's homecoming dinner." She shook her head and sighed, thinking about the catastrophe that used to be her checking account. "I still can't believe I paid eighty-five dollars for a teaspoon of caviar."

"And your idea of Domino's pizza or Chinese take-out was better?"

Annie stuck her tongue out at him. "I'm not *that* clueless when it comes to entertaining."

Collin raised an eyebrow to challenge her statement. "Here," he said, thrusting one of the steaming cups in her direction. "You can't risk having too much blood in your caffeine system today. I brought you a transfusion." When Annie took the cup, he said, "This is Latte Land's early-morning special. Triple-mocha latte. Fully leaded. A dash of cherry flavor. And with yummy cinnamon sprinkles amidst a rich whipped cream topping." He tapped his cup against hers. "Here's to homecomings. And then to multiple comings and comings, and . . ."

Annie rolled her eyes. "Forget caffeine. What I *need* is a Valium smoothie." She held a shaking hand out as proof.

Collin shook his know-it-all head. "Wrong again, sweetums. Excitement masked as anxiety does incredible things to the libido. A little anxiety will give you the energy and stamina you need later in the bedroom."

Annie groaned.

Collin leaned against his desk — his nameplate boasting *Queer Nerd* since he had been responsible for the silly titles. "Listen, lovey," he said. "Forget the nervous jitters. Just clear your mind and focus on nothing but how wonderful it's going to be after you pick Dave up at the airport. You're going to spirit him away to your apartment for a scrumptious five-star meal, already prepared exclusively by moi." He polished his nails proudly against his expensive silk shirt. "And then you're going to render that boy senseless with a multimega lovefest he'll never forget."

Annie managed a weak smile. "You're right. You've helped me plan everything perfectly."

"Right down to the designer condoms waiting on his pillow," Collin chirped.

"I know," Annie said. "I'm just nervous. Dave and I haven't seen each other in four long weeks. There's also the blasted time difference. And Dave's e-mails are strictly one-liners. Plus —"

"*Stop* it." Collin took Annie gently by the shoulders and forced her to look at him. "Now. Stand up straight. And take one long, deep, cleansing breath to calm yourself."

Annie only made it as far as standing up straight before Kathy's voice rang through the intercom. "Haz-Matt's on line one. And he wants to talk to you, Annie."

Annie automatically glanced across the room. The vacant desk hogging the window in the place of authority had *Neanderthal Nerd* on the nameplate for obvious reasons. "Haz-Matt" was the head of the creative department, Matt Abbington. The nickname, like his nameplate, was self-explanatory. Matt's tall, dark, and deadly good looks could be hazardous to a woman's better judgment, not to mention her heart.

Annie looked back at the blinking line and frowned.

She'd had her own lapse in judgment where Matt was concerned shortly after she'd first joined Paragon a year earlier. It wasn't something she was proud of. It was just one of those situations where the beauty of the moment had been strictly in the eye of the *beer* holder, for lack of a better explanation. To date, they'd both had the good sense to pretend that night never happened.

"You'd better answer that, Annie."

Annie glanced in Collin's direction. He looked anxious, playing the role of peacemaker as usual for his old college roommate. It was no secret that Matt had taken Collin right up the corporate ladder with him after designing a successful video sports game that immediately made him Paragon's wonder boy extraordinaire.

Gratitude and a close friendship kept Collin in check. But for her part, Annie was growing tired of Matt expecting his creative team to continually take a backseat to his own brilliance. Lately she and Matt had been clashing at every turn. Especially since no one had the power to jerk her chain faster than Matt Abbington.

Rattle. Rattle. Rattle.

Clang. Clang. Clang.

"*Annie.* Pick up the phone. You know Matt hates to be kept waiting."

"I know," Annie said, staring at the blinking line. But, dammit, he was going to ruin her good mood. Annie knew he would. Matt always did.

For the first time during her glorious June morning, Annie sensed black clouds slowly gathering above her head.

If Matt hated anything, it was being left on "ignore."

Annie knew it. Collin knew it. So where the hell were they?

They had their heads together oohing and aahing over some fashion magazine, most likely. Or discussing what they were going to wear to the next big function on their social calendar.

Well, screw that.

He needed to talk to Annie and he needed to talk to her *now.*

He disconnected the call and hit speed dial. "It's Matt again, Kathy," he said the second the receptionist answered. "Do I suddenly need a special password to get someone to answer the phone in my own department?"

He groaned when the shut-up-and-wait music kicked in.

Matt shook his head disgustedly. He deserved a gold medal for putting up with Collin *and* with Annie. In fact, most of the time he felt like he was living one long PMS nightmare. He, of course, was always the bad guy because he had no interest whatsoever in getting in touch with his *feminine* side.

Like that was going to happen in this lifetime.

Besides, Collin and Annie were the ones who always seemed miserable with their ultra-feminine selves. Not him. Annie, for instance, had been moping around for weeks over dickhead Dave, with whom she was supposedly having a "meaningful" relationship. As opposed to the meaning*less* overnight relationship she'd had with him.

Sure, he'd been sore at first when Annie pretended their night together never happened. As her boss, he could have used his authority to get back at her. He hadn't done that, at least not intentionally. In fact, Annie had actually done both of them a huge favor by giving him the brush-off. She was looking for happily-ever-after. He wasn't looking, period.

Now, he never let himself dwell on that near disaster. Just as he refused to dwell on Annie's little-girl grin and her body made for sin. Or her down-her-back reddish gold hair that was sexy as hell. Or those saucer-size eyes so blue a man could get lost in them.

He'd had one weak moment, that was all.

Miss Meaningful Relationship was strictly off-limits. Because the last thing this homeboy wanted was *any* type of relationship.

Relationship.

Even the word made him queasy.

Mainly because he just didn't get it.

Women claimed they wanted to be treated as equals. They demanded equal billing in the boardroom *and* in the bedroom. They even insisted they wanted carefree single lives and successful careers first, and families later. But was that enough? Nope. They just had to pull out the old relationship trump card that quickly pushed going out and having a great time together into the No-win Zone.

For a guy, that is.

Because the rules constantly changed.

Call a woman up during the day just to say hello, and you could guarantee she'd be (a) hurt, (b) confused, or (c) just mad as hell (take your pick) because you didn't call her the evening before to say goodnight. Take her to an outdoor concert on Saturday, then brace yourself for the (a) whining, (b) crying, or (c) screaming fit (again, take your pick) she'd wage on Sunday because you wanted to play golf and she assumed you would want to (a) drop by her parents' house for lunch, (b) walk through the mall looking into jewelry store windows, or (c) just spend some quality time alone with her (you get the idea).

Yup, that was just the tip of the relationship iceberg. At least from a *heterosexual* male point of view. And that's exactly why Matt intended to bob and weave his way around the No-win Zone for as long as he could hold on to his wonderfully happy single-guy life.

"Annie Long," his nemesis said brightly, as if she hadn't kept him waiting for five full minutes.

"Glad you could pull yourself away from your morning gab session with Collin to answer the phone."

"Yeah, thanks for waiting," she said right back. "We only had a few sips left of our triple-mocha lattes. It would have been a real shame to let them get cold."

"Cut the crap, Annie," Matt said. "I'm in pain. And I'm definitely not in any mood for your twisted brand of humor this morning."

"Poor baby. Hungover, are we?"

Matt didn't miss the facetious tone in her voice.

"Worse," he said. "And I swear I'll fire you, Annie, if you make one smart remark. Laughing isn't an option, either." When she didn't have a comeback, Matt took a deep breath and said, "I won't be in the office today. I pulled a groin muscle."

The instant peal of laughter told him exactly what Annie thought about his threat to fire her. "Matt pulled a groin muscle," he heard her call out to Collin between cackles. "Twenty bucks says it was that dental hygienist you told me about who likes to tie him up with her dental floss."

"Put me on speakerphone," Matt yelled. *Damn Collin.* His diarrhea of the mouth was going to get him punched out someday. And Matt was going to be first in line.

When the laughter died down long enough for Annie to switch him to the speaker, Matt said, "I hope you took that twenty-dollar bet from Miss Delusional As Usual, Collin. Not that either of you seem to care that I'm in excruciating pain, but I injured myself last night playing racquetball."

"Sure, Matt. We believe you," Annie said, but her giggle told him that she didn't.

"We do believe you and we are sorry, Matt. Honest," Collin said. "Are you okay? Is there anything we can do?" Collin's genuine show of concern appeased Matt for the moment. He tried maneuvering into a more comfortable position on the bed. Finally, he gave up. His head flopped back against the pillow with an exasperated sigh.

"There are several things you can do," he said. "Collin, I want you to get the notes on the new daredevil game we've been working on in order. And Annie, you need to attend the monthly production meeting in my place at four o'clock this afternoon."

Annie gasped.

Collin sent a terrified look in her direction.

"Excuse me?" Annie said. "You've obviously confused me with someone who doesn't have the afternoon off. You gave me the afternoon off two weeks ago, Matt. I'm picking Dave up at the airport at four o'clock this afternoon."

"Well, I'm sorry," Matt said. "But two weeks ago I wasn't lying flat on my back with ice between my legs."

"What about Collin?" Annie was *not* going to let Matt take back her time off without putting up a fight. "Why can't Collin attend the meeting in your place?"

Matt's dramatic sigh echoed through the speaker. "Because Collin can't handle the pressure of being in the same room with the CEO. He'll start acting . . ." There was a long pause before he said, "giddy."

Collin sent Annie a sheepish look. "He means I turn

into a flaming, babbling queen under pressure, Annie. Matt's just trying to be tactful."

"Collin's right, Annie. I was trying to be tactful," Matt said. "But now that we've crossed that hurdle, I think even you will agree we can't risk Collin getting nervous and describing lying in a coffin filled with poisonous snakes as a rather slithery experience with a dash of imminent death."

"Ha. Ha. Ha," Collin said, but his smile reminded Annie how close the two of them really were.

"I've already called J.B. and told him about my accident," Matt said, referring to J.B. Duncan, founder and CEO of Paragon. "J.B. knows you'll be sitting in for me, Annie. And he doesn't expect a full design document. Just get the notes in some kind of order. Type them up. Make seven copies as usual. And focus on the main objective. We want to get J.B. and the other department heads excited about the game. Any questions?"

Annie still wasn't giving up. Yet. "Any idea how I'm going to keep everyone awake while I'm making this boring presentation, Matt? Collin and I have both been telling you for weeks the daredevil idea is overdone. *You* were the one who insisted you could sell snow to an Eskimo, if I remember your analogy correctly."

"Do either of you have a better game idea?" Matt challenged. "If you do, then pitch it with my blessing."

You know we don't have a better idea.

Annie didn't even bother to comment.

"But I have to say I'm a little confused," Matt added. "I thought you'd jump at the chance to attend a monthly production meeting, Annie. You sure give me enough hell about always keeping you and Collin in the background."

Annie blushed at the truth. "And normally I would

jump at the chance," she said in her own defense. "But today —"

Matt cut her off. "Let's make this simple, okay? You attend the meeting. Collin can meet loverboy at the airport. And the guy will be waiting for you with bated breath when you get home. End of story."

Matt hung up before Annie could argue.

"Arrogant ass," she mumbled. She had no sooner pushed the button to eliminate the annoying buzz of the dead phone line when someone from their office doorway called her name.

She turned around. "I'm Annie Long."

A deliveryman walked across the room and handed her a vase filled with a dozen long-stemmed red roses and a Tyvek envelope with her name typed on the front. Annie was so surprised, it took her a second to realize the guy was patiently waiting for a tip. By the time she rummaged through her purse and handed him a couple of dollars, Collin had his nose buried in the velvet-soft scarlet petals.

"See?" Collin said with a wide grin. "Dave is obviously just as excited about him coming home as you are. So you have nothing to worry about. I'll pick Dave up at the airport and take him back to your place for one of my famous martinis." He paused for a second. "In fact, attending the meeting might be a blessing in disguise, Annie. By the time you get home, Dave will have had a chance to wind down from his trip."

Always making excuses for Matt, Annie thought as she took her own turn inhaling the scent of the fragrant bouquet. But all thoughts of Matt Abbington were erased from her mind when she said, "Don't you just *love* a romantic man?"

Collin grinned. "Every chance I get." He pointed to the envelope. "Well? Aren't you going to open it?"

Annie tore open the envelope. When she held up a videotape, Collin got a hopeful twinkle in his eye. "Hurry, let's watch it. Maybe it's X-rated."

"You wish," Annie said, but she didn't waste any time walking across the room.

One entire wall of their office housed every type of state-of-the-art electronic equipment known to modern man, used daily for the development of their game ideas. Within seconds, her adorable Dave came to life on the forty-six-inch flat plasma screen.

Annie and Collin both squealed like schoolgirls.

Dave was standing against a railing, with a spectacular view of the Golden Gate Bridge and the blue waters of the San Francisco Bay as his backdrop. He was dressed casually, and a gentle wind blew his sandy blond hair slightly back off his handsome forehead.

"Hey there, Annie," Dave said.

Collin whispered, "The man *is* gorgeous."

Annie shushed him, her eyes glued to the screen.

Dave smiled slightly. "The roses are just a small token of my appreciation for the wonderful six months we've spent together."

"My hero," Annie said with a sigh.

But then Dave added, "I hope you won't hate me, Annie, but I'm not coming back to Atlanta. I've been offered the opportunity of a lifetime here in San Francisco and I can't pass it up. A long-distance relationship wouldn't have worked for either of us."

The camera was still running when Dave pushed off from the railing. But just before the screen went blank, a distinctly female voice came through loud and clear:

"She'll understand, sweetie. How do I turn this thing off?"

Collin's hand flew to his mouth in total shock.

It took two full minutes before Annie could say a word. "Oh. My. God" came out as a whisper. But her voice recovered fully when she screamed, "That bastard just dumped me on a video. And his new girlfriend made the fucking tape!"

Collin ran across the room and slammed their office door. He hurried back in her direction in a total state of panic. "Now, Annie, we hate the F-word, remember?" He put an arm around her shoulder, trying to console her. "We think that word is lewd, crude, and totally offensive."

Annie pushed him away. "Well, excuse me for forgetting my language manners. But sometimes the F-word is the only appropriate word for the situation."

"You're right," Collin said, wringing his hands. "Getting dumped on a videotape that the new girlfriend made is *definitely* one of those situations. You have every right to be angry."

"Oh, I'm not angry," Annie said, pacing back and forth like a woman possessed. "I. Am. Wayyyy. Beyond. Angry. I'm stomp-a-mud-hole-in-Dave's-ass *livid*, is what I am."

"And a mud hole is exactly what Dave deserves in his ass," Collin said, following right along behind her with every step she took.

He actually bumped into Annie when she whirled around to face him. She pushed him out of the way, stomped to her desk, and picked up the phone. Collin reached her before she finished punching in the number for information. He finally wrestled the phone out of her hand and placed it back in the cradle.

"Annie, please. You don't want to do anything rash. Especially not while you're still so upset."

"Like what?" Annie clenched both fists at her sides. "Like flying out to San Francisco, maybe? So I can personally dangle the worthless son of a bitch upside down by his heels and drop him off his opportunity-of-a-lifetime Golden Gate Bridge?"

"Exactly like that." Collin grabbed her hand and held on tight. "I know this hurts, Annie. You feel betrayed. You feel used. You probably even feel yourself slipping into a deep, dark, dangerous state of depression."

Annie jerked her hand away. "I'm not suicidal, Collin. I'm *homicidal*, dammit."

She glared at him for a second longer. And then she collapsed onto her chair and burst into tears.

"It's okay," Collin kept saying, standing above her, patting her back supportively as she cried.

Annie only sobbed harder.

"I just can't believe I've been so stupid," she said, crying into her hands.

Stupid. Stupid. Stupid.

Maybe we should move in together when I get back stupid. I'm miserable when I'm away from you stupid. You're the best thing that's ever happened to me stupid. I'll be back as soon as possible stupid.

"You aren't stupid," Collin said, still delivering reassuring pats to her back. "Your prince just turned out to be not so F-wording charming, that's all."

"And your two-hundred-dollar gourmet meal?" Annie sniffed few times. "Who's going to eat that crap? Because you were right, Mr. Galloping Gay Gourmet. I'll take

Domino's pizza and Chinese take-out any day of the week over high-priced rotten fish eggs."

"Not to worry," Collin assured her. "I'll gallop over and eat the rotten fish eggs and the other crap myself. And I'll also personally reimburse every penny of your money."

Annie's head came up. "And the eighty-five-dollar black teddy you forced me into buying at Neiman Marcus? Do you also plan to wiggle your buff little tush into a thong-style teddy?"

Collin raised an eyebrow. He put a finger to his chin as if he were seriously contemplating the idea.

"And drop the comedy act. It isn't working." Annie sat up and made a swipe at both eyes with her fingertips. But this time she didn't push Collin away when he bent down to give her a long, supportive hug. "A video," Annie said. "The no-balls coward actually dumped me on a video."

She left her chair, walked back across the room, picked up the remote, and hit rewind. When she hit play, Dave smiled and said, "The roses are just a small token of my appreciation for the wonderful six months we've spent together." And then Annie hit pause, freezing Dave right where he stood.

"You cowardly *bastard*," she yelled at the screen. "What did I ever see in you?"

Collin walked up behind her. "Men," he snorted. "Too bad they don't come with a remote control so you can fast-forward past the heartache."

"You can say that again," Annie said.

Wait a minute, Annie thought. Then she had an *oh shit!* moment so powerful she dropped the remote.

"Annie? Are you okay?"

Annie looked past Collin with a glazed-over stare.

Why *couldn't* a woman have a man she could control with the aim of a remote or the simple tap of a mouse? A man who would never disappoint her. A man who would always be there to listen and offer support during any situation. A man who would always assure her that she was beautiful, smart, and desirable. A video-type Joe. Someone who would help her bruised ego recover after receiving one of life's little slam-you-to-the-ground lessons like this one.

"You're starting to look pale, Annie. God, don't you dare pass out on me."

Collin held his arms out prepared to catch her, but Annie grabbed him by the front of his shirt and pulled him so close they were literally nose to nose. "Did you or did you not hear Matt say that if either of us had a better game idea, we could pitch it with his blessing?"

Collin pried her fingers from his silk shirt and smoothed away her imaginary fingerprints. "Yes. But that was a rhetorical statement and you know it."

"Too bad. I'll plead temporary insanity." Annie hurried back to her desk.

"What does that mean?" Collin asked timidly. "Or do I want to know?"

Annie's laugh sounded borderline hysterical even to herself. "It means when I attend that production meeting this afternoon, it will *not* be an outline of poisonous snakes in a coffin that I place in front of our CEO."

"You're kidding, of course." Collin walked over to stand by her desk. Annie didn't miss the fact that he was fretfully chewing his bottom lip.

"No, I'm not kidding. I've never been more serious about anything in my life."

"You're scaring me, Annie."

"Take a number. I'm scaring myself." Annie placed her hands above her keyboard. She paused for a moment. And then she typed two words.

When the words came up on her computer screen, Collin asked on cue, "What's Joe Video?"

"He's going to be the perfect man. On DVD," Annie said proudly. "And there won't be any reason to fast-forward past the heartache. Joe Video is going to be the answer to a woman's prayers. He'll be her best friend. Her personal cheerleader. He'll even be her own private shrink when she needs to vent about anything or anyone screwing up her life."

"I believe Matt refers to those venting sessions as 'ass-numbing' chats," Collin said.

"And that's because Matt can be an obnoxious macho moron like most men."

Collin thought about it, then nodded in agreement.

"Oh, oh," Annie said, shaking both hands with excitement. "He'll be interactive, of course. And never clueless. Joe Video will *always* have the perfect response for any given situation."

"You mean responses like, 'No, sweetie, you don't look fat in those jeans,' and 'Don't be silly, gorgeous, you couldn't have a bad hair day if you tried'?"

"Yes. Exactly like those. Except I don't want the script to be corny. The script needs to be natural, loving, and supportive. And he won't be computer-generated, either. An actor will have to play the role. I want him to be completely realistic."

"Oh. A *realistic* fantasy man." Collin put his finger to his chin again. "Which would make him an *oxy*moron, I believe, instead of a *macho* moron."

Annie sent him a go-to-hell look. "Stop making fun of

this idea. Joe Video is going to set the video game industry on its mother-loving ear."

Collin took a deep breath and made the sign of the cross slowly over his chest.

"Oh stop it," Annie said. "You aren't even Catholic."

"Well, it certainly can't hurt," Collin wailed. "Matt's definitely going to kill us. And then he'll fire us both."

Annie blinked in surprise. "Us?"

Collin grinned and nodded.

Annie jumped up and hugged him. She looked down at her watch. It was only 9 a.m. That meant they had six hours to come up with a concept outline before they had to make copies for the meeting. Not a complete design document, Matt had said that himself. All they had to provide was enough information to get the CEO and the department heads excited about the game idea. With Collin's help, that would be doable.

So screw Matt for his smarter-than-thou attitude.

And screw Dave twice for being the coward that he was.

Annie, however, had been screwed over her last time.

This *previously* token female member of the creative department planned to be kick-ass ready for her long-awaited breakout debut when four o'clock rolled around.

CHAPTER 2

By noon Matt had counted every tile on his bedroom ceiling. He'd multiplied the tiles. He'd divided the tiles. He'd even devised a ceiling tile game of sorts that involved mentally rearranging all the tiles until they spelled out UGA, the initials of his beloved alma mater.

In other words, he was bored shitless.

He was also suffering from a slight attack of guilt. He hadn't pulled his groin muscle on purpose. *God, no.* But he also hadn't forgotten he'd given Annie the afternoon off as she'd accused him of doing earlier. How could he? Annie and Collin had been planning Dave's big homecoming party nonstop for the last two weeks. He wasn't deaf.

Hell, when he thought about it, he could practically recite Collin's five-star gourmet menu word for word.

And okay, so maybe he had derived a tiny bit of pleasure out of assigning Annie to attend the meeting so she wouldn't be able to pick her Mr. Wonderful up at the airport. But not because he was jealous. Annie could date anyone she wanted. He'd just never liked Dave. The guy had shifty eyes, the kind that never made direct eye contact. He also had a wimpy handshake. Shifty eyes were bad enough. But shifty eyes *plus* a wimpy handshake equaled one thing: a guy who couldn't be trusted.

Matt just hoped Annie figured the dude out for herself sooner instead of later. He and Annie might have their differences, but if the jerk hurt her, old Davey boy would have to answer to *him*.

"What the hell?" Matt grabbed the corner of the bedsheet to cover his nude body when his cleaning lady suddenly burst into his bedroom unannounced. "Jesus, Lil. Have you ever heard of knocking? I'm not exactly decent here."

"That's the understatement of the century," Lil said in a gravelly voice compliments of too much whiskey and Marlboro cigarettes. "And don't flatter yourself, toots. You're not my type."

In spite of her rude behavior, Matt had to smile. When he'd signed up with the cleaning service used by most of the residents in his exclusive Midtown apartment complex, he'd envisioned some sweet thing in a sexy maid's costume showing up every Friday to tidy up the place in case he decided to do a little "entertaining" over the weekend. What he'd gotten instead was a sixty-year-old hellcat, five feet tall, with bleached-blonde hair and a closet full of polyester.

And Matt adored her completely.

He eased himself up into a sitting position with his back resting against the headboard and lifted the sheet to take a look. The ice bag was still resting against his right inner thigh. Surprisingly, his sitting-up maneuver had caused little pain.

"What are you doing home, anyway?" Lil frowned at him over her shoulder for a second, then continued scurrying around the room like a white tornado.

Matt started to tell her. But after the teasing he'd just received from Annie, there was no way he was going to tell Lil about his pulled groin muscle.

"I hurt myself playing racquetball yesterday."

Lil glanced over her shoulder again. "Maybe that's a sign an old man like you ought to slow down."

Matt made an ugly gesture with his middle finger.

Lil made the same one right back.

"And maybe you should ask the college kid who called me 'Grandpa' at the racquetball club yesterday whether or not I need to slow down. I beat the little punk like a yard dog."

"Good idea," Lil said. "Let's call the kid. Maybe he'll come over and help me change Grandpa's bedpan."

"Hey," Matt protested. "I'm only thirty-five years old. I'm just now reaching my prime."

"Keep telling yourself that, sweet pea," Lil said and went about her business.

Matt pouted for a few minutes before he said, "Just curious. But what *is* your type, old woman? For some reason I picture you on the back of a Harley with a big, burly biker at the wheel."

Lil stopped swatting at the vertical blinds on his bedroom window long enough to point her feather duster in his direction. "I don't like bikers. And I don't like dark-haired men with muscles out the yazoo and scratchy, hairy chests like you. I go for slender blond men with hairless bodies and pretty-boy faces." She grinned when she added, "Like your friend Collin. Now, *there* is one good-looking man."

"Well, too bad for you. *Women* aren't Collin's type."

"Yeah, I know. Such a waste." She shook her head

sadly, hit the blinds a few more times, then started collecting the clothes littering his bedroom floor.

Matt mumbled, "Haven't had any complaints about my muscles or my scratchy, hairy chest yet."

Lil laughed her gravelly laugh. "And how would you know? According to Collin your idea of a long-term relationship is two dates in a row."

"Collin has a big mouth."

Jeez.

What was it about women and gay men, anyway? That instant connection women and gay men seemed to have with each other?

Until Annie joined their team, he and Collin had practically been inseparable. Lately, he was lucky if Collin even showed up at the gym. His best friend was too busy planning menus and going off shopping with her.

Not that he was jealous. Collin could hang out with Annie if he wanted. It was just another irritating example of how Matt always seemed to be standing on the outside looking in where Annie and Collin were concerned.

He frowned.

But would he really want to fit into that inner little chick-clique of theirs? He tried to imagine himself clapping his hands with glee at the thought of rushing off to some big midnight madness sale. Or getting all teary-eyed watching Oprah or Dr. Phil.

No way.

Not in a million frigging years.

"Okay, bucko," Lil said, standing above him with her hands on her bony hips. "If you want your sheets changed you'd better haul your rusty butt out of that bed."

"And unless you want a good look at my rusty butt, you'd better give me some privacy," Matt threatened.

She laughed. "I'm a tough old girl, Matt, but even I'm not that tough."

Matt moved his eyebrows up and down. "One look might change your mind about dark-haired, hairy-chested men."

She cast her eyes to the ceiling, then pointed to his bedside clock with a nicotine-stained finger. "I have about thirty minutes left in the kitchen. Get showered and dressed before I get back."

When Lil closed the bedroom door behind her, Matt took a deep breath and tested his endurance for pain a little further. He moved his right leg slowly from side to side. Sore, sure. But nothing like the double-over-I'm-gonna-puke pain he'd felt yesterday at the racquetball club.

He grabbed the ice bag and tossed it to the foot of the bed, proud of himself for taking the sports trainer's advice and staying off his feet as long as possible. Easing his legs over the side of the bed, he held to the corner of his bedside table and stood up. Again, the pain was tolerable.

When he managed to make it into the bathroom with only a slight limp, Matt decided he was in much better shape than he'd ever expected. In fact, he figured that, after a hot shower, he might even feel like going into the office after all. At least in time for the monthly production meeting.

Like it or not, Annie had probably been right about the bore-into-snore reaction J.B. and the other department heads were going to have when she presented what they had so far on the daredevil game idea. *Crap.* He knew the whole concept was lacking. He'd just been confident he could wing it at the meeting. Later is when he would come up with something to make the game stellar and creative.

He really didn't have much choice. He hadn't told Annie and Collin, but the daredevil idea was one J.B. had crammed down his throat. But then, who could blame him for not sharing that information? There wasn't a guy alive who liked to admit he had to play kiss-ass now and then to stay in the boss's good graces.

Stepping into the shower, Matt adjusted the water as hot as he could stand it, congratulating himself on his decision — belated that it was — to do the right thing. J.B. had the potential to eat Annie alive if he happened to be in one of his moods. Annie didn't deserve being devoured at her first production meeting — especially over a game idea she hated anyway. And whether he personally liked Dave or not, Annie shouldn't have to change her plans because he'd challenged some college punk on the racquetball court.

However.

Had it been worth pulling a groin muscle to beat the little jerk hands down?

You betcha.

Matt stuck his head under the pulsating stream coming from the showerhead, wondering why his ego had kicked into overdrive over the last few months. He'd never felt the need to prove himself to anyone in the past. *Maybe because Annie and Collin think you're a total ass most of the time?* Yeah. That was a possibility.

But he really wasn't the bad guy Annie and Collin made him out to be. The measure of any good department head was the ability to recognize the strengths of the members of the team and make good use of them. Collin was a genius when it came to logic and detail. Annie had an imagination and drive that rivaled his own. If you asked him, the three of them made one hell of a fine creative team.

Maybe that was the problem.

Maybe he really was too much of a hard-ass most of the time. It wouldn't kill him to tell Collin and Annie more often what a great job they were doing. Give them praise where praise was due. Prove his own commitment to the team.

Solidarity, man.

That's what they needed.

Why hadn't he realized this before? A guy could lighten up without getting all touchy-feely, couldn't he? So what if he didn't have any interest in their shopping and their menu planning? What was wrong with inviting the two of them out for an occasional beer? On his turf. Any great sports bar would do.

Maybe throw darts and shoot a few games of pool. Collin had always been an excellent darts player. And knowing Annie, she would probably end up beating both him and Collin at any game they played.

That's it.

They needed to do more things together as a team.

And as long as Collin was with them, he and Annie couldn't possibly get into trouble like that one night when they'd bumped into each other in Underground Atlanta.

When he stepped out of the shower, Matt toweled himself off, feeling better by the minute. He'd hit some burger joint first, he decided. Grab a bite to eat. And then he'd show up at the office in time to save Annie so she could rush off and meet old shifty Dave at the airport.

Matt smiled, slapping shaving cream on both cheeks.

Yup. From here on out, no more Mr. Hard-Ass.

As of today, he was turning over a new leaf.

He couldn't wait to see the look on Annie's face when he showed up unexpectedly like the knight in shining armor he was going to become for the sake of the team.

Rah. Rah. Rah.

Go team! Go!

"Five, six, seven," Collin counted as he walked back from the copy room with a stack of blue binders in the crook of his arm. He placed them in a neat stack on the corner of Annie's desk. "You're sure? You really want to go through with this?"

Annie sent him a well-duh look. "Like I have a choice now? It's three o'clock, Collin. We couldn't get the daredevil material together if our lives depended on it."

Collin gave her a shrug. "Okay, then. It's time to get you ready for center stage."

"I beg your pardon?"

"Well, you can't go into your first production meeting looking like *that*. You've cried off all your makeup. And your hair's a complete mess."

Annie sent him a perturbed look. "Gee, thanks for boosting my confidence."

Collin held his hand out, wiggling his fingers. "Give me your makeup bag."

Annie laughed. "This is *me* you're talking to, remember?"

Collin pursed his lips in a prim pout, then reached over and punched the intercom button. "Kathy, it's Collin. Annie needs an emergency makeover. Hurry. Bring everything you have."

When he turned back around, Annie was trying to stuff a few fallen strands of hair back into her not-so-poofy-now swoop. Collin smacked her hand away. "No, no, that won't do," he fussed. "Your hair needs to be down. Loose. Reckless and untamed. Like the type of woman who would buy Joe Video because she's out of patience with the toads who keep hopping through her life."

He was still pulling pins out of Annie's hair in a frenzy that would have put Edward Scissorhands to shame when Kathy rushed into the room with a makeup bag the size of a shopping bag. Annie took a second look. *Yikes*. It *was* a shopping bag. From Elizabeth Arden.

"Sorry about that loser Dave, sweetie," Kathy said, giving Annie's shoulder a sympathetic squeeze after Collin pushed her down onto her chair.

Annie looked up at Collin and frowned. *Damn him.* The "most famous mouth in the South" title Collin was always bragging about fit him in more ways than one.

"Do something bold but subtle with her eye makeup," Collin ordered, and Kathy started plowing through her shopping bag. "Bring out the innocent blue of her eyes."

He grabbed a hair brush from Kathy's stash and ran it through Annie's hair several times, making her yelp. Then he started a grab-a-handful-and-scrunch ritual that made Annie's eyes cross.

"Her lipstick needs to be more kiss-me pink than kiss-off red," Collin insisted. "Feminine and persuasive, not brazen and negative."

Annie squirmed. She sputtered a few times as Kathy ran a dozen different brushes up and down and back and forth across her face. And after what felt like hours of torture, Annie finally said, "*Enough, already.*"

She fought her way out of a cloud of hairspray that was threatening to asphyxiate her and jumped up, ready to escape. Kathy and Collin, however, were both looking at her, not fully satisfied.

"Her hair and makeup look great. The dress and shoes are perfect. But something is missing," Kathy said, shaking her head in concern.

"Cleavage!" Collin exclaimed. "Other than Gretchen from art and filming, there will be five men sitting in that boardroom. It's a known fact straight men go stone deaf and agree to anything the second they see a bodacious pair of millennium domes. We have to have cleavage. It will be the perfect diversion."

Annie frowned. "Well, I hate to disappoint you, but I couldn't achieve diversion-quality cleavage even if I *superglued* both of my nipples together. Trust me."

Collin clicked his tongue. "'Trust me' is déjà *moo*, Annie. We've both been hearing that *bullshit* line from men all our lives." He walked across the room, grabbed the tissue box from his desk, and held it up. "Time to stuff and fluff, lovey. You'll be boobylicious."

Annie crossed her arms, trying to hide her cleavage-less chest. "You've got to be kidding me."

Collin and Kathy both sent her a look that said no one was kidding.

"Fine," Annie huffed. "Give me the tissue box."

She was just about to start stuffing when their office door opened. Annie almost fainted when Matt limped in.

The only thing Matt could think to say was, "What the hell is going on in here?"

His office looked like one giant cosmetic sale gone bad. Brushes, lipsticks, and more makeup paraphernalia than any man should have to witness in a lifetime were strewn all over the place. The heavy scent of hairspray caused him to sneeze twice.

With a wide-eyed expression, Annie said, "*I'm* getting ready for the production meeting *you* insisted I needed to attend in your place. What are you and your pulled groin muscle doing here?"

Matt said with complete sincerity, "I'm here because it wasn't fair to make you change your plans, Annie." He looked down at his watch. "It's only three-twenty." And with a hitch of his thumb, he motioned to the door. "Go pick Dave up at the airport. And whether you believe me or not, I hope you have a great evening together."

Instead of the look of gratitude he'd expected, Annie looked as if he'd slapped her.

Matt glanced over at her two buddies.

Collin and Kathy also looked as if he'd just dropped a giant cockroach into the employee water cooler.

Matt frowned. "Okay. Let me repeat myself. What's going on? And why am I *not* going to like it?"

Kathy zipped past him, still stuffing things into her shopping bag. Collin stood by, wringing his hands the way he always did when he was anxious about something. And Annie sent him a pleading look.

"I'm so sorry, Matt. Let me explain," she said.

Matt's newly turned-over leaf blew out the window.

He could already feel the heat creeping past the crisp collar of his starched Brooks Brothers shirt. He steeled himself. Whatever it was, it had to be *bad*.

"Start explaining, Annie," he said. "You have my undivided attention."

Collin jumped in ahead of her with a high-pitched giggle. "Matt, you're not going to believe this. But everything that's happened here this morning really is satire at its finest. You know, tragedy with a comical twist? You, of all people, have a great sense of humor, Matt. I've always told you that. And —"

Matt cut him off. "You're babbling, Collin." He looked down at his watch, then back at Annie. "The clock's ticking, Annie. Your turn."

Annie opened her mouth to speak, but Collin cut in again. "Don't pick on Annie, Matt. She's suffered a horrible shock. It all started when Dave sent her roses and a videotape . . ." He shot Annie an apologetic look before he looked back at Matt and said, "The jerk dumped Annie on the videotape, Matt. And then *I* said, 'Wouldn't it be wonderful if men came with a remote control so you could fast-forward past the heartache.' And then *Annie* had this incredible woo-woo moment that almost made her pass out. And *you* had told us earlier that if we had a better game idea to pitch at the production meeting, we could pitch it with your blessing, and —"

"Stop!" Matt held his hand up. He glared at Annie. "And I guess that's where you come in. Right?"

He could swear he thought he saw her gulp. She walked over, picked up the top binder from a stack on the corner of her desk, then walked back and handed it to him.

Matt flipped the binder open and saw two words: *Joe Video*. "Undamnbelievable," he shouted. "I leave you two alone for one morning and Woo-woo and Foo-foo decide to score a coup d'état."

"It really wasn't like that, Matt. Not really," Annie said.

He cut her off with, "And what the hell's Joe Video?"

Her chin came up. She crossed her arms stubbornly across her chest and said, "Joe Video is the perfect man.

On DVD. And he's going to open the video game industry to an entire new target audience of women."

Matt was dumbfounded.

He glared at Collin. "Tell me she's kidding, Collin. And you'd better tell me you had nothing to do with this."

Collin blanched. "But Annie's idea really is a fab concept, Matt. Seriously."

Matt exploded. "A fab concept?" He shook his head and glared back and forth from one to the other. "You two slay me." He pointed to his mouth and said, "Read. My. Lips. Men aren't perfect, boys and girls. And guess what? We don't care. And do you know *why* we don't care? Because a woman's definition of the perfect man *today* always does a complete one-eighty when tomorrow rolls around."

Collin frowned. "Well, I don't know if many women would agree with that statement, Matt."

And Matt shouted, "Stuff it, Collin. You're the most fickle woman I know." He looked back at Annie. "Well? You can jump in any time, Annie."

She tossed her head, distracting him for a moment when her long, silky hair swished back over her shoulder. He hadn't noticed, but her hair was down and loose today, instead of pulled back in a tomboy ponytail the way she usually wore it. It was also the first time he'd noticed that she wasn't wearing slacks, but a short sundress that showed off her long, shapely legs to perfection.

Matt's *yow-za* factor kicked in for a second.

Until his pulled groin muscle begged for mercy.

If Annie could have fast-forwarded herself right out of the room, that's exactly what she would have done at that very moment. She couldn't possibly feel any more guilty about going behind Matt's back with her idea than she already did. However, his showing up before the meeting was just another example of his irritating superior attitude.

He'd ordered her to attend the meeting. And then he'd strolled into the office in that Hugo Boss oyster-colored suit that always kicked her heartbeat up a notch because the cut fit him perfectly and made his shoulders look twice as broad as they actually were.

Wait.

Was she nuts?

Matt had just taken a giant bite out of her butt with a five-minute ass-chewing and she was thinking about how great he looked in his oyster-colored Hugo Boss suit?

She shook her head and let her anger take her right back to the heart of the matter. Not for one minute did she believe Matt had shown up for the meeting so she wouldn't have to change her plans. *Or* because he wanted her to have a really great evening with Dave. Matt thought Dave was a two-faced pussy — his own words, according to Collin.

Annie gulped.

Crap! Matt's right.

But forget Dave.

It was obvious Matt had shown up for the meeting for one reason only. He didn't think she was capable of doing her job. And regardless of feeling guilty about going behind his back and switching his idea for hers, his total lack of confidence in her ability really pissed her off.

Forcing herself to remain calm, Annie adopted her own snotty attitude. "I've already told you I was sorry, Matt. But you're not going to lure me into a no-win argument about men not being perfect and women being fickle."

His dark eyes took on a deeper level of coldness.

"And," she added, "regardless of what you think about my Joe Video concept, it couldn't be any more lame than the one you expected me to try and salvage at the production meeting. Besides, you said yourself if we had a better idea, we could pitch it, and —"

"Bullshit. You both knew I didn't mean that literally." He stood there, hands at his waist, his expression cold and threatening — like a shiver looking for a spine to run up. "Did it ever occur to either of you that I might have had a valid reason for sticking with such a lame idea? Like the fact that the idea was an order straight from the top? That J.B. himself is hell-bent on jumping on the daredevil bandwagon, regardless of how hard I've tried to talk him out of it?"

Annie's mouth dropped open.

Collin dropped down onto his chair, limp as a rag doll.

Matt smiled cynically. "Is that tidbit of information 'woo-woo' enough to suit the two of you?"

He limped across the room, slammed the binder down on his desk, then lowered himself onto his chair with a groan that Annie feared had more to do with his disappointment in her and Collin than with his pulled groin muscle.

What in the hell have I done? she thought.

"I can't tell you how sorry I am," she said. "I couldn't be any more serious than I am right now."

Poor Collin had his head nodding in agreement so fast he looked like a bobbing dashboard figure.

Matt refused to acknowledge either of them.

Annie finally walked over to stand in front of his desk. Fighting to hold back the tears, she said, "I take full responsibility, Matt. For everything. Before you fire me, I'll go into the boardroom myself and tell Mr. Duncan face-to-face why his daredevil idea isn't ready to be discussed at today's production meeting."

Matt still wouldn't look in her direction.

After a few moments of agonizing silence, Annie gave up and turned to leave. She prayed her bowed head and her shoulders slumped in defeat made him feel better.

"Wait," he called out before she reached the door.

Her back stiffened. Then Annie turned around.

His expression was still cold and passive. "I know you think I'm a total ass, Annie. And I know you think I hold you and Collin back on purpose. But I want to set the record straight. Okay?"

Annie nodded obediently.

"A good department head doesn't push an assistant out into the main arena unless he knows that assistant will succeed. Personally, I haven't felt you were ready to go solo with any of your own game ideas yet. But since you've pushed the envelope completely off the ledge today, I guess it's time for both of us to see just how ready you are."

Annie forced herself to ask, "Meaning what?"

Matt looked down at his watch. "Meaning it's almost showtime, Madam Psychic." He struggled to his feet. "I expect you to join me in the boardroom in ten minutes. I want to personally introduce you before you present your *fab* new *woo-woo* concept to our CEO at the production meeting."

Annie moved aside when Matt half limped and half

stomped past her. When he slammed their office door behind him, Annie grabbed for a tissue.

"Don't cry now," Collin shrieked. "We don't have
time for a makeup repair."

He held up both hands when Annie shot him a don't-
screw-with-me look.

"Damn Matt," Annie said and sniffed into the tissue
again. "He's the only person I know who can make me
feel like Benedict Arnold one minute, and Lizzie Borden
the next." And that's exactly how she felt. Guilty for be-
traying him. Yet ready to look around for an ax for his
making fun of her idea.

Collin said, "It might be wise if you stuffed your bra
this time." He pushed the tissue box closer.

Annie pushed the box away. "Would you stop it with
your boob obsession already? The only thing I'm going
to 'stuff' is my idea when I push it through the hoop in a
slam-dunk sale to the CEO."

"That's the spirit," said Collin, but he added, "still,
flashing your hooters at the old man couldn't hurt."

Annie ignored him and pushed her hair back away
from her face. "Just get the binders ready, Foo-foo," she
told him. "Woo-woo needs a second to collect her
thoughts."

When Collin gave her some space, Annie squared her
shoulders and took a deep breath to calm herself the way
Collin had instructed her to do hours ago. It didn't help.
She was still shaking uncontrollably inside and out.

God, she'd never seen Matt so angry.

Not without good reason, granted. She'd admit it. She
deserved the "Shittiest Employee of the Year" award,
hands down. She'd been so furious over the unforgivable

stunt weasel Dave pulled, she'd directed all of her anger toward Matt — mainly because he happened to be within striking distance and Dave didn't.

Not a mature thing to do.

Of course, if Matt had told them up front that the daredevil idea had come straight from the top, she never would have pushed her freaking envelope off the ledge, as Matt so aptly put it. But did it really matter who had come up with the idea?

Nope.

Not one iota.

The fact remained that Matt was at the helm of the boat she could end up sinking with her selfish it's-all-about-me attitude. Matt was responsible for calling all the shots. And Matt had deserved both her and Collin's full cooperation when he made the decision to go with the CEO's idea.

God, could I possibly feel any more guilty?

No wonder Matt didn't think she was ready to go solo on any game design ideas. She'd been acting like a spoiled brat for months, pissing and moaning because big, bad Matt wouldn't let little crybaby her be the leader.

In all reality, Matt should have fired her on the spot.

Unfortunately, the fact that he hadn't fired her was a double-edged sword. Annie was immensely relieved in one respect, and borderline terrified in the other. She just couldn't shake off the coldness in those ink black eyes of his. *Petrifying*.

It had to make her wonder if Matt was simply giving her enough rope to hang herself at the meeting. Or had he decided to be the bigger person and let her finish what she'd started, despite that she'd gone behind his back to do it?

Damn. Damn. Damn.

She never should have gone behind his back like that. *Never.*

Especially not after their accidental night together. No matter how much they both tried to pretend otherwise, things had been strained between them ever since that one regrettable night. But talk about hot sex! *Whew.* Annie absently fanned her face with her hand. Matt had stripped her down to nothing and made her beg for things she never even knew she wanted.

At least she'd awakened first the next morning and slipped quietly out of his apartment while he was still asleep. She'd fully expected him to take her aside on Monday morning and give her a long speech about it being bad company policy for the boss to date his employees, blah blah blah. Instead, Mr. Cool had chosen to pretend the night never happened. Basically, end of story, as Matt was so fond of saying.

And after this meeting, it probably will be the end of the story for me at Paragon.

Annie sighed when Collin walked up beside her and handed over the binders. "You'd better go, Annie. The last thing you want to be is late."

Annie nodded. "Wish me luck. If Matt fires me after the meeting, promise me you'll keep in touch."

Collin scrunched her hair a few more times and gave her a quick peck on the cheek. "You wouldn't be going to this meeting if Matt were going to fire you," he assured her. "Just remember two things. Screw 'em if they don't like Joe Video. And take no prisoners."

"Take no prisoners," Annie repeated.

She took a deep breath and wobbled in the direction of the boardroom on her four-inch-heel Manolos, a silent prayer on her lips that after the meeting she would still be able to afford an occasional pair of three-hundred-and-fifty-dollar shoes.

CHAPTER 3

It had taken some fast talking, but Matt had made it through phase one of damage control by the time the other department heads started showing up for the monthly production meeting. He'd appeased J.B. temporarily by assuring him the daredevil game was coming along nicely. And then he'd told J.B. another bald-faced lie.

He'd told his boss that Annie's idea was so unique he needed J.B.'s expertise and input before he gave Annie permission to waste any more time on the concept.

The unique part had piqued J.B.'s interest.

The asking for his help part had stroked J.B.'s ego.

Would you deliver a truck filled with snow to Alaska COD, please?

Matt looked across the room at the imposing man talking with some of the other department heads. J.B. Duncan could easily pass for Colonel Sanders's twin both in looks and in shrewd business sense. With the exception that J.B. always wore Armani instead of plantation white and string bow ties. And that J.B. was so health-conscious he wouldn't have eaten a piece of fried chicken if someone held a gun to his head.

God, I hated lying to the old man like that.

As rigid and stubborn as J.B. could be, he was a fair man who always stood behind his employees and constantly urged them to reach their full potential. Matt tried to clear his conscience by reminding himself he was doing the same thing for Annie — standing behind her decision, even if she had made it behind his back. That might have worked, had he still not been so angry with her.

He should have fired her. That's what he should have done. Now there was a chance they both might be fired after this meeting. There was no way J.B. Duncan was going to go along with Annie's off-the-charts idea.

Joe Video.

What a joke.

That's the main reason he'd wanted Annie to attend this meeting. She'd get the picture real quick. There was nothing glamorous about having your idea chewed up, spit out, and thrown back in your face. He should know. Been there. Done that. More times than he cared to remember.

Matt smiled to himself, thinking how Annie would react when they all started firing questions at her at once.

They'll rip her apart like a pack of pit bulls.

But he wouldn't let them tear Annie completely to shreds. Even if she did deserve it. He wasn't that heartless.

"Okay, people. It's meeting time," J.B. announced.

Matt panicked when J.B. started walking toward the head of the boardroom table. The old man was a stickler for punctuality.

Where the hell is Annie?

She'd better not have walked out on him. What she'd

better do was to have the decency to walk through that door and clean up the mess she'd gotten them both into.

I'm a dead man, Matt thought when J.B. sat down.

But his rescue squad arrived wearing four-inch heels.

Under the circumstances, Annie didn't expect even a lukewarm reception from Matt when she walked into the boardroom. But when he smiled one of his dazzling smiles and welcomed her like a long-lost friend, Annie knew the fight was on.

She stiffened when he hurried to her side and placed a hand lightly on her shoulder. She felt like punching the crap out of him when he kept it there.

"I'm sure everyone recognizes Annie," he said, smiling as he looked around the room.

This is where the lukewarm reception came in.

Most of the department heads didn't even look in her direction. J.B. Duncan at least had enough manners to nod politely. But then he dismissively turned back to the guy sitting on his right to continue the conversation they'd been having when she first walked into the room.

Matt whispered out of the corner of his mouth, "Friendly bunch, huh?"

Wonderful, Annie thought. *Maybe I should have stuffed and fluffed.*

Matt started up again. "I asked Annie to attend the production meeting this month because . . ." He stopped and chuckled slightly. Then he shook his dark head a few times. Finally, he threw his hands up in the air dramatically. "To tell you the truth, guys," he said, halfway apologizing, "I asked Annie to give you a brief outline of the idea she's come up with because the concept is so *unique* we're really not sure how marketable it will be. Right,

Annie?" He gave her shoulder a squeeze that wasn't very friendly.

Annie was only one second away from giving a quick knee-jab to a certain pulled groin muscle when Matt made the wise choice and removed his hand from her shoulder.

"And that's where you guys come in," he continued, rubbing his hands together. "We need your input. We encourage you to bombard Annie with questions. And we hope you can point us in the right direction with Annie's, well, *unusual* idea."

Furious didn't even touch what Annie was feeling. Matt left her side and walked around the table. As luck would have it, he took a seat directly across from the only place left for her to sit.

So that's how he's going to play it, is he?

Her idea had suddenly gone from "woo-woo" to "*unique*." And good old nurturing department head Matt was just trying to help his bumbling little fledgling leave the nest and find the right direction for this ridiculous idea of hers.

Well, she could play at that game, too.

Annie smiled and said, "Before I give each of you an outline, I want to thank Matt personally for recognizing that my idea does bring something new to the table. *And* for giving me the opportunity to present it to you at this monthly meeting."

She felt a few daggers from his cold black eyes whiz past her cheek.

"Because my idea isn't your usual cookie-cutter type of game," she added, "I hope everyone will keep an open mind and think outside the box while you evaluate its marketing potential." She smiled purposely at Matt before she said, "Or, as we like to say in the creative department, push that envelope completely off the ledge. Right, Matt?"

The look on Matt's face reminded Annie she needed to make a last will and testament.

She ignored him and walked around the room placing binders in front of everyone seated. She also placed a binder in front of Matt, even though his unexpected attendance at the meeting meant she wouldn't have a copy of the outline for herself. She seated herself at the table, trying to look confident, as she clasped her hands in her lap to keep them from shaking.

"Shall we begin?" J.B. Duncan said. "Joe Video," he read aloud before he impaled Annie with a look that made her sit up straight. "Why don't you start by giving us a thumbnail sketch of exactly what the Joe Video game concept is, Miss Long?"

Annie didn't falter. "Joe Video is the perfect man. On DVD. Or to put it simply, sir, Joe Video is going to open the video game industry to a new audience."

Everyone at the table sent her a blank stare.

Matt only smiled.

Annie tried again. "Let me ask you this. What gender buys most video games?"

"Male," several guys at the table said in unison.

"Do you realize why video games are such a guy thing?"

Everyone still looked puzzled.

"Because men are visual," Annie said. "But women are verbal. Women want to talk about things that are happening in their lives. When they talk about issues important to them, they want someone to listen and validate those issues with a supportive and positive response."

When no one commented, Annie said, "Think about it. Technology has always been focused entirely on the male perspective. That's why we have a female market out there just waiting to be tapped into. Joe Video will be everything a woman wants. He'll listen when she wants him to listen. He'll talk when she wants him to talk. He'll always have the perfect response for any given situation. And he won't make a mess or leave the toilet seat up."

Gretchen, the tall, gangly redhead from art and filming, was the only one who laughed at her last statement, but it gave Annie the confidence she needed to continue.

"The fact is, we live in a techno-fanatic society today," Annie said. "Instant gratification isn't fast enough. Dial-up was too slow, so we now have high-speed online services. Cell phones were boring, so we added video screens and text messaging. And how dare anyone suggest we wait even one hour to have film developed. Digital cameras eliminated that pesky problem."

She glanced at J.B. Duncan. He was leaning back in his chair, tapping a pencil against the table with one hand and stroking his manicured white beard with the other.

Annie said, "Whether we like it or not, patience has become a lost virtue in today's society. So my question is, why not be the first to give women the instant perfect man?"

J.B. Duncan paused for a moment before he said, "My main concern is that you've been talking about techno *conveniences*, Miss Long. Convince me why you think the female population would embrace a techno *fake* boyfriend."

Annie glanced at Matt. She was surprised that he didn't jump to his feet and do a few excited backflips down the boardroom table.

She turned her attention back to her CEO and smiled. "I understand your concern, sir. But women have certainly embraced"— she held up one hand as she ticked off on three fingers —"fake tans, fake nails, and fake boobs."

"And what about those fake hair extensions women use?" the guy from the sound department asked.

"Men have hair plugs, too," Gretchen was quick to remind her male counterparts.

"Collagen injections, Botox, and liposuction." Annie continued.

"And don't forget Viagra," Bill from the programming department said with a laugh. "That's one instant motivator you can't live without when you reach my age."

Everyone laughed this time.

Annie spoke up again. "I'm not trying to paint a grim picture of life as we know it today, sir. I'm only trying to prove there is a place in today's market for Joe Video. He'll be exactly what a woman wants — the ideal substitute until her real Mr. Perfect comes along."

Greg Wilson from advertising snickered. "I'm not trying to be crude, Annie, but the substitute market *has* already been tapped into. You can buy those substitutes in all shapes and sizes and with batteries included."

"But have you ever seen any of those devices that could talk back to you, Greg?" Annie challenged.

Greg's big grin disappeared. "Don't tell me you intend to give a whole new meaning to the term 'joystick.'"

Annie laughed. "No, of course, not. But Joe Video does offer a 'Pleasure Me' option."

That comment sent everyone thumbing through the binder in a hurry. For the first time, Matt even turned a few pages.

Annie waited until everyone found the page before she

said, "The basis for this option is actually a relaxation technique I learned in a sensitivity class I took back in college." Tongue-in-cheek, she added, "Of course, with a hunky guy's sultry voice leading you through the process of discovering the pleasure points of your own body, how a lady uses this exercise will be up to her."

Gretchen said, "Explain the 'Striptease Aerobics' option outlined on page four."

There was no way Annie was going to admit she and Collin had taken lessons from a gay male stripper last summer when Collin was trying to win an amateur striptease contest at Backstreet, his favorite gay bar. But both of them had been sore for weeks after they'd taken those lessons. Annie had even lost five pounds.

What she did say was, "Our goal is to give a woman everything she wants all in one package with this game, Gretchen. With Joe Video, she won't need Pilates or a dozen other exercise tapes. Striptease aerobics will get her in touch with her sensuous side, and work her booty off at the same time."

"It works for me," Gretchen said.

Annie was mentally congratulating herself on how well everything was going when questions started flying at her from all directions.

Yes. She thought the game should be marketed for every venue possible. PCs, of course, and laptops. PlayStation 2 and Xbox, since what mom didn't have access to those when she put Junior to bed? Now that the portable game players were becoming so popular, a woman on the go would never have to be without her best friend, Joe.

No. A computer-generated format simply wouldn't do. An actor needed to play the role of Joe Video. Preferably someone unknown. Someone who wouldn't expect an outrageous commission and who would be glad for the exposure. But gorgeous, of course. A cross between Antonio Banderas and Fabio, with a sexy accent. The kind of guy women everywhere fantasized about while their hubby or their boyfriend lay stretched out on the sofa with the remote in his hand.

Annie couldn't resist sending Matt a sweet little smile when she finished making *that* statement.

When he glared back at her, Annie decided she definitely needed to make her will.

The questions continued for several more minutes. When they finally stopped coming, Annie was more than ready to make her run for the checkered flag waiting for her at the finish line.

On your mark.

Get set.

Go!

She'd almost made it when Matt stuck his leg out and tripped her. "Before Annie closes," he said, "I'd like to bring up a few points of my own about Joe Video."

Kudos to Annie, Matt thought sullenly. She'd managed to make her first run through the gauntlet without so much as a scratch.

So far.

But his ass was on the line here, too. Matt didn't intend to become the laughingstock of the entire video game industry without at least putting up a good fight.

He looked around the room and grinned. "For the men in this room who are probably having a harder time than Annie and Gretchen understanding this female-focused concept, I thought in all fairness I should bring up a few points about this game from the male point of view."

He almost laughed when Annie's eyes narrowed.

He pointed to Bill from programming. "Bill, you're married, right?"

"For the last twenty-five years," Bill said with wan enthusiasm.

"Does the wife ever get irritated because she decides to tell you something about her sister's neighbor's cousin's brother, and you couldn't keep up with the conversation even if you *weren't* trying to watch a Braves game on the tube?"

"For the last twenty-five years," Bill repeated.

Everyone but Annie laughed.

Matt held up a finger. "But. Think about it, Bill. What if your wife had Joe Video? Joe would be the one listening and validating her concerns with those perfect responses Annie was talking about. And you'd be stretched out on your recliner munching chips and tossing back a few cold ones while you watched the game in peace."

Bill's face erupted into a wide grin. "How soon can we start production on this game?"

Everyone laughed again.

Except Annie.

Matt couldn't resist. He smiled at her and winked.

He said, "I'm trying to point out that even though Joe Video is going to be targeted for women, he might turn out to be *man's* best friend instead. Annie said it herself. Men aren't verbal. So let Joe Video do the talking. Let him make all of those perfect responses. If you ask me, every husband and boyfriend on the planet should run out to buy Joe Video the second the game hits the shelves. He might finally get some peace and quiet."

"Thank you, *Matt*," Annie said, "for giving us another perspective on Joe Video, exaggerated as it was."

Matt winked at her again. "Always glad to help."

She dismissed him with a toss of her head and looked directly at J.B. Duncan. "Paragon has always had the reputation for being first when it comes to new and innovative game ideas, Mr. Duncan. Being a woman, I see Joe Video becoming today's answer to the self-help craze of the eighties and the nineties. Only with Joe Video women won't have to look in the mirror repeating positive statements to themselves. They'll have a personal virtual soul mate to boost their ego for them."

Back up the trolley, sweetheart.

Matt intended to have his final say, too.

"That's our big dilemma, J.B.," he said. "Being a man, I can't see anything but the humorous side of this concept. My concern is that if Paragon does market this game, it could end up being the biggest joke in video game history."

The silence was deafening.

It seemed like an eternity before J.B. Duncan looked in Matt's direction. "Well, being the *businessman* I am, Matt, I don't see your dilemma. Whether women embrace this game as their salvation, or whether men buy it for their ladies as a gag gift, sales are sales are sales." He looked around the table. "High-concept. Cutting-edge. Brilliant. Joe Video is all that and a bag of chips, people." He looked back at Matt. "I want you to forget the daredevil idea for now, Matt. Take the ball and run with Joe Video before someone else gets wind of this concept."

Speechless, Matt looked across the table at Annie.

Annie looked as shocked as he felt.

But before Matt could argue, J.B. pointed to him and said, "Stand up a minute, Matt."

Matt slowly rose to his feet, his head aching far worse than his pulled groin muscle ever had.

"Heads up, people," J.B. said. "You are looking at the type of department head each and every one of you should aspire to be. I've always known Matt was a visionary. And he proved it here today. Not only did he recognize a great concept, but it's obvious he's looking ahead and grooming his staff to step effortlessly into his shoes when he makes the next big move up in this company. That's vision, people. Learn from it."

What?

Annie couldn't believe her ears.

Matt could fall into a shit-filled vat and still come out smelling like one of Dave's kiss-off roses that she'd thrown in the trash. Was she crazy? Or had the freaking CEO all but given Matt the promise of a big promotion for *her* high-concept, cutting-edge, brilliant idea?

I'm going to be sick.

She was going to throw up all over the place if she didn't get out of that boardroom. And who would even notice? Everyone else had gathered around Matt in suck-up mode the second J.B. finished his speech. J.B. even had his arm around Matt's shoulder now. And Matt was laughing heartily at something unhappily-married-for-twenty-five-years Bill was saying. More good ol' boy jokes about Joe Video, no doubt.

I'm definitely going to be sick.

Annie bolted from the boardroom and ran past Kathy, who sent a startled look in her direction. She barely made it into the women's bathroom and one of the stalls in time to keep from ruining the Manolos she'd worried might be her last pair ever. By the time she'd stumbled back to the bathroom sink to splash cold water on her face, Collin burst into the women's bathroom as if he belonged there.

"Are you okay, Annie? Kathy said you ran out of the boardroom. Don't tell me those bastards fired you."

Annie jerked a paper towel from the dispenser. "Fire me?" She tried to laugh, but it came out as a croak. "Don't be silly. J.B. was so thrilled with *my* Joe Video idea, he all but handed *Matt* the freaking key to the executive bathroom."

Collin grimaced.

"Oh? And do you want to hear another lovely little twist? J.B. more or less gave Matt permission to market Joe Video as a gag gift. Sales are sales are sales, you know."

Collin groaned. "Oh Annie. I'm so sorry."

Annie squeezed her eyes shut, shaking her hands in front of her face as if that would keep her from crying. "Don't console me, Collin. I can't take it right now."

When she finally got herself back together, she said, "Would you please go get my purse? I'm so emotionally drained my head might cave in. I don't want to see Matt. Maybe not ever. But definitely not right now."

When Collin left to get her purse, Annie leaned against the wall and banged her forehead against the cold tile, testing her cave-in theory. Talk about a day going to hell in a handbasket in a hurry. She'd been on an emotional roller coaster from the moment she'd arrived. First Dave's betrayal. And now she'd been betrayed again by Matt and her CEO, who were determined to turn her idea into the gag gift of the century.

How much more can one person take?

"Here," Collin said rushing back in to hand over her purse. "You don't have to worry about bumping into Matt. Kathy said he just left with J.B. The old man's taking Matt to dinner to celebrate."

Annie's envelope went over the ledge for real.

"It's just so unfair," she sobbed against Collin's willing shoulder. "*I'm* the one who's supposed to be celebrating tonight. Not Dave with some new girlfriend. And definitely not Matt getting credit for *my* idea."

"I know," Collin mumbled as he stroked her hair.

Annie pushed away from him. "Oh God, Collin. I just thought of something else. I can't go home. Not to all the candles and the champagne and that stupid robe I bought for Dave spread out on my bed next to that damn black teddy I might as well throw in the trash."

"You don't have to go home," Collin promised. "You'll get to wear that teddy later for someone a lot more deserving than Dave."

Annie shook her head. "No way. I'm through with men for the rest of my life. Trust me."

"Déjà *moo*," Collin warned.

Annie almost managed a smile.

"Come on, sweet cheeks," Collin said, putting his arm around her shoulder. "I'm taking you to Backstreet. If there's anything you need right now, it's a tequila shooter to get you in a better frame of mind."

Annie shook her head. "You know I always feel uncomfortable at Backstreet. I'll really feel uncomfortable the way I'm dressed today. Look at me. I'll stand out like Martha Stewart at a Spice Girls convention." But she didn't resist when Collin put his hands on her shoulders and pushed her toward the bathroom door.

"You look gorgeous," Collin said as he kept pushing

her toward the elevator. "Blatantly straight, yes. But that will keep me from having to babysit you every minute if someone happens to catch my eye."

Annie cut her puffy eyes sideways in his direction. "But you wouldn't run off with some hunk and leave me at Backstreet by myself, would you?"

Collin pushed the button that would take them to the parking garage. "Don't be ridiculous. I'd never leave you in a million years and you know it."

"Okay. But you can forget about any to-kill-ya shooters," Annie said. "Tequila makes me crazy."

Collin waved his hand in the air to pooh-pooh her statement. "After the day you've had? You're *already* crazy, Annie. That gives you the freedom to drink whatever you want. I'll drive and we'll take the Black Knight," he said, referring to the name he had given his sleek new black Mercedes sedan.

"You're not listening, Collin. I don't do drunk well."

The elevator doors opened. When they stepped into the parking garage Annie said, "All I need is one glass of white wine to take the edge off." She grabbed Collin's arm. "Promise me, Collin. One glass of wine. Then you'll take me to your place and let me crash."

"Promise," Collin said. "Trust me."

CHAPTER 4

When Annie opened her eyes on Saturday morning, the first thing she thought was, *Who is that horrible-looking creature plastered to the ceiling?*

When her fuzzy brain cleared, she realized she was looking at her own reflection in the mirrored canopy above Collin's extravagant French provincial four-poster bed.

She gasped.

And not just because she looked like a wild-eyed raccoon wearing a hideous frizzed-all-over clown wig. Something was moving beneath the covers.

And it isn't me!

Annie held her breath.

She blew it out again when a familiar head popped out from beneath Collin's elaborate designer comforter.

However.

The relieved blast from her morning-after-too-many-tequila-shooters breath caused Collin's terror of a Chihuahua to wrinkle his little black nose in disgust, throw his head back, and howl loud enough to wake the dead.

"Elton John. *Hush*," Annie begged, pressing against her throbbing temples. But she couldn't really blame the poor pooch. Without a doubt, sometime during the night something had crawled inside her mouth, curled up, and *died* there.

Probably after I got hit by the truck, she thought, still too groggy to remember any specific details from the night before. But if your breath smelled like roadkill and your body ached all over, getting hit by a truck had to be the only explanation.

She pushed herself up on her elbows, her head still pounding like a bass drum in a marching band. When she pushed back the covers, she would have blushed if all the blood in her body hadn't already been participating in the lively parade marching back and forth between her temples.

Poor Collin had obviously undressed her himself. She was wearing one of his Ralph Lauren pajama tops.

"Owwwww." Could her head possibly hurt any worse?

Her loud moaning gave Elton John reason for another eardrum-piercing yap before he jumped off the bed and scurried out of the room. As slight as the movement from the tiny terror was, the parade turned the corner and marched straight to the center of her stomach.

Annie managed to pull herself up, then hobbled in the direction of Collin's adjoining bathroom, hand over her mouth and a searing pain radiating from her right foot all the way up to her periwinkle blue thong. But it wasn't until she bent over at the toilet that she screamed loud enough to bring Collin running to the bathroom door, a terrified look on his face.

"What's wrong?" He had an apron tied around his slim waist and a dishtowel in his hand.

"*That*," Annie said, forgetting her nausea as she

pointed down at her right foot. "Please tell me that isn't a . . . a . . ."

Collin looked down at her foot, then back up at her. "A *toe*too? Or at least that's what you insisted on calling it last night when you decided to let some stranger make a permanent mark on your body with an ink-filled needle."

Annie was mortified. She sank down onto the toilet seat, staring at the bright red heart tattooed on her sore little piggy. The little piggy next to her big toe, gone-to-market piggy. The little piggy that was supposed to stay *home*!

"You took me to a tattoo parlor?" she shrieked.

"Don't you *dare* try to blame it on me." Collin lifted his nose in the air and slung the dishtowel over his shoulder. "After enough tequila shooters, you were the one who insisted those wearing-your-heart-on-your-sleeve days were over. That you wanted your heart tattooed permanently on your toe so another bastard like Dave wouldn't be able to find it."

Annie squeezed her eyes shut, massaging her temples again. "You promised you wouldn't let me drink tequila."

"I didn't *let* you. When I left you at the bar, you were quietly sipping your glass of white wine and telling that lesbian couple sitting next to you how lucky they were that they didn't have to put up with low-life lying cowards like Dave."

"You said you wouldn't leave me, either," Annie reminded him.

"I didn't *leave* you. I was on the dance floor. Six feet away. And the next thing I knew, you and your new best friends were having a pound-'em-back, we-hate-men tequila shooter contest."

"And then what?" Annie wailed. "You let the lesbians hold me down and tattoo a freaking heart on my toe?"

Collin rolled his eyes. "Noooo. You got the tattoo at Amazing Al's Tattoo Parlor in Little Five Points."

Little Five Points? Annie gasped — not an area of Atlanta she or Collin usually frequented. "What in the hell were you thinking taking me to Little Five Points?"

Collin frowned. "You mean what was I thinking when you decided you were going to Little Five Points with or without me?"

When Annie frowned, he said, "You wanted to go to the funkiest place in Atlanta, you kept saying. You kept insisting that Little Five Points was better than San Francisco's Haight-Ashbury district on its worst day."

"You couldn't have just driven me home?"

"Since you were already in the car with the lesbians, and *I* wasn't the one driving, not hardly."

Collin walked to the linen closet, grabbed a washcloth, ran it under the cold water faucet several times, then handed it over. "Here. Wash that mascara off your face. I'm having flashbacks from my Kiss obsession days. You look like Gene Simmons, bad hair and all."

Annie took the washcloth and buried her face into the coolness, then placed the damp cloth on her forehead. "Please tell me you at least chose a *clean* tattoo parlor."

"Yes, the tattoo parlor was clean," Collin said. "And I made sure the tattoo needle was sterile. But I didn't choose the place. You hooked up with Amazing Al on your own. At the salsa bar."

Annie's head jerked up. "The salsa bar?"

Oh God. Bits and pieces were beginning to come back to her. *Amazing Al.* Yes, she did remember him. He was a skinny little guy who barely came to her five-foot-seven shoulder, with a ring through his nose and a peace sign tattooed in the middle of his forehead. *But God could that man dance.*

"I see I'm not the only one having flashbacks," Collin chided. "So? Now do you remember why you were so adamant about going to the salsa bar in Little Five Points? You were going to find the perfect guy to play Joe Video, you kept insisting." He paused. "This is a direct tequila quote from you, Annie: 'I want to find my own Joe Video before Matt drags some bubba into art and filming wearing bib overalls and no shirt and with a front tooth missing.' Yes, I'm pretty sure that's exactly how you put it."

Annie winced as a smooth, chiseled, and handsome face instantly appeared in her mind. Hunkability factor right off the charts. Tall, muscled, ink black hair. Chocolate brown eyes. A low, sexy voice laced with a thick Cuban accent. "The bartender," Annie finally whispered.

Collin nodded. He folded his arms across his chest rather snootily as he leaned against the bathroom doorjamb. "But not just any bartender, Annie. The bartender whose family owns the salsa bar. The bartender you told everyone there you were going to make an instant star when he played Joe Video. *And* the same bartender whose two older brothers got so excited at your wonderful news, they not only bought a round of drinks for the house, they also hoisted you on top of the bar to make a toast exclusively to you."

Annie buried her face into the washcloth again,

trying to stop the chanting —*Maravilloso, Annie! Bravo, Annie!*

"Oh, in case you're still wondering," Collin said, "it had to be sometime *after* the toast and *during* the merengue that you talked Amazing Al into opening his tattoo parlor around the corner so you could get your hidden-heart *toe*too."

Annie didn't know whether to cry or throw up. At the moment she was close to doing both. "Collin, I am so sorry," she said, the tears in her eyes genuine. "There's no worse punishment than taking care of a drunk friend. I owe you. Big-time."

She was hoping for a comforting I-forgive-you hug, but Collin said instead, "Yes, you do owe me big-time. And that's why you can't say one word about me inviting Matt over to have brunch with us at eleven."

Annie put her hand over her mouth, unsure how much longer she could avoid the inevitable with that bit of news.

"Don't get your hopes up," Collin continued. "Matt's already agreed to come. He thinks I'm right. You need to clear the air between you before we start working on Joe Video come Monday morning."

That does it.

Annie slid off the toilet seat and lifted the lid as Collin scooted out of the bathroom.

He remained outside the bathroom door long enough to say, "I'm headed to your apartment now for that two-hundred-dollar meal we aren't going to waste whether you like it or not. I'll get you some clean clothes while I'm there. So, that means you have about an hour to puke, take a shower, and pull yourself together before Matt shows up."

Annie groaned.

The thought of facing Matt was bad enough.

But the reminder of those damn rotten fish eggs helped her successfully accomplish the first of the Saturday morning assignments Collin had just given her.

The one thing Enrique Romero had wanted since childhood was to be an actor. A dream his sainted padre, God rest his soul, had put to an end when he slapped Rico's eighteen-year-old cheeks and shamed him in front of the family by saying, "You will forget the acting. And you will work hard in the taberna with your faithful brothers to provide for this family. Se acaba el tema!" The subject is finished.

Being the youngest male, and also a faithful son, Rico had never again thought about doing anything other than what Papa expected. Until last evening when a beautiful stranger walked into their family-owned Cabaña Club.

Un bebé caliente!

She was one hot babe.

She had given Rico a wake-up call with the first curl of her polished finger. For the first time since dear Papa's departure to heaven only a few months earlier, Rico realized he could finally do exactly as he pleased.

He flexed his muscles, striking several poses as he admired himself in the bathroom mirror. The loud banging and the insults his younger sister screamed through the bathroom door didn't even faze him.

"Cerdo arrogante. Femenino. Hombre gay."

Rico only smiled. He didn't consider himself an arrogant pig. Nor was he the least bit effeminate. And he certainly wasn't gay. Most of the available — and some not-so-available — women around Little Five Points could certainly attest to that fact.

He struck a few more poses, then reached out and ran his finger over the raised letters of the business card he'd temporarily stuck between the bathroom mirror and its metal frame. That Annie. She definitely was a looker. But her business address impressed him more.

Bank of America Plaza.

Tallest building in the entire Southeast.

How many times had he gazed toward downtown? Looking at that building standing tall and straight against the Atlanta skyline, its twenty-four-karat gold spire glowing both day and night? He had looked at that building wondering what his life would have been like had he not been born the son of an immigrant who ruled his family with an iron fist. A man too proud of his heritage to abandon old customs that should have been put aside when he brought his family from Cuba to America when Rico was fourteen years old.

But those times were in the past.

Now he, Rico Romero, had been summoned to that very building first thing on Monday morning so he could take his first step into stardom. Destiny had come knocking. And now that it had, Rico intended to open the door wide and embrace his new future.

Unfortunately, his sister had also come knocking — again on the bathroom door.

Too bad. He would get out of the bathroom when he was good and ready and not one second before.

Still admiring himself, Rico ran a comb through his thick black hair, then flashed a smile at the mirror,

proud of his even white teeth. Then he turned his head
from one side to the other, checking out his profile.

"This man is going to be my Antonio Banderas," the
pretty woman with hair the color of a summer sunset
had told her blond male friend when she'd pointed in his
direction.

Well, he had news for this Annie. *She* was going to
be his Melanie Griffith — his ticket out of Little Five
Points and into a lifestyle enjoyed by the rich and
famous.

Rico flexed his muscles again, thinking how his two
older brothers had rubbed their greedy hands together at
the prospect of his fame and fortune. "We will postpone
announcing your engagement for now," his oldest
brother, Ernesto, had declared. "I will meet with your
intended's uncle and explain. And then you will do what
this fancy lady says."

Ernesto had said this, then slapped him upside the
head after they closed the bar last night. Manuel had
nodded in agreement like the spineless puppet that he
was.

"You let this woman make you a big star in this city,"
Ernesto had told him. "Our pockets will overflow with
money and our business will go derecho a traves de la
azotea." Ernesto had pointed his finger straight to the
ceiling.

Rico spit into the sink. "Bastardos."

Little minds with no ambition, his brothers.

Always causing him trouble.

It had been Ernesto, taking his new role as head of
the family seriously, who had declared shortly after
Papa's death that it was time Rico should marry and
start a family. And still following old customs, Ernesto

had picked his bride for him, the niece of a man who had prospered in America and had become relatively wealthy like his own family. A niece who had been sent from Cuba to live with her uncle so her prosperous uncle could find her a prosperous young husband.

For weeks, Rico had protested this marriage.

Until he came face-to-face with sexy Helena Gonzalez.

Rico felt himself stir with desire at the thought of Helena now. She was the kind of woman no man could resist. All softness and curves. All sweet and giving. But passionate? *Demasiado caliente dirigir!* She was too hot to handle, that one.

Unless your name happens to be Rico Romero, Rico thought, smiling to himself. There had never been a woman born too hot for him to handle.

Helena he could handle. Even about the postponement of their engagement. It was the uncle that made Rico worry.

Ernesto had assured him the uncle would not be concerned that the engagement was postponed temporarily. He would have to trust Ernesto about this. He really had no choice. Unless he wanted to end up an old man, still swabbing bar for his demanding older brothers who were just like his papa. Everything for the family. Always for the family.

Rico turned around, looking in the mirror at the scratches on his back. Helena had put them there during their lovemaking the night before. Her love for him was just as fierce as her passion.

Helena would wait for him.

Of that, he was certain.

Just as Annie, with her connections, would help him climb the stairway to success.

"Nada perder, todo a ganar," Rico said aloud, proud to be using his dear papa's favorite expression.

Nothing to lose, everything to gain.

Matt waited for the security guard crossing arm to lift, then drove his newly washed black Jeep Cherokee out of the parking lot situated below his high-rise Midtown apartment building. His newly washed classic 1956 white Corvette was still sitting in the reserved space he paid extra for every month, its thick canvas cover secured safely in place.

He only drove *that* baby on special occasions.

Going to Collin's to clear the air with Annie wasn't one of them.

He headed down Colonial Homes Drive in the direction of historic Inman Park and Collin's circa 1890 two-story Victorian home that old family money had bought before the turn of the century. The same old family money that provided Collin with monthly trust fund stipends so staggering, keeping the old house in tip-top shape didn't put so much as a wrinkle in Collin's fair-skinned brow.

Matt had often wondered why Collin bothered working at all. Especially since he would solely inherit the Adair Carpet Mills fortune when his widowed mother passed on. The estimated value of the estate today was somewhere in excess of seventy-five million dollars. Matt knew this only because Collin's rather flamboyant "Mumsey," as Collin called her, let you know exactly *with whom* you were dealing.

Matt had even had the nerve to ask Collin once why he bothered with a paycheck that was far less than any of his monthly trust fund checks. Collin's indignant reply had been, "I'm not some kind of loser, Matt. I intend to work for a living just like everyone else."

Collin's family money explained why the constant power struggle had always been strictly between Matt and Annie. Unlike Collin, he and Annie weren't so privileged. They were both hungry for financial freedom. That hunger translated into getting to the top and staying there. And getting to the top and staying there was the reason he'd been so eager to take Collin up on his invitation for brunch.

Dinner with J.B. the previous evening had been the equivalent of dangling a juicy carrot in front of Matt's wascally-wabbit-that-he-was face. He only hoped Annie's mouth would salivate with equal expectancy when they had their little heart-to-heart that Collin had stepped in and arranged for them.

Of course, there was a good chance she was going to have the big hangover Collin expected when she finally rolled out of bed — something she still hadn't done when Collin tracked him down on his cell phone during Matt's second trip to the car wash at 9 a.m.

According to Collin, Annie had gotten pretty trashed. Which certainly wasn't like her. But who could really blame her? First, she'd had the big Dave disappointment. Then she'd had the big praise disappointment from J.B. Tough break. For anyone.

Matt knew he'd have to tread carefully to make Annie see the light. He would say, yes, that it had been wrong of J.B. to give him all the credit for her idea. And yes, life wasn't fair, it sucked most of the time. But he'd also point out that it was a dog-eat-dog business world out there. That like it or not, there was an unwritten chain of command the business world followed as faithfully as America followed *Monday Night Football*.

Yeah. Good analogy.

He'd point out that J.B. himself would ultimately be hailed the all-mighty video game king if Joe Video did turn out to a big success. Certainly not a lowly department head like him, nor a lowly creative assistant like Annie. The only way *their* names would ever pass through lips in the video game industry is if Joe Video became a big flop.

So, basically, they had two choices.

They could either work together for success. Or they could go down in flames as the two idiots who cost Paragon big bucks with a video soul mate game that never left the shelves.

Matt smiled.

After he got Annie straight on the whole "life isn't fair" scenario, he would hopefully lift her spirits with the good news. And the good news was that he'd never seen J.B. so excited about any game idea during the ten years he'd worked for the man. In fact, J.B. was borderline jubilant.

He just wasn't sure how he was going to break it to her that J.B.'s excitement had little to do with the game itself. It was the age-old man versus woman controversy that J.B. believed equaled enough buzz factor to have consumers eager to buy the game before the first copy was ready for distribution.

"The world thrives on controversy, Matt, don't ever doubt it," J.B. had told him.

"Controversy," Matt mumbled to himself, thinking about the controversy that would damn near explode when he told Annie the marketing strategy J.B. had in mind for the two of them.

Yeah. That's when the fistfight is going to start.

He felt like a real jerk, but Matt halfway hoped Annie did have a wicked hangover. He needed any advantage he could get when he delivered the giant reality check J.B had written out with both of their names on it.

Collin's arm snaked around the bathroom door, Annie's clean clothes in hand just as he'd promised.

A humble thank-you almost made it past her lips. But Annie swallowed those words when she realized what Collin had brought for her to wear. "Are you kidding me? Out of my entire closet, you brought me this?"

His head popped around the door. "And you have a problem because?" He pointed to the bundle she held in her hands. "You big silly. I was with you when you bought those adorable hip-hugger khakis. And I personally picked out that to-die-for orange crop-top with the peekaboo off-the-shoulder sleeves. Orange, orange, orange, Annie. I've told you a million times, it's in, in, in."

"You didn't stop to think I'd look less provocative if I came downstairs for brunch wearing nothing but this towel?" Annie shook her head in disbelief. "I'm still in the frame of mind to punch Matt *out*, Collin, not try to turn him *on*."

Collin actually looked surprised. "Well, I doubt you have to worry about turning Matt on, Annie." He kept looking at her as if that were the craziest thing he'd ever heard. "If you walked downstairs buck naked with a six-pack under your arm, *then* you might turn Matt on."

Annie pursed her lips in a pout. Collin was probably right, but he didn't have to say it.

"No," Collin decided. "Make that buck *nekkid*, as Matt so crudely pronounces the word, with a six-pack under your arm and duct tape over your mouth."

"*Okay.* I didn't mean to flatter myself." She looked down and haughtily flipped through the clothes. Clean panties and her favorite pair of sandals were there, although today she would have preferred tennis shoes to hide the blasted "toetoo" she'd spend the rest of her life regretting. "Any particular reason why you didn't bring me a strapless bra? Other than your sudden boob envy, I mean."

Collin sent her a mischievous grin. "Sorry. Totally slipped my mind about the bra." He sent her a cute ta-ta wave and closed the bathroom door.

"Liar," Annie grumbled. About the bra. About his choice in clothing. And about her ability to turn Matt on, although Collin had no way of knowing that.

The secret night she'd spent with Matt was something she'd *never* be brainless enough to share with motormouth Collin. She knew Matt evidently felt the same way or everyone in Atlanta and the rest of the free world would have already heard ages ago that she and Matt had done the dirty deed.

Still, Collin didn't fool her. The little sneak had known exactly what he was doing conveniently forgetting her bra. More of his so-called diversionary tactics, no doubt.

Please.

Annie sighed as she stepped into her panties, then pulled on the khakis that hit her dangerously just above her pelvic bone. Next she struggled into the orange-is-in top with the peekaboo sleeves that were called such for a very good reason. Not only wouldn't the sleeves stay up, but they weren't comfortable when they slid down on her arms to rest just above her elbows.

Peek-a-frickety-boo.

She opened the top drawer and rummaged through Collin's elaborate Victorian-style vanity until she finally found a styling brush, then bent over and took her frustration out on her long, tangled hair.

Brush. Brush. Brush.

Yeow. Yeow. Yeow.

But by the time the painful detangling regimen was completed, Annie had come to a few firm conclusions. First, she was glad Collin had taken the initiative to clear the air between her and Matt before they showed up for business as usual on Monday. Second, she wasn't going to put Matt on the defensive in any way, shape, or form, regardless of how hard he tried his usual chain-rattling routine. And third, she was going to conduct herself in a totally professional manner.

She was going to prove that she really wasn't the psycho chick Matt probably thought she was after the stupid stunt she'd pulled with Joe Video. Basically, she was going to try her best — for once — to meet Matt on some kind of common ground.

Common ground. Yes. That's good.

She would simply point out that while he did deserve one hundred percent of the credit for allowing her to present her idea, Joe Video was still her vision. She'd say she realized he wasn't keen on the concept. She'd tell Matt she could even see why, from his point of view, he might consider the game one big joke. But she'd also plead to his sense of fair play and ask permission to develop the game for the female audience she had in mind and give the sales record a chance to speak for itself.

Satisfied that her game plan was solidly in place, Annie opened several other vanity drawers before she finally found the Advil and popped more than the recommended dosage into her mouth. She might have pushed the envelope, but Matt had been the one who literally pushed her off the ledge to sink or swim.

Annie smiled. He had no way of knowing she'd been the captain of her eighth-grade swim team.

CHAPTER 5

The second Collin opened the door to Magnolia
Haven — the name of the house, according to Inman
Park's Historical Society register — Matt asked, "Well? Is
Cruella — I mean *Tequila* De Vil awake and moving
around yet?"

Collin sent him a drop-the-attitude look. The little
ankle-biter perched in the crook of Collin's arm wrinkled
his nose and growled low and mean.

Matt growled back.

Collin pursed his lips and stepped aside, allowing Matt
to enter. "Do you have to start irritating Elton John before
you even walk through the door? You know being a
latchkey dog keeps his nerves on edge."

"Me?" Matt sent a mean look at the tiny terror who
had nailed him with those needle-sharp teeth too many
times to still be alive. "Face it, Collin. The mutt hates me.
Why don't you let me get you a *real* dog?"

"And why don't you refrain from mentioning the most
hated villain known to modern dog in front of Elton
John?"

"Right. The dog knows exactly who Cruella De Vil is."

In rebuttal, the latchkey canine threw his head back and let out a long, woeful howl.

"And you were saying?" Collin challenged.

Matt sent Elton John a suspicious look. "I was asking whether or not Annie was more alive than dead today."

Collin ignored his question and motioned for him to follow. Matt obediently fell in behind his host. He followed Collin through the impressive foyer with the classic *Gone with the Wind* staircase. Then they headed down a hallway to the left, adorned with antique frames and pictures of relatives a long time dead.

A few more steps and they walked into the large kitchen that still had turn-of-the-century-charm but was fully equipped with the most up-to-date cooking utensils and appliances available. Finally, they passed through what Collin called old-world French cottage doors and out onto a climate-controlled gazebo-style sunporch.

Even Matt had to admit that the view of Collin's blue ribbon first-place garden — named such by the Inman Park Garden Club for several years in a row — was spectacular. He wasn't surprised that, like the garden's twenty-thousand-dollar sparkling waterfall, Collin had gone overboard in what he would insist were only "simple" preparations.

The spread was laid out upper-crust Southern style with tons of sterling silver, Collin's treasured bone china, and crisp linen napkins the same color as the plush emerald cushions of the antique white wicker chairs. Matt made his way to the chair where Collin indicated he should sit, and Collin took a seat across from him, placing the damnable yapster on his lap.

Elton John instantly bared his teeth and so did Matt.

They stared each other down across the large white wicker table.

Only then did Collin decide to answer Matt's original question. "Yes, Annie is awake," he said. "She's getting dressed, and should be down in a minute."

"And the hangover?"

"Not severe enough that you can push her around, if that's what you're getting at."

Again, Matt protested. "Me?"

Collin rolled his eyes. "Don't pretend you weren't hoping Annie's hangover might give you some kind of an edge. You're talking to me, Matt. I know you inside and out."

Smart-ass, Matt thought. "I don't know what you're talking about."

Collin raised an eyebrow. "Really? No particular reason why you were so eager to come over and make amends with Annie? No hidden agenda, maybe? No urgency to win Annie over to your way of thinking after your big celebration dinner with J.B. last night?"

Make that arrogant smart-ass.

But before Matt could come up with another pointless lie, Annie strolled through the old-world French cottage doors and out onto the sunporch.

Swallowing a big gulp, Matt stifled a painful moan when her sexy walk toward the table reminded him he could almost fit his hands around the tiny waist that was fully exposed between her neon orange top and the nonexistent waistband of her hip-hugger khakis.

She even had her hair down again, which was always a big distraction for him. Every time Annie wore her hair down, Matt couldn't keep himself from remembering how those long, silky strands had fallen across his face that night when he'd pulled her magnificent body on top of his, put his hands around that tiny waist of hers, and . . .

Stop!

His eyes locked with hers for a brief second.

And then Annie pulled the dirtiest trick of all.

She seated her bod made for sin in the chair next to his and disarmed him completely with a heart-stealing grin.

Annie stuck her hand out. "Truce?"

She was still trying to interpret the weird look on Matt's face. Not a grimace, exactly. But not relief that she was trying to be cordial, either. More surprise with a dab of anguish, as Collin would put it.

Drat.

Maybe she should have just punched him out and gotten it over with.

Matt finally made a skeptical reach for her hand, but Collin called out, "Nothing doing. A trivial handshake isn't enough."

He scooted his chair back, placed Elton John on the cushion, and was standing behind them before Annie could protest. "This truce calls for a hug." He grabbed each of them under the arm, pulled them to their feet, and pushed them together.

The hug was forced and awkward. But for a fleeting moment Annie felt Matt hug her back. And, no — having Matt's arms around her didn't produce any of those romance book reactions. Electricity didn't instantly surge through her body. No tingling chills ran up and down the full length of her spine. She didn't even feel a white-hot heat spreading straight to the center of her quivering loins.

Her reaction was much more subtle.

Having Matt's arms around her was nothing but a sad reminder that they would never be anything more than semi-good friends.

Alrighty, then, Annie thought when everyone was seated at the table again. She removed the celery stick from the Bloody Mary sitting in front of her. Munched on the celery. But she wisely left the Bloody Mary alone.

She said, "I'm really glad you were willing to come for brunch, Matt. I wanted to tell you myself I'm not upset. About anything. You gave me the opportunity to present my idea, and you deserved the credit for doing that. You are, after all, the head of our department. And that's something I won't forget again."

He was still staring at her with that goofy look on his face. Maybe, Annie decided, he needed more proof that she was being sincere.

"I also owe you an apology for acting like a spoiled two-year-old with her lip pooched out for the last few months," she admitted. "And I don't blame you for doubting I was ready to run with my own game idea."

Still no response.

"In fact, you should have fired me on the spot for going behind your back with Joe Video. I'm grateful that you didn't, of course," Annie added quickly, "especially since J.B. really seemed to like the idea. I just hope we can reach some kind of common ground when it comes to the marketing strategy."

The lights seemed to be on.

Was anybody home?

Hell-ooooooooooo? Annie felt like screaming.

Collin saved her the trouble. "Scotty? Could you beam

Matt up, please?" he said. "The poor boy seems to be lost in another galaxy."

Collin's sarcastic comment snapped Matt out of his Annie-induced trance. *Damn.* The second Annie strolled through the door his own reality check had bounced. Then Collin's stupid hug idea had caused a different muscle in his groin to throb to attention. And to top things off, Annie had quickly taken control of the conversation more effectively than if she'd been holding him captive with a multi-round Uzi under her arm.

Matt almost wished she did have a machine gun.

He'd beg for mercy and ask her to put him out of his misery. Especially since those sleeves of her skimpy top kept playing havoc with his concentration every time she pushed them up only to let them slide seductively off her slender shoulders again.

Focus, he told himself and reached for his Bloody Mary. He ignored the celery stick that poked him in the eye and practically drained the glass with one long gulp. Collin frowned at his table manners and pointed to his napkin, as if Matt would be uncouth enough to wipe his mouth with the back of his hand.

To annoy Collin, that's exactly what he did.

His two cohorts were still staring at him as if he needed to quit wasting oxygen. What had happened to his usual razor-sharp edge? He was used to dealing with disgruntled employee Annie. But had anyone ever met a *gruntled* employee before?

"You've left me speechless, Annie," Matt finally said. He sent her a friendly smile. "Here I was, dreading coming over here because I was afraid you were going to scratch my eyes out, and instead you've blown me away with your incredible insight. I can't tell you how relieved I am that you've already thought this whole situation through from start to finish."

He wasn't sure she was buying it, but she sent him a semi-friendly smile back.

"Especially the part about me being the department head. *And* that you'll never forget it again."

Oops. There goes the smile.

"Chain of command," Matt said, deciding maybe he could salvage his original speech after all. "That's something we all have to be reminded of now and then."

Fading, fading. Outta here!

"Like last night at dinner with J.B., for instance," Matt said. "The longer he talked about the outrageous marketing idea he has in mind for Joe Video, the more I had to keep reminding myself that J.B. was the boss. That he signed my paycheck. And that unless I wanted to let ten years of hard work at Paragon go right down the drain, I was going to have to carry out his orders whether I agreed with them or not."

He paused, giving Annie a chance to absorb his statement.

She didn't hesitate to ask, "Exactly what kind of ridiculous marketing idea are you talking about?"

Matt sent her a sympathetic look. "You aren't going to like it, Annie. Not one little bit."

Her chin came up. "Try me."

Matt hiked his shoulder up in a you-asked-for-it shrug. "J.B. is smart enough to realize this game concept is going to need a custom-made marketing campaign. The female audience you want to target doesn't subscribe to the video trade magazines. The male audience that does depend on our usual ads in trade magazines wouldn't get past the first line of a blurb announcing the perfect man on DVD. I'm sorry, Annie, but J.B. could care less about the game itself. It's the buzz factor he's so excited about."

"Buzz factor?"

Matt nodded. "J.B.'s convinced the key to this game's success is going to be the age-old controversy between man and woman. He believes if we get the buzz started as soon as possible, we'll have orders pouring in for Joe Video before we even start production."

Collin held his hand up like a student in a classroom. "Excuse me? Do you mind filling the clueless homo in on this age-old man versus woman controversy? I'm not sure I understand what you mean."

Matt laughed. "Do the names Adam and Eve ring a bell?"

"Oh please," Annie said. "Bringing up Adam and Eve is a big stretch in anyone's imagination."

"I was referring to man and woman and sex in general," Matt said. "Man spends half of his time thinking about sex. And he spends the other half begging woman to have sex with him. If that's not controversy, I don't know what is."

"Good point," Collin said.

Matt said, "Joe Video is going to be in your face with one big Mars and Venus standoff. And unless your head is in Uranus, you have to admit it's a brilliant marketing strategy."

Cute, Annie thought, frowning at Matt's little play on words. Yet something told her the worst was yet to come. "So? What type of in-your-face advertising does J.B. have in mind?"

The look on Matt's face told her she wasn't going to

like it. "For starters," he said, "ever hear of a local morning television program called *City Singles*?"

"I love that show!" Collin exclaimed.

"I've seen it a few times," Annie admitted.

Matt held her gaze. "That's where the old man wants to start."

Annie forced herself to ask, "And the catch?"

Matt finally dropped the bomb. "It's going to be me and you, Annie. He said, she said. On local TV. In front of Atlanta's three million-plus viewing audience."

Collin burst out laughing.

Annie didn't. "That is *so* not funny, Matt."

"Do you see me laughing?" He shook his head. "I told J.B. up front I wasn't interested in appearing on TV and I knew you would feel the same way. But being the shrewd businessman that he is, J.B. upped the stakes."

Annie braced herself. "Meaning he'll fire us if we refuse," she said matter-of-factly.

Matt shook his head. "J.B. has too much integrity to threaten his employees." He leaned back in his chair, his expression serious when he looked at Annie and said, "If we can make Joe Video the huge success J.B. thinks it can be, he'll promote me to executive vice president in charge of production. And he'll promote you to the head of the creative department."

Annie was astounded.

She immediately sent a guilty look across the table at Collin. She'd only been with the company a little over a year. Collin had ten years under his belt, just like Matt.

"Don't worry about Collin," Matt threw in, reading her mind. "Collin isn't going to be available to take over the creative department. He'll be going with me to the front office with an impressive executive assistant title."

Annie looked at Collin.

Collin looked back.

She was sure they were both thinking the same thing. All three of their salaries would basically double, without even figuring in the perks. Joe Video's success would be a win-win situation for all three of them.

She needed to move.

She needed a few minutes to take it all in.

Pushing back from the table, Annie rose to her feet and started pacing around the sunporch. She knew Matt and Collin were both waiting patiently for her response. Matt maybe not as patiently as Collin, since Annie knew Collin could care less about the money. An impressive title he could flaunt in front of his wealthy A-Gay Club members would be his reward.

Pace. Pace. Pace.

Think. Think. Think.

She should have been savoring this tiny bit of power she had while their futures hung in the balance, pending her decision. And maybe she would have savored the moment if she really had a decision to make. Essentially, it was a no-brainer. Being unemployed in an already sluggish economy certainly wasn't something she could risk. Nor would she ever be able to live with herself if she walked out and purposely tried to ruin Matt and Collin's chances for a big promotion.

Sales are sales are sales.

She had to get that through her thick skull.

As long as she had the opportunity to promote a serious version of Joe Video, why should she really care what idiocy Matt came up with?

Annie stopped pacing.

She walked back to where Matt was sitting, planted

both hands palms down on the wicker table, and leaned forward so close he scooted back in his chair to get her out of his space.

"I know you're the department head, Matt, but I want full control in the development of Joe Video. Script. Choosing the actor. Everything. Right down to the wording on the packaging cover."

"You've got it," Matt said without hesitation.

"And if J.B. does insist that we go through with the he-said, she-said act, I intend to match you word for word. Gloves off. No holding back."

"Ditto," Matt said with a challenging grin. "Anything else?"

Annie stood up. "Yeah. I guess a situation like this one is where that line 'all's fair in love and war' comes from."

"And which would this be, kiddies?" Collin spoke up. "Love? Or war?"

Annie and Matt both sent their host a kiss-off look.

Collin closed his laptop and looked down at his watch. "Okay, children. It's nine p.m. You can stay here all night and keep working on the development schedule. But *I* have a nightlife reputation to uphold."

He looked over at Annie, who was curled up on the opposite end of his new chofa, and grinned. "Remember that pilot I told you about? The one I know has a crush on me, but is playing hard-to-get? Swedish. Tall, blond, and —"

"Whoa!" Matt protested. "Way more information than I want to know."

He wasn't homophobic, but a guy had to draw the line somewhere. Besides, he knew Collin often amused himself seeing just how close to that line Matt could be pushed.

After he and Annie had settled their differences, the three of them had been working nonstop, laying down a game development schedule. They still had a few kinks to work out, but Collin was right. It was time to call it a day.

Still lying on his back on the floor of Collin's den, Matt sat up and stretched. He glanced in Annie's direction, still amazed she was being so agreeable about everything.

She was sitting on one end of Collin's newly purchased "chofa"—a cross between a chair and a sofa, made popular by the *Queer Eye* boys who had become Collin's new to-live-by idols. At the moment, she had an overstuffed pillow hugged to her chest, spoiling his view of her bare midriff. But it wasn't until she unwound her long legs from beneath her and stood up that he noticed the new addition to her right foot that Collin had mentioned when he first phoned Matt earlier that morning.

"Nice *toe*too," Matt said with an overstated smirk.

Her cheeks flushed. "Thanks."

Thanks? Was that the only rise he could get out of her? Matt wasn't sure what was going on, but knew he didn't like it. From the moment he'd arrived, Annie had been way too agreeable. And definitely too calm. Even about the television program.

It was downright scary.

Call him crazy, but he liked her much better in combat mode. At least he was safe when they were at odds with each other. It kept him from seeing Annie as anything other than the giant pain in his ass that she usually was.

"You need to drop me off at Paragon to pick up my

car," she told Collin, stepping around Matt and ignoring him completely as she headed out of the room.

"I'll drop you off," Matt called out. "It's on my way."

He'd offered only because he knew Annie would refuse. There was no way she'd agree to being alone with him. One-on-one? With the chance he might bring up the night they'd spent together? She wouldn't let that happen. He'd bet his promotion on it.

He smiled inwardly when she turned back around to look at him.

Until she said, "Great. Give me a few minutes to get my things."

Here she was. Sitting in the front seat of his Jeep Cherokee. An arms-length away from Haz-Matt. Making a painfully silent trip to get her car.

Her only consolation was that at least it was dark. Which meant Annie really couldn't ogle him. She'd had a few weak moments after brunch when they'd headed to Collin's den to work out the details of their game development schedule.

Matt had stretched out on the floor, arms above his head as he kept playing catch with a chewed-up ball, probably just to annoy Elton John, who growled every time Matt tossed his toy into the air. To say she hadn't noticed that his Muscles "R" Matt polo shirt kept riding up to expose his hard, bronzed stomach would have been a lie. Just as it would have been a lie to say her eyes hadn't repeatedly followed the trickle of black hair that disappeared into the waistband of his tight-fitting jeans.

Damn.

Who was she kidding?

Matt was make-you-drool sexy.

And make-you-a-fool dangerous, Annie reminded herself.

Just like now. Talk about feeling foolish. They were two grown adults on the verge of getting big promotions that would change their lives and further their careers. Yet they were both acting like children, too stubborn to talk about the one underlying subject that could keep them from reaching the very goal they'd both agreed to pursue.

Annie was tempted to make Matt pull over and stop the car. Then she would grab him by the shoulders, shake the living crap out of him, and scream, "Matt! We had one night of mind-blowing sex. Stop pretending we didn't. We both need to get past it."

She was actually looking for a likely place to pull over and talk when Matt broke the silence.

"I think this is a good time to talk about —"

"Thank God," Annie said before he finished his sentence.

His head jerked in her direction. "I beg your pardon?"

Annie panicked for a second. "Please tell me you didn't mean something work-related."

His eyes returned to the busy street ahead of him. "No. I meant . . . the night we spent together."

Finally. The subject was out in the open. No more pretending. No going back. They were finally going to have the conversation they'd been avoiding for over a year.

"I'm glad you brought it up," Annie said. "We need to stop pretending that night never happened. We need to talk it out and get past it. That's the only way we'll ever be able to survive working on Joe Video together."

"Get past it?" he echoed, glancing at her. "I assumed you were past it when you left without saying good-bye the next morning."

Was he for real? He knew damn well they'd been playing the you-don't-exist-for-me game for over a year now. Unlike when she'd first joined the team. Then, they'd acted like all men and women act when they're attracted to each other. They'd tossed the witty come-on comments back and forth. They'd made eye contact at every opportunity with those hidden-agenda, I-want-you-like-crazy gazes. Not to mention the shameless preening that would have put two proud peacocks to strut-your-stuff shame.

Well, forget that. She wasn't going to let Matt get away with pretending he hadn't been purposely ignoring her just as much as she'd been purposely ignoring him.

"I left without saying good-bye," Annie informed him, "to save you the trouble of giving me the boss-shouldn't-date-employees speech. Whether you'll admit it or not, I know you were relieved that I did leave while you were still asleep."

He glanced sideways again. "That's what you really expected from me? A dating protocol speech?"

"Oh, puh-leeze," Annie said. "Miss Delusional As Usual has never been *that* delusional. A boss having a personal relationship with one of his employees is never a good idea. We had one night of scrape-you-off-the-ceiling sex. Let's leave it at that and move on."

There was a hint of surprise in his voice when he said, "Scrape-you-off-the-ceiling sex? Really? That's how you'd rate it?"

Annie groaned. "What a typical male response. Forget trying to have a mature conversation here. Let's focus on the performance factor instead."

"Yeah, let's do." He glanced in her direction with a devilish grin this time. "Just curious. But what would scrape-you-off-the-ceiling sex rate on a scale of one to ten? Definitely more than a six, I'd imagine. More than a measly eight. Not exactly a —"

"Not important," Annie insisted. "I was only trying to make a point. We were attracted to each other when we first met and we acted on it. But as great as the sex was, we both had enough sense to know it could never work between us. I'm not interested in an occasional booty call. And you're not a relationship type of guy." For good measure Annie threw in, "End of story," it being Matt's all-time favorite expression.

He let out a long sigh.

"What?" Annie demanded. "Please don't insult my intelligence by trying to pretend that everything I just said isn't one hundred percent truth."

"No, everything you just said is true," he admitted. "And that's what really irks me. Why can't two consenting adults go out, have a great time together, and even enjoy great sex without automatically landing on the relationship doorstep?"

Annie turned sideways in her seat to face him. "I'm not sure I understand the question. Isn't that exactly what we did?"

He thought it over for a second. "Well, yeah. *But.* Say we'd decided to see each other again. That's the rub. That's where things would have gotten complicated with all that relationship bullcrap women like to beat a guy over the head with."

Annie clenched her teeth together. *Should I start sharpening the ax?* Lizzie Borden whispered in her ear.

"Well, I'm sorry, Matt, but yes, if we'd continued seeing each other, even for a good time and great sex, we'd still be in a relationship. A *casual* relationship, at best. But a relationship just the same. And that goes back to my original statement. *I* want more than a casual relationship. You don't."

When he didn't answer, Annie said, "You can make fun of me forever, but I seriously want a real-life Joe Video. I want to be cherished and adored. Twenty-four-seven — three-sixty-five — until death do us part."

He had the nerve to laugh. "You're kidding yourself, Annie. You'd be bored to death if some guy adored you twenty-four-seven. No conflict? No sparks? No challenge? Sounds like a pretty dull existence to me."

"You're wrong," Annie told him, relieved they were finally pulling into the Bank of America Plaza parking garage. "I'll take being bored and adored any day of the week. I've had enough conflict in the relationship department to last me a lifetime. The next time around, I'm going for Olympic relationship gold. Nothing less."

Matt swiped his employee card and drove through the parking gate when the arm lifted. Obviously sensing she was thinking about her most recent "Dumpee of the Year" bronze medal, he said, "Dave's a jerk, Annie. At least you weren't in love with him."

Annie looked in his direction. "How do you know?"

Matt pulled up beside her VW and switched off the engine. He turned to face her. "Well? Were you? In love with Dave?"

Annie sighed. "No. But I thought there might be a possibility we could eventually head down the road to love. I guess that's why the sudden detour took me by such surprise."

Matt actually sent her a sympathetic look. "Look on the bright side. Dave's detour gave you the brainstorm for Joe Video. You have nowhere to go but up. Career-wise, anyway."

They kept staring at each other, the lights from the parking garage allowing Annie to see the sincere expression on his face. The fact that he was actually trying to comfort her made Annie realize how little she really knew about Matt. Other than what Collin had told her, that is.

She found herself asking, "And what about you, Matt? Aside from your career? Don't you ever see yourself married someday? Kids? A house in the suburbs?"

He grinned. "I won't say *never*. But I have three older brothers. All of them are married with children. Not one of them fails to tell me on a regular basis that I need to hold on to my single life as long as possible."

Annie smiled back. "Collin has a theory, you know, about what he calls your relationship procrastination."

"Collin has a theory about everything," Matt said. "But I'm game. Let's hear it."

"You're holding out because you've already had the all-American family. The football coach dad, proud of his four strapping all-male sons. The Betty Crocker mom, who doted on all of you completely. You grew up in a secure and loving environment. That's why you don't feel the pressure to hurry and find someone to share your life. You have no reason to believe you won't have that same all-American dream when you do decide to settle down."

His look was thoughtful. "As opposed to you and Collin, you mean? Who didn't grow up in an all-American family?"

Annie nodded. "You have to admit it makes sense. Collin's father died when he was five, and he grew up being cared for by a string of nannies while his mother jet-setted here and there. Knowing Collin as we both do,

I'm sure he's already told you about my incredibly dysfunctional family tree."

His rather embarrassed expression told Annie her assumption was correct.

He was tactful enough to say, "I know your mother is a prominent civil liberties attorney here in Atlanta. And that she's a bit of a feminist."

Annie laughed. "That's a nice way of putting it, Matt. But praying to a Gloria Steinem icon on a daily basis makes my mother more than just a *bit* of a feminist."

If he knew about her mother, that meant Collin couldn't have kept himself from telling Matt about her father. About the man who had been much older than her twenty-two-year-old campus activist mother. An esteemed professor of philosophy at Cornell University. Sixty-four years old, to be exact. Who'd had a massive heart attack at a nuclear energy protest and left the starry-eyed-in-love-with-her-professor Beverly Sue Long both unmarried and pregnant with a daughter who had been nothing but a big disappointment to her. Mainly, Annie knew, because Annie refused to live by her mother and Gloria Steinem's famous motto: A woman needs a man like a fish needs a bicycle.

When Matt squirmed slightly in his seat, Annie suspected he feared she *would* bring up the uncomfortable subject of the man who'd unintentionally but ultimately made her a bastard. She decided to let him off the hook.

"Let's go back to the original subject about the differences between you and me when it comes to relationships," Annie said. "You're anti-relationship for now, so you think my quest to be cherished and adored is dull and boring. I'm pro-relationship, so I think your single-guy life sounds dreadfully sad and extremely *lonely*."

"That's where you're wrong," Matt said and winked. "I'm seldom ever lonely. If you get my drift."

There. That was the Matt she knew. The cocky, self-assured I-love-being-a-player Matt. It was safer, Annie decided, if she didn't try to scratch beneath the surface, didn't try to uncover another side of Matt. Let him be satisfied with a lifetime of one-night stands. What did she care? Her first new order of business in the relationship department was going to be installing a frog-proof filter for her dating pool. And a guy like Matt would be bounced out of the pond before he could charm her with his first throaty suck-you-in ribbet.

"Well," Annie said, hoping he would take the hint.

He did. "Yeah," he said, looking down at his watch. "It's getting late. We'd both better get going."

Implying what? That he had some hot overnight date? *Well, to hell with him.* She couldn't care less.

He was out of the Jeep and opening her passenger-side door before Annie had time to prepare herself for his hand on her arm as he helped her step down from the Jeep. When he released her, he closed the door. Though she truly wished he hadn't, he started walking with her across the short space to her VW bug.

He propped up against her convertible, his elbow resting on the ragtop roof, and the cocky grin on his face reminding Annie why she should be thankful they'd both agreed they had no future together.

"Think a new car might be in your future when you get your promotion?" he teased. "Department head image? All that."

Annie purposely glanced over at his Jeep. "Upgrade to the current department head's Jeep? Thanks but no thanks. I'll stick with my punch buggy."

He laughed. "I was only kidding, Annie. Your purple punch buggy suits you."

Annie raised an eyebrow. "I'm going to take that as a compliment."

He grinned. "I meant it as a compliment. I have a classic car myself. I wouldn't part with it for anything."

Referring, of course, to his babe-magnet Corvette.

Ribbet. Ribbet. Ribbet.

She needed to get out of Haz-Matt's deadly range.

Fast.

"Thanks for the ride," Annie said. They were, after all, alone in the depths of the parking garage, nothing to keep her from turning toward him if he gave her any inclination that he might want —

God. Wrap this up and do it quickly.

"I'm glad we cleared the air about everything," she said, never once looking up at him as she fumbled through her purse for her keys.

He drummed his fingers on the top of her car. "Yeah, me too," he said, obviously reflecting back over the conversation himself. "You were right. It was time we talked everything out. We'll work much better together as teammates. I mean, now that we don't have any personal . . ." He paused for a second. "What is Collin's favorite word? *Issues?*"

Annie only nodded, still afraid to look directly at him. She unlocked her car door and tossed her purse and the bag with her dirty clothing in the back. She was only one second away from sliding behind the wheel to safety when Matt said, "Annie."

She tensed. But she forced herself to look at him. He was way too close for comfort. She could smell the heady scent of his cologne. Even feel the heat from his body.

Almost taste his lips against hers. Her brain was terrified he would tell her to call him if she changed her mind about an occasional booty call. And her heart was terrified that he wouldn't.

"I just want you to remember one thing," he said, his eyes searching her face.

Annie held her breath.

"If we do put on the gloves in front of the TV cameras, remember it's just business. Nothing personal."

"Nothing personal," Annie repeated.

She was still repeating those two cold and hopelessly impersonal words to herself as Matt followed closely behind her out of the parking garage.

CHAPTER 6

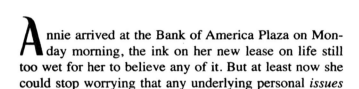

Annie arrived at the Bank of America Plaza on Monday morning, the ink on her new lease on life still too wet for her to believe any of it. But at least now she could stop worrying that any underlying personal *issues* she had with Mr. Nothing Personal would keep them from achieving their goal.

Once they did achieve their goal, she'd be rid of Matt anyway. Except for one of those occasional nods in the hallway maybe, and a monthly production meeting.

End of *that* story.

But thankfully, the beginning of a new one.

She'd already decided she would give up her postage-stamp-size loft apartment. Scale up to something maybe not that much larger, but classy. In a singles complex this time. With neighbors she'd actually want to spend time with. A complex that would have all of the amenities anyone could ask for. A twenty-four-hour fitness center. A killer clubroom. Indoor and outdoor pools.

No more sitting around the pool war zone at her current building while the Carson twins, Joey and Johnny, tried to outsplash each other in a cannonball competition. No more emergency lifeguard duty because elderly Mrs. Simpson tottered too close to the edge of the pool and instantly sank to the bottom because she wouldn't let go of her walker.

Maybe she *would* buy herself a new car.

Or not.

The thought of giving up her signature VW bug quickly pushed that idea to the back of her mind. She *loved* that car. Ridiculous purple paint and all. It was paid for. It was in perfect running order. You didn't have to take out a loan for a trip to the gas pump.

No, I'm not giving up my purple punch buggy, no matter how much money I make.

She would travel instead. Take one of those singles cruises. She was footloose and fancy-free again, wasn't she? She'd even send loser Dave a postcard from some romantic tropical island — Having a great time. *Glad* you're not here!

Annie was still smiling over the possible postcard opportunity when she walked into Paragon's reception area. Kathy stood up from behind her desk the second she saw her walk through the door. By the time Annie reached her desk, Kathy had her in a bear hug.

"I'm so proud of you, Annie," Kathy gushed. "You'll be the first woman ever to head up the creative department at Paragon."

Annie frowned when Kathy let her go. "I see Collin has already made his rounds this morning."

Kathy grinned. "What gave you that idea?"

"I wish I could say I'm as optimistic as our company cub reporter," Annie said with a sigh. "A lot could still go wrong with the entire project."

"Don't talk like that," Kathy said. "You have to think positive. And you're certainly dressed for success again today. Makeup and all."

Annie frowned. "Did I really look that horrible on a daily basis?"

"No, of course, not," Kathy said. "I'm just saying you're smart to move a step up on the office appearance ladder, Annie. J.B. has his eye on you now. And believe me, that man doesn't miss anything."

"Thanks for the warning."

Kathy nodded and looked her up and down again. "That navy suit really does look good on you. The skirt is short enough to show off your legs. And that orange blouse really perks. It's bold. Fresh. A perfect department head fashion statement, if you ask me."

"Yeah. Orange is in, in, in," Annie mumbled, then tossed her hand in the air and headed down the hallway to her office.

Dammit, she decided. Collin's daily gossip report needed to stop. She was just the person to see that it did. However, when she walked into their office and found Collin bustling around the room watering his plants, all she could think about was what a close friend he really was to her.

He smiled when he looked up and saw her. "Good morning, sunshine."

Annie walked directly to him and gave him a big hug. "You didn't tell me you took time to rid my apartment of any sign of Dave's homecoming when you went to pick up my clothes. But thank you, Collin. I don't think I could have faced going home to that reminder, even on Saturday."

He hugged her back. "No problem. You'll be happy to know I found a good Swedish home for the robe. And I put your black teddy in your bottom bureau drawer for future use."

Annie pushed away from him. "Get out! About the robe, I mean. I thought you said the pilot ignored you every time you got around him."

Collin batted his eyelashes dramatically and placed the watering can on his desk. "He did always ignore me," he said, hitching a hip to sit on the corner of his desk. "Until I showed up at Backstreet with Trey Saturday night."

"Trey? As in William's gorgeous partner Trey?"

Collin nodded. "But Lars didn't know Trey and I were just good friends. He was livid. Practically threw me over his shoulder and carried me off the dance floor." Collin grinned. "Take notes, lovey. There's nothing like the green-eyed monster to bring out the beast in a man."

"Just please tell me this guy's name really isn't Lars."

"Ya. It is Lars. Lars Svenson."

Annie laughed. "If you were trying for a passable Swedish accent, you're going to need a lot of practice."

"Oh, I plan to spend plenty of time practicing with Lars," Collin teased. He reached out and took her hand when he added, "But I'm serious, Annie. I really, really, really like this guy. Really."

Annie squeezed his hand. "Just be careful, okay? Proceed with caution. Safeguard your heart from the very beginning."

"Get my own hidden-heart toetoo?"

Annie shook her finger at him. "My toetoo is nobody's business, Collin Adair. That means running your mouth about it here at the office or anywhere else is strictly off-limits. Got it?"

Collin's hand flew to his mouth. "Oops," he said. "Too late."

*   *   *

Matt looked to the left, then to the right. When he was sure he didn't see a single soul he knew, he ducked into Latte Land.

The line of people waiting, however, was long enough that his mind wandered back to the air-clearing discussion he'd had with Annie on Saturday night.

The fact that occasional scrape-you-off-the-ceiling sex wasn't going to be in their future was actually a relief. It was best if they did keep their relationship platonic and businesslike. Annie had told him herself she was going for Olympic relationship gold. He wasn't even ready to try out for the qualifying team.

But he'd thought about her the entire time he worked on his short game at his favorite golf course Sunday morning. And about Collin's know-it-all theory. Could it really be that simple? Was the reason Collin and Annie were both so adamant about their personal relationship hunt merely some subconscious yearning to belong?

Collin had told him all about Annie's famous father who died before he could marry Annie's mother and before Annie was born. Tough break for any kid.

He tried to imagine life without both of his own parents and he couldn't. They'd both always been such a big part of his life. He always called and checked on his folks every Sunday. Last night, his mom had asked him the same question she asked him every Sunday: "When are you going to bring a nice girl home for us to meet, Matt?"

Funny, but this time when his mom asked that question, he thought of Annie. Maybe because Annie was exactly the type of woman he *would* want when the time came for him to settle down. She was smart, had a terrific sense of humor, and was gorgeous, of course. But something more. Annie had the uncanny ability to make him wonder — briefly — if maybe he *was* cheating himself by holding on to his single-guy life.

Briefly being the key word in that train of thought.

Besides, Annie wanted a lapdog kind of guy who would follow her around like a lovesick puppy. Adoring her twenty-four-seven, didn't she say? Well, sorry, but he wasn't the guy for the job.

However, they needed to be friends to work well as teammates. That was the reason he was standing uncomfortably in line at Latte Land now — Annie and Collin's favorite new get-me-started-in-the-morning pit stop.

He frowned, thinking how Collin had died laughing when he'd called Collin earlier to say Latte Land would be his treat today. Matt had finally hung up on him. Now he understood why Collin had thought his stopping by Latte Land was so damn funny. This was not a place he planned to be caught in again, team player or not.

When he left Latte Land, Matt was still praying no one he knew would see him. He walked quickly toward the nearest group of elevators with a latte in each hand.

But wait a minute.

As he got closer, Matt realized there were three extremely pretty women waiting in front of the elevator, all literally beaming in his direction. Matt squared his shoulders and sent them his best *how-you-doin'* smile.

Man, oh, man.

How lucky could a guy get?

Standing right in front of him were a blonde, a brunette *and* a redhead. All in the same group. What were the odds of that happening?

If this was the type of reaction he got by being brave enough to stroll through the lobby of the Bank of America Plaza with a latte in each hand, maybe getting in touch with his feminine side wasn't such a bad idea.

"Good morning, ladies," Matt was about to say when it registered that they were looking *past* him. Not *at* him. In fact, all three of the incredibly gorgeous women ignored him completely when he walked up and stopped beside them in front of the elevator.

Out of curiosity, he craned his neck around, looking for the source. He found it when the tall blonde said, "Now that's the type of man women fantasize about."

Matt frowned. The guy was tall, dressed fit to kill, and had his jet black hair slicked back and bound in a Steven Segal queue at the nape of his neck. He was okay-looking except for the hair, Matt supposed, not that he was accustomed to checking out other guys. But the type of man women fantasize about?

Matt frowned again.

He'd heard that expression all too recently from Annie during their infamous production meeting.

Jeez.

Was he imagining it? Or did all three of the women actually sigh when the guy smiled back at them? Luckily the guy had the good sense to keep walking farther down the corridor to another elevator. The way these women were acting, the poor dude never would have made it out alive if he'd gotten into the elevator with them.

"I bet he's famous," the brunette gushed.

"If he isn't, he should be," the redhead said.

Give me a f-ing break, Matt felt like saying. But when the bell dinged and the elevator doors slid open, Matt offered another bright smile and said instead, "After you, ladies."

They didn't even look in his direction.

The blonde motioned to the brunette, who grabbed the redhead's arm. In a flash, all three women headed off to where the guy was still standing, saliva practically dripping from their skillfully painted lips.

"Women," Matt mumbled and barely made it through the elevator doors with only an inch to spare before the doors closed behind him.

He poked the button for the thirty-second floor with his elbow, then stepped to the back of the elevator. Not only was it the first time he'd ridden up to the thirty-second floor carrying two foo-foo lattes, but it was also the first time he could ever remember riding in any Bank of America Plaza elevator alone.

"Women," he mumbled aloud again.

But he wondered in spite of himself if the blonde, the brunette, and the redhead were acting out their fantasies three elevator cars away.

When Matt walked into the creative department, a Latte Land cup in each hand, Collin looked at Annie and held out his hand.

"If I hadn't seen it with my own eyes, I never would have believed it," Annie said. She grabbed a ten-dollar bill lying on the top of her desk and slapped it into Collin's upturned palm.

"I'm the one who should be paid," Matt grumbled. "For the dignity I lost going into that place." He handed over a cup to each of them.

He was ready to launch into a rant when Kathy appeared in the doorway of their office, all aflutter.

"There's a guy up front claiming he has an appointment with you, Annie." Her puzzled look drew her eyebrows together in a straight line. "I didn't know what to tell him. When did *you* start taking appointments?"

Good question, Matt thought.

"The bartender," Annie and Collin said at the same time.

"What bartender?" Matt asked.

They both looked in his direction.

"The bartender Annie met at the salsa bar on Friday night. She wants him to be Joe Video," Collin said, as if that made perfect sense.

Matt frowned and looked at Annie. "How much tequila did you drink Friday night?"

Annie said, "I never dreamed the guy would take me seriously, Matt. Honest."

Matt glanced at Collin again. Now Collin looked confused. "I take it you don't agree with Annie's statement?"

Collin grimaced. "Sorry, Annie, but you *were* pretty convincing. You even had the whole bar cheering because you assured the bartender you were going to make him a huge video game star."

Matt shook his head and looked at Annie. "A bartender turned video game star. Another one of your *fab* concepts, I suppose."

"Oh stop it. Both of you," Annie said. "You've heard of a Kodak moment? Well, I had a tequila moment. What do you want me to do? Call the hasty inebriated decision police and turn myself in?"

"What I want you to do is get rid of the guy," Matt said a little too sharply. "There's too much at stake to drag a bartender in off the street and expect him to double as a professional actor."

Her buzz-off look told Matt he should have been more tactful.

She pointed her finger at him. "We made an agreement. You agreed I had full control when it came to the development of the game. Even choosing the actor to play Joe Video."

"*Actor*, Annie. Not some bartender," Matt reminded her.

"Guys," Kathy pleaded. "Would you please stop arguing and tell me what I'm supposed to do? I need to get back to the front desk."

"Send him in, Kathy," Annie said, tossing Matt a look that challenged him to say differently.

"Yes, Kathy, by all means send the bartender in," Matt said. "Lucy here has some 'splainin' to do to her bartender about the tequila moment she had last Friday night."

When Kathy hurried off, Matt walked over to his desk and dropped down onto his chair. "What?" he said when Annie and Collin both kept glaring at him.

"Let me handle this," Annie said, her hands on her hips now. "This is my mistake and I'll correct it."

"My lips are zipped." He made the motion with his fingers across his mouth.

"Keep it that way," Annie told him.

When the bartender walked into the room a few seconds later, Matt was glad no one expected him to utter a single word.

He couldn't have.

He'd been shocked into silence.

Annie's bartender was the guy from the lobby.

*   *   *

"Holy guacamole," Collin muttered loud enough for Annie to send him a stern look.

But Collin's reaction to the tall, dark, and handsome man walking toward her was dead-on. The last thing this man looked like was a bartender. He was one wicked hot hunk with all the Armani and Gucci trimmings.

Thank you, José Cuervo!

Hasty inebriated decision or not, Annie knew she'd made the right one.

"Good morning," she said, extending her hand as her brain scrambled around trying to come up with his name.

He saved her the embarrassment. "Enrique Romero at your service. As you requested."

He took her hand and touched it lightly to his lips, the smoldering look in his chocolate brown eyes telling her he was at her service for anything she had in mind. Which would be nothing more than a contract to star in her video game. Annie made that decision the split second he kissed her hand.

Either this guy was trying to prove he really could act, or he'd spent too much time watching the I-can-be-suave bachelors on reality TV. Either way, the kiss on the hand was too clichéd for Annie to take seriously.

"Thank you for coming, Enrique," Annie said, easing her hand out of his grip.

"Call me Rico. Please."

His sexy Cuban accent reminded her how perfect he would be for Joe Video. But gorgeous as he was, he was still *so* not her type.

She knew it was crazy, but the minute she met a guy, the boink factor kicked in and automatically filed him in one of three categories. Boinkable. Possibly boinkable. Not in a million years boinkable.

Looks weren't the only thing her quirky brain took into consideration when making this decision. It could be attitude. Hairline. Fingernails. Even something as ridiculous as hand kissing. *Or—* his name.

Shallow?

Extremely.

But even if he hadn't kissed her hand, Annie tried to imagine her extremely shallow self, her head thrown back in ecstasy, moaning, "Give it to me, Rico. Give it to me!" She just couldn't do it.

She couldn't.

"Rico," Annie said, as he took his place in her never-in-a-million-years-boinkable file, "you've already met my associate, Collin Adair, I believe."

Collin stepped forward and offered his hand slightly too high for a customary handshake. He looked disappointed when Rico managed to shake it anyway.

"And," Annie said, motioning toward Matt. "This is our department head, Matt Abbington. Matt will also be working on the video game with us."

Annie noticed the muscle in Matt's jaw jump at the "us" part. He'd have to get over it. She would never find a man more perfect for Joe Video than the one standing beside her.

To her relief, Matt walked over to give Rico what appeared to be an amicable handshake.

And what a sight that was.

Two incredibly sexy men. Standing eye to eye and toe to toe. *But uh-oh.* From the looks of things, they were also sizing each other up. The vibes bouncing around the room weren't exactly friendly.

"Collin," Annie said, alarmed at the hint of hostility already brewing between Matt and her new protégé. "Will you please check with Kathy and see if the board-room is available? We'll be more comfortable if we can sit down and explain to Rico exactly what we have in mind for the video game we're developing."

Good. Her request had broken up the macho standoff. At least for the moment. Unfortunately, Rico was now practically undressing her with an appraising look.

"The boardroom is free and clear," Collin announced.

But Matt said, "Collin, why don't you escort Mr. Romero to the boardroom? I need a few minutes alone with Annie before we join you."

Are all men annoying? Annie thought. She braced herself for Matt's outburst. It arrived the second Collin ushered her unexpected guest out of the room.

"Why are you wasting this guy's time?" Matt demanded. "Not to mention ours?"

"I'm not wasting anyone's time, Matt," Annie said. "I admit I never expected the guy to take me seriously, but now that I've seen him again, I know he's right for the part."

Matt shook his head. "What happened to your idea of calling that old boyfriend filmmaker of yours and seeing if he knew any struggling male actors who might be interested in playing Joe Video?"

Annie refused to be intimidated. "There's no reason to call Dan now. Rico has the look, Matt. That's what it's going to take to sell this game. I'm positive he'll be perfect for the Joe Video role."

"Oh come on, Annie." His face was beginning to turn a tad red. "Even if you do like his looks, the guy's a fake.

The hair? The hand kissing? *And* the fake goo-goo eyes? You can't be serious."

Aw. Did the big bad hunk let some air out of your overinflated ego?

"I thought the hand kissing was touching," Annie lied. "And terribly romantic."

Matt's face turned deep blood-red at that comment.

Oh, what fun she was having watching Matt squirm. A mental payback for his dismissive "nothing personal" comment? *Probably.* But still, having a little fun at his expense was something she just couldn't pass up.

He ran his hand through his short dark hair and shook his head. "Whatever. Just don't expect me not to say I told you so when this whole thing blows up in your face."

Annie said, "Deal," and she stuck her hand under his nose in the perfect position to be kissed.

"Not funny," Matt said.

He pushed her hand away and he definitely didn't kiss it.

Matt had already decided he didn't like the guy, but he couldn't help but feel sorry for him when they arrived in the boardroom to find Collin babbling about the only *correct* way to make an absolute perfect martini. His compassion evaporated, however, when Chico, or whatever the hell his name was, ignored him completely and immediately sent Annie the same kind of smile that made the women in the lobby sigh.

Matt almost laughed at the dramatics until the bartender pulled another dirty chivalrous trick and pulled out the chair next to his, waiting dutifully for Annie to seat herself.

Which she happily did.

Yes, dammit, with an adoring little sigh of her own.

Okay. He'd admit it. He didn't run around kissing Annie's hand and pulling out her chair. But he also hadn't seen even the slightest spark of personal interest in Annie's eyes when she looked at this guy. The type of spark that sometimes appeared — if only for a second — when he and Annie were in one of their usual face-off squabbles.

Or?

Did I just miss it?

He pulled out a chair across the table from Annie and her new admirer, and he did so on purpose. He could scrutinize the interaction between the two of them more closely from this position. Study their body language. See if Annie's interest in this guy was merely business, the way it needed to be with all of their careers at stake.

But he really should give Annie more credit than that. Despite her claim that she wanted to be cherished and adored, she would never fall for a cheesy guy like this one.

Would she?

She needed to be focusing on the video game, not some hand-licking Romeo. This was definitely not the time for Annie to get suckered in by another worthless jerk. Not now. Not with so much at stake.

Matt tuned in to the conversation in time to hear Annie say, "You definitely have the look we want, Rico. Unfortunately, it will be next week before I can give you the exact figure for the monetary compensation you would receive if you decide to take the position."

She paused for a second. "But can I be candid?"

The guy nodded.

"I'll tell you up front that the sum will be a modest one. I wanted you to know that in case money is a big factor in your decision."

Matt expected him to sprint for the door at that remark. Instead he leaned back in his chair and sent Annie a slow, come-on smile. "The money. It is not important."

Yeah, sure it isn't, Matt thought. Yup, Annie would see right through that blatant lie.

"But the publicity?" The jerk smiled. "It is my business that will benefit. This is what I am hoping."

This is what I am hoping, Matt fumed — *that Annie will see through your bullshit act and find someone qualified for the job!*

Unfortunately, the approving look on Annie's face told Matt that wasn't likely to happen.

"Wonderful," she said. "Then I guess we'll get back to you the first of next week, Rico."

She stood up.

So did Matt, along with Collin and Mr. Queue.

And when she held her hand out, Matt's mind kept chanting, *Kiss it, kiss it, kiss it.* Annie might have thought one hand kiss was touching, but a second was bound to break the spell.

He frowned when Mr. Marvelous only folded Annie's hand in both of his for what he was sure Miss Isn't-He-Romantic would think was a freaking *touching* squeeze. "Until next week, Annie."

Except his pronunciation of her name came out "Ah-nee."

"Let me walk you out," Ah-nee literally bubbled, and Matt frowned again.

"Gentlemen," he said with a dismissive nod, first to Collin, last to Matt.

The second the happy couple waltzed out of the boardroom, Collin sighed dramatically. "Be still my beating heart."

"Don't make me puke," Matt said.

"What?" Collin asked innocently.

"The guy's as fake as his martial arts ponytail. Not interested in the money? Right. He's a bartender, for Christ's sake."

"No. He's the bar *owner*," Collin corrected. "And he's obviously smart enough to realize how much free publicity his club will get with the game." Collin paused. "But what's really going on with you, Matt? If I didn't know better, I'd think you were jealous."

"Jealous?" Matt thundered. "Of what?"

"You tell me," Collin said with an inquiring smirk.

"There's nothing to tell," Matt said.

But he walked out of the boardroom before his see-all, hear-all, and tell-all best friend could probe any further.

Rico stole a sideways glance at the woman he'd come to conquer as they walked side by side down the long hallway. He was going to have his work cut out for him. Of that, he was certain. He'd known it within minutes of walking into her office.

He was, after all, a master in the study of human behavior. His position behind his family's bar had been invaluable in that respect. He'd spent most of his life watching people. Watching people and determining who they really were and what they were really all about.

This Matt, he knew, would be his enemy. A past with Annie? Most likely. But to Rico it did not matter. The past was in the past. And Rico intended for Annie's future to be all about him. At least until she introduced him to the right people.

That will be the hard part.

Winning Annie over.

He'd seen the new breed of American women like Annie come and go at the Cabaña Club. All polished and successful on the outside, yet sadly jaded on the inside. Women who had given up. Women who had accepted the fact that romance was dead, that passion was fleeting, and that the best they could hope for in life was a lifetime of being ignored by a career-focused husband with a fat portfolio.

Wasn't Annie's obvious desire for romance, even on a video game, not proof of this?

He'd seen the surprise in her eyes the second he'd kissed her hand. That he'd caught her off guard with such a simple romantic gesture amused him. But when her body language told him she doubted his sincerity, Rico had known exactly what his strategy was going to be.

He would bombard her with grand gestures. Show her romance was indeed still vibrantly alive even in such a fast-paced world. He would break down her wall of defenses by being exactly the type of man she had outlined in her video. A real-life fantasy man. A man who would fulfill each and every one of her little-girl dreams.

With that thought in mind, Rico turned to Annie when they reached the elevator, brought her hand to his lips, and gently kissed it again. "A pity," he said, holding her gaze, "that romantic customs such as this one are no longer common. Sí?"

She blushed slightly and quickly pulled her hand away. "Yes. It is a pity."

Rico chuckled. "Forgive me, please, if I embarrass you. It is not my intention. I am just, as they say, anticuado. Old-fashioned. It is something I cannot help. Something I feel here," he said, touching the place over his heart.

Much better, Rico decided when his comments left her at an obvious loss for words. He took one of the Cabaña Club business cards from his inside jacket pocket and handed it to her. "I have written my cell phone number on the back. It is best if you reach me at that number."

She nodded. Before she had time to say anything else, the elevator doors opened and Rico quickly stepped inside the elevator car.

He smiled inwardly, knowing she hadn't missed the approving looks several women in the elevator were already giving him.

She held her hand up to her ear, her pinkie and her thumb sticking out from the fingers curled into her palm, indicating she would call him.

Rico nodded politely.

But being the skillful master of human behavior that he was, he purposely waited until the elevator doors almost closed completely. And then Rico smiled — so that the last thing Annie would remember was the final charming smile he'd reserved only for her.

Annie remained standing in front of the elevator for a second, trying to wrap her brain around the interaction that had just taken place.

She couldn't.

Not completely.

But the ick factor where Rico was concerned was fading. *Fast*. Especially after his line about lost romantic customs. Could this guy be for real? Aside from being just about the hottest guy she'd ever laid eyes on, was he really as sensitive and sincere as he pretended?

She turned and walked back down the hallway, reminding herself that any interest she had in him had to remain business-oriented. *Period*. Getting involved with Rico personally wasn't an option even if he'd had a first name that *did* fit into her head-thrown-back-in-ecstasy scenario.

But her gut feeling also told her with this undeniable hunk in front of the camera, her promotion was guaranteed to be signed, sealed, and delivered. That was her goal. Getting her promotion.

My only goal.

She smiled. She'd seen how every woman on the elevator practically stopped breathing the second Rico stepped into the car with them. Yes, Rico's mesmerizing hold-your-attention goo-goo eyes, as Matt had called them, were going to translate perfectly through the eyes of the camera. Unfortunately, remembering she still had to deal with Matt wiped the smile right off her face.

Maybe she should try and appease Matt. Just this once. If for nothing else but the sake of their agreement to work together as teammates. Would it really hurt her to find a few real actors to also interview for the role? Wouldn't that be the type of wise business decision a responsible department head would make?

That's what Annie was thinking when she walked back into Paragon's reception area.

Until Kathy said, "Talk about one hot gorgeous specimen of manhood!" She fanned her face, then looked back over her shoulder. "I didn't want to say anything in front of Collin. You know how he is. It would be all over the office that I practically wet my pants just looking at the guy." She looked back over her shoulder again. "But seriously, Annie. If that's the guy who's going to play your Joe Video, I want to place my order *now*."

"That's the guy."

There.

She'd said it.

Forget appeasing Matt.

Her decision was final.

CHAPTER 7

"Y our bouquet del día, señorita," Collin said as he placed a vase filled with a freshly cut flower arrangement on the corner of her desk. "Just as they have been delivered every workday for how long now? The last three weeks?"

"Long enough that this office is starting to look like a damn funeral parlor," Matt grumbled, being his usual wise-ass self.

Annie sent Matt a look that said a funeral parlor could be his next stop.

"Shall I read today's card?" Collin plucked the card from the card holder before Annie could snatch it away from him. "Fairy tales can come true. Dine with me tonight and let me prove it. Love, Rico."

Collin sighed wistfully. "Now this is what I call a romantic man."

Annie wasn't so enthused.

Her bouquet of the day was becoming annoying.

In fact, had she known hiring Rico would make her the immediate object of his obsession, she might not have made such a hasty decision. Especially since most of the buzz Rico had been creating around Paragon for the last three weeks had nothing to do with his role as Joe Video.

His ardent pursuit had her coworkers whispering behind their hands and behind *her* back. *Not* what she needed while she was trying to prove she was a smart, professional businesswoman deserving of a big promotion.

She'd hoped to nip his daily flower delivery in the bud (pardon the pun) the day he'd returned to Paragon for a photo shoot and to sign his contract. She'd taken Rico to lunch. And she'd told him up front that business was her *only* interest where he was concerned.

He'd responded by sending her a slow, playful smile and saying, "I am glad business is your only interest, Annie. Because I intend to become your business."

Dammit.

How did a woman respond to an answer like that one?

Especially considering her overall state of mind. In the short span of a few weeks, she'd been dumped, almost fired, promised a big promotion, and now she was being pursued by the same Cuban hottie she'd proclaimed herself as every woman's frickin' fantasy.

Overwhelming?

Flattering?

Wickedly confusing?

All of the above.

In particular the confusing part. She'd been telling herself her entire life that all she needed to make her existence complete was an adoring man. She hadn't even dared to hope for a sexy, too-gorgeous-to-be-true, romantic type of man like Rico. Yet Annie felt like a little kid finding out there wasn't any Santa Claus. Her lifelong belief in if-only-he-adored-me was threatening to be shattered. Worse yet, Matt's hateful adored and bored theory was staring her directly in the face.

But it wasn't so much about Matt possibly being right

as it was about her possibly being so wrong. Now that this gorgeous, sexy, and adoring man had finally come along, why couldn't she enjoy the lavish attention? Better yet, why wasn't she jumping at the chance to see where a relationship with a hunk like Rico might really take her?

It didn't help matters that Collin kept chastising her on a daily basis. "What more could you ask for in a guy?" he kept insisting. "It's obvious Rico's crazy about you, Annie. He never even looks at another woman."

That part is true.

In addition to the daily flower delivery, Rico had managed to materialize at her office almost every day to take her to lunch. One of the drawbacks, she guessed, of being pursued by a man whose days were free since he worked at his family-owned bar at night.

It hadn't surprised her that regardless of where they went for lunch, female heads always turned. Many women didn't even try to pretend they weren't giving Rico the eye with Annie sitting right beside him. What had surprised her was that never once had Rico given Annie any indication that he had eyes for anyone but her.

Whatever.

He'd also boldly said he would not be discouraged. That he wanted more intimate time with her than just lunch. She'd been successful stalling him so far, but she could sense he was growing impatient.

Did she risk pissing Rico off when they were only days away from filming Joe Video? Or should she give in and at least go to dinner with him — for the sake of the team?

"Rico is on line one for you, Annie," Kathy announced over the intercom.

Damn. Thinking about him scared him up.
This time Annie did sigh dramatically.

"Oh stop it," Collin scolded as usual. "Would you give the poor guy a break? Let him take you to dinner. Then take him back to your place. Have wild uninhibited monkey sex with the man. And see where you go from there."

Annie's eyes locked with Matt's for a moment. They both knew exactly where you went from wild uninhibited monkey sex. Directly to "nothing personal."

Matt was still holding her gaze when he said, "Don't you get it, Collin? Annie's already bored to death with this guy."

Annie felt her hackles rise. "That is *so* not true. I just don't think dating Rico is the professional thing to do while I'm being considered for a possible promotion."

"Well, I disagree," Collin said. "We've already decided Rico will be saying his lines directly to you when we start filming next week. I say give the guy a good reason to stare longingly at you."

Annie sent Collin a mean look. "Well, thank you for sharing your opinion, Mr. Suddenly Turned Pimp."

Matt quickly chimed in. "I don't see why anyone would have a problem with you dating Rico." He flashed Annie a grin that said he knew she was lying through her teeth about her reason for not dating Rico. "Rico isn't an employee here at Paragon." He paused for a second. "Come to think of it, what would you call him? A freelance bartender? Or a freelance wanna-be actor?"

Annie grabbed the phone and jabbed the button. "Hello," she said, more sharply than she'd intended.

"I have caught you at a bad time. Sí?"

Annie swiveled around in her chair, turning her back on her tormenters. "Not a bad time," she said, "just busy."

"All work and no play can make for a sad soul," Rico said with a husky chuckle. "Which is why you should come out and play with me. But not for lunch, Annie. Tonight. For dinner. Not a fancy place, but quaint. A place I know where we can sip wine and gaze at the stars together."

At the moment, sipping wine and stargazing sounds pretty damn good, Annie thought. Wild monkey sex didn't sound so bad, either. "I'd love to have dinner with you, Rico," she said before she changed her mind.

There was a long pause. "You are serious?"

"Completely," Annie assured him. She gave Rico her address and finished with, "I'll see you at seven."

When Annie turned back around Collin brought his hands together for four loud, measured claps. "Thank God," he said. "I was beginning to think something was seriously wrong with you." He walked over and gave her a quick hug. "Good to have you back amongst the happy, horny, and hopeful, lovey."

Annie didn't bother to tell Collin that "lovey" was anything *but* happy with herself at the moment. Rico was a nice guy. A really nice guy. And he didn't deserve her agreeing to dinner mainly because Matt had provoked her into accepting the invitation.

How was it, exactly, that Matt always managed to have her number?

But maybe it was a good thing Matt had goaded her into accepting the date, Annie kept thinking. Maybe over dinner she could convince Rico to at least stop with the daily flower delivery. And if she were lucky, she could also make him understand that friendship was the only thing she had to offer him.

And she did want them to become friends.

They were going to be working closely together over the next few weeks during filming. The last thing they needed was any friction between them. She had enough friction in her life already.

She automatically glanced in Matt's direction.

He had his back to her now, seemingly engrossed in his computer screen. She felt like picking up her stapler and throwing it at him.

"Where are you going for dinner?"

"Huh?" Annie wasn't even sure what Collin had asked her. She'd been too busy worrying that if Matt kept pushing her buttons, anger management classes might be in her immediate future.

Collin looked perturbed. "I asked where Rico was taking you for dinner. Ritzy and glitzy? Or normal and not formal?"

Annie shrugged. "I'm not sure. He said 'nothing fancy.'"

"Imagine that," came a reply from what was quickly becoming the endangered-species side of the room.

"Rico said the place was *quaint*," Annie said, raising her voice slightly as she glared at the back of Matt's head. "A place where we could sip wine and gaze at the stars together."

Matt mumbled something else, but Collin drowned him out with, "Ooooh, I know just the outfit."

Annie stifled a groan. Either Collin was oblivious to the hostility that surrounded him or he was used to it.

"Wear those cute royal blue capri pants," Collin said. "Wear them with that vamp cowl-neck chartreuse top. And remember that multicolored glass-beaded belt you bought on our last big shopping trip? Wear that. The belt will bring the colors together and go perfectly with those glass-beaded sandals we found at Pizzazz. I'll write it all down for you," he added. "And please, Annie, humor me and wear your hair down. Okay? Not pulled back with that dreadful clip the way you have it now."

It was on the tip of Annie's tongue to remind Collin that she wasn't an imbecile. That she was perfectly capable of choosing her own wardrobe. And that she'd wear her hair any damn dreadful way she pleased.

Fortunately for Collin, Gretchen from art and filming saved him from the verbal abuse when she walked into the office grinning from ear to ear.

She placed a folder on Annie's desk. "I finally got the proofs back from Rico's photo shoot. The camera loves this guy, Annie. And he's going to look just as fabulous on film."

Annie opened the folder. When she finished spreading the top four photos out on her desk, Collin said, "Ooh la la, Rico."

Her soon-to-be Joe Video was shirtless in all of them, wearing faded jeans and barefoot. There was a shot of Rico spread out like a hot lunch on a stark white chaise longue. There was Rico propped against a doorjamb, his thumb hooked in the waistband of his jeans, his ink black hair falling forward over one eye and a provocative smile on his lips. There was Rico leaning back against a brick wall, his hands clasped behind his head, emphasizing his incredible biceps and six-pack abs. And there was Rico with his muscled back to the camera, legs spread and hands up against the brick wall like a naughty prisoner awaiting a hands-on pat-down.

"Now that's an award-winning buns pose if I've ever seen one," Collin said, practically drooling. "Matt," he called out. "Come look at Rico's amazing buns."

Annie looked up at Collin when he punched her with his elbow. He winked. Annie decided her mischievous gay friend might not be as oblivious to the rivalry between her and Matt as she assumed.

"I'll leave Rico's amazing buns to *your* wishful thinking," Matt called back, "and to Annie's big date tonight."

Yeah, right. Like he was going to bolt over to check out some guy's ass. How about kick Rico's ass, instead? Now *that* he could go for.

But he did feel guilty about pushing Annie too far with the teasing. Except for one fact. When exactly had Annie ever done anything he had suggested? How about like, say — *never*!

He'd expected to push her in the opposite direction by suggesting she should date Rico. What he got instead was Annie agreeing to a dinner date that had the potential for Mr. Amazing Buns to be served wild monkey sex for dessert.

Matt pushed the monkey sex possibility to the back of his mind. *Dammit.* The thought of Annie having sex with the guy really bothered him. It was an ego thing. That's all. He was only human. What guy wouldn't feel a little less confident about himself under the circumstances?

He'd seen for himself women in the lobby practically knocking each other down trying to get a glimpse of Rico. For the last three weeks everyone around him had talked incessantly about little else but Rico's sex appeal.

Give a guy a break already.

Now he guessed he'd have to endure a day's worth of amazing-bun chitchat. Between long discussions of Annie's wardrobe and hairstyles, that is. But if Collin brought up that wild monkey sex crap again, he was going to . . .

"Let's go show Kathy the proofs," Collin said, and Matt waited until Collin and Gretchen left the office before he turned his chair all the way around to face Annie.

She ignored him and pretended to be working on something at her desk.

"Annie," he said.

She looked up.

"I'm sorry."

"Excuse me?"

Damn, Matt thought. She wasn't going to make this easy. "I'm sorry for teasing you. I know you only accepted the date because of me. Call Rico back. Tell him you changed your mind."

Now the chin came up. "Get over yourself, Matt."

Matt tried counting slowly to ten. He only made it to three. "Come on, Annie. Don't sit there and tell me you accepted the date for any other reason except you're too stubborn to give me the satisfaction of saying I told you so about being adored and bored."

He didn't like the way she was caressing her stapler.

"Are you really that self-absorbed?" Her chin jutted even higher. "You actually think I would be that idiotic and immature and go out with Rico just to keep *you* from saying I told you so?"

Matt frowned. "Don't twist my words around. I didn't say you were idiotic and immature. But *I'm* not stupid, either. And I know it's had to cross your mind that I was right about being adored and bored. That's just the way it is, Annie. The badda-boom doesn't work without the badda-bing. And whether Rico adores you or not, admit it. There's no *badda-damn-bing*."

Was he imagining it, or did her laugh sound maniacal?

"Well, thank you so much for setting me straight, Matt," she said. "Silly me. Here I was, thinking maybe the fact I'd been dumped on a videotape only a few weeks ago might be the reason I was being cautious where Rico was concerned. But it's a *bing* thing. Who knew?"

Damn.

This conversation was not going well.

At all.

"Okay," Matt said, taking a deep breath. "Let's start over. I didn't mean to make you mad."

"Too late!" She stood up from her desk.

Matt stood up as well.

But their face-off was interrupted when Greg Wilson from the advertising department walked into the room.

Annie looked in Greg's direction. If anyone was asked to identify an advertising executive in a lineup, they wouldn't hesitate to point a finger at Greg. The tailored suit. The power tie. His blond hair only long enough to be fashionable. He was the kind of guy who would definitely be in her boinkable file had he not been happily married with an adorable two-year-old son.

Greg looked first at her, then Matt, and grinned. "Hey. You guys look like you're ready to put on the gloves and come out swinging."

When neither she nor Matt commented, he said, "Which isn't necessarily a bad thing. I hate this is such short notice, guys, but I've finally sealed the deal for your appearance on *City Singles*."

Annie lowered herself back onto her seat. She'd been hoping against hope the deal wouldn't go through. Greg had told them earlier there was a problem. The morning show already had guest appearances lined up way past the time where it would have been beneficial to promote Joe Video. She should have known J.B. Duncan wasn't the type of man to take no for an answer.

"Define short notice," Matt said, sitting back down himself.

"I need you guys at WAGA-TV bright and early in the morning," Greg said. "Six a.m. early," he added, twisting the cold knife of dread piercing Annie's stomach further. "The show's live and it airs at seven. They'll need to run you both through makeup first. Then Claire Winslow likes to have a few minutes with her guests before air-time."

Annie glared at Matt.

Matt glared back.

"Just one word of caution," Greg said. "Claire is a shark in the water, guys. She likes to draw blood. She'll do anything in her power to see if she can't make you slip up and say something you might regret later. Be prepared for anything." He grinned again. "Remember, Big Brother — a.k.a. J.B. — will be watching."

Matt asked a few more questions, but Annie tuned him out. She was still fuming over the argument Greg had interrupted. How *dare* Matt assume he knew her so well. Even if he did. The very nerve of him telling her to call Rico back and call off the date. Like it was *his* decision instead of hers. So maybe she was being idiotic, imma-ture, and stubborn. She didn't care. She would handle her problem with Rico her own way. And she didn't need any input from Matt. *Period*.

Besides, Greg's shocking announcement had brought a more pressing problem to the forefront. There was someone else on Annie's mind. The second Greg left their office, she took her purse from her bottom desk drawer and told Matt rather than asked him, "I'm taking an early lunch."

"Okay," he said. "But don't be gone too long. Greg said we needed to be prepared for anything. We'll need to spend the rest of the day coming up with a foolproof game plan, and rehearsing our he-said, she-said act."

Right. Like you and I need practice getting in each other's face.

Annie left without saying a word.

She didn't even acknowledge Collin and Gretchen, who were still huddled over Kathy's desk admiring Rico's photos. But by the time she reached the elevators, she had her cell phone to her ear.

"Mother? I know this is short notice, but could you meet me for an early lunch? I'll come to you. Meet me at Gino's around the corner from your office."

Annie squeezed her eyes shut. "Yes, it's important, Mother. If it weren't, I wouldn't be calling."

She snapped her cell phone shut and stepped into the elevator when the doors opened. But she couldn't keep from shuddering. Her respected, card-carrying Feminist Majority mother was going to be mortified.

She'll probably even disown me.

And why wouldn't she?

Activist Beverly Long's hopeless maleaholic daughter was about to appear on local TV — professing to women all over Atlanta that all they needed to make their lives complete was a video version of the perfect man.

CHAPTER 8

Annie made it across town in record time and parked her VW bug on the street in front of Gino's, a small Italian bistro that had an outside seating area on the sidewalk. She knew outside was where she'd find her mother, despite the unbearable July heat that sent heat waves up from the sidewalk, blurring her vision. That her mother could be such a die-hard defender of political correctness and still be a smoker was a mystery to her. But then, the woman called "Ball-buster Bev" by the unlucky opponents who happened to come up against her in court had always been a mystery to Annie.

For instance, what in the world could a twenty-two-year old have possibly seen in a man old enough to be her grandfather?

At least her mother had never lied to her about her father. From the time Annie was old enough to question why she didn't have a dad like other kids Bev had told her that esteemed professor Thaddeus Dick had been a man with a brilliant mind. A man who had contributed immensely to the field of philosophy with his papers and essays, many of which were still used as examples in college classrooms throughout the world today. The same papers Annie had read herself over and over a zillion times. Words, brilliant as they were, on a lifeless page.

A poor substitute, if you asked Annie, for a full-time father.

But it hadn't been until Annie turned ten, about the same age all kids started looking up curse words in the dictionary, that she came across the word "bastard." Even now, she still remembered the outrage she'd felt.

She'd stomped into the kitchen, her thumb safely securing the dictionary's "bastard" page, and she'd yelled at the top of her lungs, "Thank you, Beverly Sue Long, for making me a bastard!"

Her mother had only looked calmly over her wire-rimmed glasses and said, "'Bastard' is a vile and ugly word. The fact that your father and I never married is irrelevant. Our love created you. You are a love child, Annie. Not a bastard."

Then her mother had wiped away the tears streaming down Annie's ten-year-old face and said, "If you like, I can file a document with the court so you can also carry your father's surname. Women do it all the time and separate the two last names with a hyphen."

Face the world as Annie Long-Dick?

Not an option.

From that moment on, she'd become Annie Sue Long, love child. She'd never brought the subject up again.

"Annie. Over here," her mother called out, waving as if Annie wasn't going to recognize her.

Perfect, Mother, call attention to yourself, Annie thought. *It will give the other customers even more reason to gawk at us later when you throw a fit on me.*

She squeezed her way through the crowded tables on the sidewalk. At least Bev had chosen a table closest to the building, shaded by the green-and-white awning running across the front of the restaurant.

Bev could easily have been a model instead of an attorney sitting at that table. Her long strawberry blonde mane was loose and fanned out around her shoulders, instead of pulled back like Annie had her own hair now. And though the sixties look was popular again, Annie knew the faded turquoise gauze sundress Bev was wearing today was almost as old as Annie herself.

People often mistook them for sisters which was a comfort in one way, but a curse in another. Bev's youthful appearance at her almost-fifty age told Annie she could expect to age as well herself. But it was Bev's ever-sharp feminist tongue that always embarrassed Annie if some unlucky man happened to approach them.

She reached the table and took the seat next to her mother on purpose. With her back to the brick restaurant wall, she could scan the crowd sitting outside on the sidewalk. To her relief, all of the people dining were couples, or groups of women. There wasn't a single guy in sight.

"Well? What's so important?" Bev quizzed, smoke snaking from the brown cigarillo she held skillfully between two slender fingers.

"Could I at least order first?" Annie looked around for a menu.

"I've already ordered," Bev informed her. "I have to be in court soon. I ordered the sausage calzone we always split."

"Fine." Annie reached for her water glass.

Bev took a slow drag from the cigarillo and blew the smoke into the air as gracefully as any classic silver-screen movie star. "How's Doug?" she asked, fishing, and Annie knew it.

"You know perfectly well his name is Dave, Mother." Who was Bev kidding? The woman had a memory like an elephant for names and faces. Annie paused before she added, "Dave moved to San Francisco three weeks ago."

"I'm sorry." Bev sounded sincere, but she erased the goodwill when she added, "Don't tell me you've already replaced Doug before his pillow had time to get cold."

"As a matter of fact, I have," Annie said right back, and metaphorically speaking, it wasn't a lie.

Bev rolled her eyes. "Maybe we should wait until after we eat before we continue this conversation. I have a feeling whatever you came to tell me is going to give me indigestion."

"Whatever," Annie snipped.

Bev made a big production of putting out the cigarillo. She snapped her napkin open and placed it in her lap. "Oh, go ahead and tell me what's going on," she said with a sigh. "The sausage gives me indigestion anyway."

"Then why did you order it?"

"Because it's your favorite."

"It isn't *my* favorite," Annie said. "I thought it was yours."

"I'm beginning to think we have a communication problem," Bev said.

And Annie said, "That isn't a news flash, Mother."

They both stared at the indigestion-producing entrée as the waiter suddenly appeared and placed the plate on the table between them.

"Anything else, ladies?" he asked, smiling.

Bev looked at Annie, then back at the waiter. "Yes," she said. "We'll have two caesar salads, please."

Annie laughed in spite of herself.

After she'd finished telling her mother the saga that had become her life over the last few weeks, Annie felt as if she'd regressed back to her childhood — waiting while Bev looked over her report card. She'd started at the beginning, with her getting dumped by Dave on the videotape. Then having the Joe Video brainstorm and being forced by Matt to present the idea. And finally, the promise of her big promotion, which, Annie explained, was the reason she was allowing herself to be railroaded by the CEO into creating the buzz for the game on local TV.

She'd left out the part about her current problem with Rico's unwanted affection, however, only mentioning that she'd found a guy with mega sex appeal to play the role. Though she was ashamed of herself for doing it, she'd also made it a point to mention Rico's name. Bev had always been a fierce minority advocate. Under the circumstances, Annie was shamefully trying to score points with her mother any way she could.

Annie looked down at her watch. It had been exactly two full minutes since she'd finished her story. As yet, Bev hadn't so much as looked up from her caesar salad.

Annie couldn't take it any longer. "Would you please say something, Mother? Scream if you want. Throw something if you have to. Just don't give me the silent treatment. You know I hate that."

Bev looked up, seemingly surprised. "Oh. I'm sorry. I was still in process mode thinking about your perfect man concept."

"And?" Annie urged, one second away from grabbing her mother's shoulders and shaking her silly.

Bev put her fork down. "I think your concept is brilliant, Annie."

"What?" Annie croaked.

Bev looked puzzled. "Why do you find that so hard to believe?"

"Hell-o? Defender of the sisterhood? Resistant to a male-controlled world? Disgusted by men-dependent women everywhere? You tell me, Mother. Why do *you* think I'm so astonished that you would think my concept of creating a perfect man on DVD is brilliant?"

"Oh, stop being so dramatic." Bev picked up her fork and waved it through the air before she dug into her salad again. "Whether you realize it or not, your concept is actually overtly feminist. How else could a perfect man exist? Unless a woman created one on DVD?"

Annie put her elbows on the table, dropped her head into her hands, and pressed against her temples. *Great.* Just what she needed. Another opinion about her concept. *She'd* seen Joe Video as an important self-help tool. *Matt* had seen the game as a good ol' boy gag gift. And now her mother was giving Joe Video a glowing endorsement as recruitment material for the frickin' Feminist Majority.

"How rude," she heard Bev huff.

Annie kept her eyes closed and pressed harder against her temples. "I'm not trying to be rude, Mother. I suddenly have a headache."

"Not you," Bev said, nudging Annie with her elbow. "That man over there who keeps staring at us."

Annie's eyes snapped open she found herself staring directly into the dark eyes of Rico's uncle. He'd introduced himself to her the morning he'd delivered the first of Rico's daily bouquets to her office. He had a flower shop, he'd said, not far from the Plaza. Umberto? Was that his name? Yes, she was sure that was it.

Oh no. He's walking in our direction.

"Don't be militant, Mother, I know him," Annie said before Bev pulled out a spray can of Mace.

He wasn't that much older than Rico, possibly late thirties, and he was almost as handsome. He was dressed simply in faded jeans, and his pale blue polo shirt only emphasized a deep tan that Annie suspected he had acquired out-of-doors and not in some tanning bed. He smiled when he came to a stop at their table, reminding Annie how strong the family resemblance really was. Like Rico, his teeth were dazzling white and perfectly straight.

Annie didn't chance even the slightest hesitation before she said, "Umberto. I was just telling my mother how fortunate we are to have Rico on board at Paragon. Mother, this is Rico's uncle, Umberto Romero. Umberto, my mother, Beverly Long."

Oh God. Oh God. Oh God.

Before Annie could scream for Umberto to run for his life, he stepped forward and kissed her mother's outstretched hand. Annie almost fell out of her chair when all Bev did was smile.

"It is an honor," he said, and maybe Annie only imagined it, but he seemed to be holding on to her mother's hand a little bit longer than necessary.

Well. The Romero men certainly are a hand-kissing bunch, Annie mused. Lucky for this old-fashioned Romero, her mother was in a surprisingly good mood today.

"Umberto Romero," Bev repeated, gazing at him intently. "I knew your name sounded familiar. I just read a feature article about you in the paper a few weeks ago. You're the singing gardener. The man who sings opera to his plants."

He laughed and held his hands up. "I am guilty as charged," he said. "Loco to some. Not so loco to others."

"Won't you join us?" Bev asked.

Annie jumped in and said, "Remember you have court, Mother."

Bev ignored her and pulled a chair out for Umberto. Umberto wasted no time in accepting her offer.

What the hell is going on here?

Annie couldn't figure it out. Her usually check-her-watch-every-second mother? Taking time out to chat up a man who sang opera to his plants?

Unbelievable.

"I've always been a huge opera fan myself," Bev said, actually smiling at him.

Why couldn't Umberto have been a rapper? Annie thought disgustedly. If her mother got started on opera, they could be there all day.

"And a favorite of yours would be?" Umberto urged.

"Pavarotti. An aria from *Tosca*. It always makes me weep." Bev actually sighed.

This heat makes me want to weep, Annie felt like saying as a trickle of sweat slid down her back.

Umberto touched his heart. "One of my favorites, also." He was now staring just as intently at her mother.

Do something! Annie's mind screamed.

"Did Rico tell you we're going to start filming next week?" she broke in. She had to change the subject before both of them started reciting every flipping aria near and dear to their opera-loving hearts.

"Yes, Rico told me about the filming," Umberto said, but he was still staring directly at Bev. "My nephew," he said, "he is very smitten with your beautiful daughter."

He finally glanced over at Annie for the first time since he'd taken a seat at their table.

Busted.

And it's my own damn fault.

"Oh really?" Bev raised an eyebrow as she looked in Annie's direction.

Annie was still grasping for something to say when Umberto looked back at her mother and said, "Just as I am sure Annie's father is smitten with her beautiful mother."

"Yes. Very smitten," Annie spoke up, hoping to steer Umberto away from that touchy topic as quickly as possible.

"Annie's father died a long time ago," Bev said, to Annie's surprise. She usually didn't like talking about the past. Especially not about esteemed professor Thaddeus Dick.

"I am sorry for your loss," Umberto said sincerely.

Bev smiled. "Thank you. But as I said, that was a long time ago."

Okay. This entire conversation is making me way too nervous. Besides, Annie knew the sooner she got her mother out of there, the less time Bev would have to pump Umberto for more information about his smitten nephew.

"Well, I hate to break this up," Annie said, scribbling her name across the bottom of the check. She slipped her credit card back into her purse. "But I need to get back to the office. Mother, didn't you say you had to be in court early this afternoon?"

Bev laughed and said, "I'm an attorney, Umberto. Not a criminal. Just in case you were wondering why my daughter is so adamant about me not missing court."

Umberto laughed, too.

Annie didn't.

Now Bev's making corny jokes?

If she didn't know better, she'd think her mother was actually flirting with this man. But that was ridiculous. Umberto had to be, what, at least ten years younger? Maybe even more?

Bev finally pushed her chair back and stood up. Umberto and Annie did the same.

"I've enjoyed meeting you, Umberto," Bev said. "Now I can brag at the courthouse that I've actually met the singing gardener."

.   Umberto smiled. "I am flattered. And, please. Both of you. Come visit my shop. You are always welcome there." He took a business card from his shirt pocket and handed it to Bev.

The second they said their good-byes, Annie nudged her mother toward her VW that was waiting at the curb farther down the sidewalk.

"I'll drop you off at the courthouse, Mother."

Bev nodded, but she looked back over her shoulder one last time. "Nice man."

"Nice and *young*," Annie said, putting emphasis on the age difference. "Really, Mother. Did you realize you were almost flirting with him?"

"You told me not to be militant," Bev said as she opened the passenger-side door of Annie's convertible.

Annie opened the driver's side door and slid behind the wheel. "That didn't mean for you to go to the other extreme and give him your phone number."

"I didn't give him my phone number. He gave me his." Bev held up his business card.

"Very funny." Annie started the car and roared away from the curb.

"And his nephew, Rico?" Bev asked a few seconds later, just as Annie knew she would. "Are you just as smitten with him as he is with you?"

Annie shook her head. "Sadly, no. I'm not smitten with Rico at all. I hope I can finally convince him of that tonight when I have dinner with him."

Despite Matt's order to hurry back from lunch, Annie didn't return to the office after she dropped her mother off at the courthouse. She'd called Collin instead, and asked him to do her dirty work for her.

"Tell Matt if he wants me at the TV studio in the morning, I need the rest of the day to get ready," she'd told Collin. "Tell him it's a chick thing. That always confuses him."

She'd spent the remainder of the day getting ready for her big television debut. She'd had a manicure and a pedicure, toetoo and all. She'd even managed to pick out — all by herself — a great black-and-white DKNY skirt, jacket, and blouse ensemble to wear when she made her big appearance on *City Singles*.

But out of respect for her fashion guru's wishes, she'd worn the exact outfit Collin had chosen when she got ready for her date with Rico later that evening. She even had her hair down and properly scrunched, exactly as Collin had instructed.

Now Annie found herself being whisked away in a classy silver Lotus, by a Cuban heartthrob who obviously had plenty of badda-boom, but sadly for her, no badda-freaking-bing.

"The place we are going, it is a well-kept secret," Rico

said, turning to look at her. "A secret I am happy to share with someone as beautiful as you."

Annie forced a smile.

She had to admit Rico was, without a doubt, one damn fine-looking man.

Like her, he wasn't overdressed or underdressed tonight. He was wearing simple black dress slacks, a slate gray shirt with a tiny white pinstripe running through the fabric, and, as usual, expensive Italian loafers. He, too, had skipped the ponytail. Annie kept waiting for a lock of ink black shiny hair to fall forward over one eye like in the photo shoot proofs. He reached up and pushed his hair back away from his forehead, as if he'd been waiting for the same thing.

"You have eaten Cuban cuisine before?"

"No," Annie said, deciding it wouldn't kill her to help him out a little with the small talk. "At least not authentic Cuban cuisine. I'm anxious to try it, though."

"Bueno," he said and smiled one of his slow, sexy smiles.

The restaurant turned out to be one of those lovable little hole-in-the-wall restaurants on a quiet residential street in Midtown Atlanta. The type of place where you knew immediately that most of the customers were regulars and that the service would always be friendly.

Rico spoke or nodded to almost every person there as he escorted Annie through the restaurant and out onto a wonderful outdoor patio that was large and spacious, unlike most outdoor eating areas in Atlanta. Tall potted trees were placed strategically around the patio, giving each table a feeling of privacy. Tiny white lights strung throughout the tree branches twinkled like a thousand brilliant stars, perfect for gazing.

The second they were both seated at one of the wrought-iron tables, Annie said, "You have definitely impressed me, Rico. I never knew such a marvelous place existed right here in Midtown."

Rico brought a finger to his lips. "Shhhhh. It is our little secret. Remember?"

God. Could he be any more charming?
Dammit. Dammit. Dammit.

The guy was perfect. The setting was perfect. Even the weather was perfect. Not a cloud in the sky. They even had a made-to-order full moon looming overhead. And a refreshing breeze was stirring through what normally would have been an armpit-sticky Hot-lanta end-of-July night.

Annie suppressed a sigh. How many times had she dreamed of a setting exactly like this one?

Only all my life!

So what, dammit, was wrong with her? What more could she possibly want? What more could she possibly ask for? What more could she possibly hope for?

What . . . the hell?

Startled, Annie gaped at the young waiter who had suddenly sprinted to their table. Despite the language barrier, the tone of the Spanish flying back and forth between the waiter and Rico made Annie realize that something was seriously wrong.

Rico jumped up. "You go with Diego," he said, slipping his hand under Annie's right arm and practically lifting her out of her chair. "Go now. I will explain to you later."

"What's going on?" Annie tried to protest, but she barely had time to grab her purse before Diego grabbed her hand and started leading her off through the maze of potted trees.

"I do not find this one bit amusing," Annie informed Diego as he led her around the back of the restaurant to a screen door. "I would appreciate it, if you would *unhand* me." She jerked her hand from his.

"So, so sorry, señorita," Diego said, motioning for her to follow him through the kitchen area.

Annie ignored the surprised looks coming from the kitchen staff, held her head high, and followed after him. Only after Diego had pushed open the swinging kitchen door and looked out did he motion her forward. After one more quick turn down a hallway, Annie found herself standing in front of the women's restroom.

"You wait. In there," Diego instructed, nodding frantically for her to agree.

Annie shook her head, telling him she did *not* agree. "I will not wait *anywhere* until I know what's going on."

He looked nervously over his shoulder and Annie couldn't help but feel sorry for him. He was no more than a kid, maybe nineteen, if that. His eyes were wide with excitement and his hands were moving as fast as he was spitting out the Spanish she didn't understand.

Annie shook her head again, even though he kept motioning frantically for her to hurry. "No Española," she told him and threw her hands up in the air, indicating she didn't understand.

Diego held up one finger. Then he opened the bathroom door himself and gently pushed her inside.

Annie held up one finger and pointed it at him. "You tell Rico he has exactly five minutes before I walk right out of this restaurant." She held up all five fingers. "Five minutes. That's all. Understand?"

Diego nodded and quickly closed the door in her face.
"This is ridiculous," Annie complained to no one, then
looked around the small bathroom.

There were only two bathroom stalls, but at least the
place was spotlessly clean. Diego had kept saying, "Tornado! Tornado!" But that was impossible. The weather
outside was as clear as a bell.

However.

When the bathroom door suddenly blew open and
Miss Hell-Hath-No-Fury twisted inside, Annie changed
her mind about the possibility of an unexpected tornado.

Miss Twister slammed the door behind her with a
wall-shaking bang. She was Hispanic, incredibly beautiful, and obviously mad as hell. And she looked, Annie
decided, like a walking advertisement for a spandex commercial.

Her bright pink spandex halter top barely covered her
voluptuous bosom. *Talk about diversionary cleavage!*
Collin would have had a coronary. Her shiny black spandex capri pants showed off her tiny waist, her flat stomach, and her long, slender legs. Her long black hair
reached well past her tanned exposed shoulders.

She was in-your-face breathtaking.

Annie suspected she was very well aware of it too.

She looked Annie up and down with a cool, dismissive
glance, her black eyes dancing with mischief and flashing
with anger.

I'm glad I'm not the one who pissed her off, Annie
thought.

Until.

Someone pounded loudly on the bathroom door.

A voice Annie recognized as Rico's yelled, "Helena!

Something, something, something, something. Annie.
Now!"

Helena's answer was to toss a cascade of jet black
curls over one shoulder, smile a deadly smile, and lock
the bathroom door.

Oh. My. God.

"I am Helena," she announced, as if Annie hadn't already figured that out for herself. "You steal my Rico?"
She made a slicing motion across her jugular with a four-
inch red talon. "I *sleet* your throat."

Annie gulped.

Having her throat *sleeted* was not at the top of her list
of things to do anytime soon. Nor, for that matter, was
being locked in a bathroom with a Hispanic spitfire who
was evidently the scorned lover of a man Annie didn't
want anyway.

The throat sleeter took a threatening step in Annie's direction. Annie's hand flew to her neck for her own pro-
tection. "I know karate," she warned. *And a few other
Japanese words.* She was definitely about to get her butt
kicked. Big-time.

"Rico! You'd better put an end to this," Annie screamed
toward the door.

The banging started up again. Helena wheeled around
and started banging on the door just as forcefully from
the inside of the bathroom. The yelling continued back
and forth between them for several seconds before Helena turned to Annie and said, "You tell Rico to go away.
Now. And I will not hurt you."

Annie laughed. "Do I really look that stupid?"

One raised eyebrow was Helena's answer.

"Look," Annie said. "I'm not trying to steal Rico. It's
only business. Nothing personal."

Helena's hands immediately flew to her shapely hips. "Not personal? Ha!" She spit toward Annie's feet. "To Rico's fiancée"— she poked her bulging bosom with her thumb —"it is *personal*."

Annie was speechless. "His fiancée?"

Helena looked at Annie for a second.

Then Rico's fiancée burst into tears.

"Annie. What is happening?" Rico yelled, pounding on the door again.

"Go away," Annie yelled back. "We'll be out in a minute."

What a freaking nightmare.

Annie turned and grabbed a towel from the dispenser and ran it under the water facet. She guided the sobbing Helena into one of the bathroom stalls, waited until she took a seat on the toilet, then handed her the dampened paper towel. Helena accepted it without question.

"Helena. What I said earlier. About it being nothing personal. I was only trying to explain I have no personal interest in Rico."

She dabbed at her eyes. "It does not matter. It is you he wants now. He told me the day after you come to the Cabaña Club he would not honor our engagement."

"He broke your engagement after I came to the club?" Annie felt her heart lurch at the thought of how she would feel if the tables were turned.

Helena dabbed at her eyes a few more times. "I am Rico's *intended* fiancée. Chosen by his family. A custom the old Rico would have honored. This new Rico"— she waved her hand in the air —"his head is now filled with big dreams. He is restless. Confused."

Annie leaned against the stall, thinking what a common bond she had with Helena, even if the woman *had* threatened to slit her throat only a few minutes earlier. Annie had been dumped herself so many times, it was amazing there weren't billboards all over Atlanta — her picture, standing stoically, holding up a Hefty bag with giant block letters that said: *Got Dumped?*

Annie reached out and touched Helena's shoulder. "I'm sorry, Helena. I mean that."

Helena's head popped up like a jack-in-the-box. "How sorry?"

The sudden gleam in her shining black eyes told Annie she was going to regret those words. She sent Helena a suspicious look. "What do you mean, how sorry?"

"Sorry enough to help me get my Rico back?" Helena's expression had now turned from hopeless to hopeful.

Annie said, "Exactly how would I go about doing that?"

This time, Helena's beautiful smile lit up her entire face. "Right now, you are pushing Rico away, sí? So, Rico, he only wants you more. But we will trick him. Like the movie. Where the guy, he gets lost in ten days. Everything Rico does not want in a woman, I know it. I will tell you. And then you will pretend to be a woman Rico would not want. This will work. I am sure of it."

Annie couldn't believe she was actually taking time to think over everything Helena had just said, but she was. Maybe because Helena had been right about one thing. Her own plan definitely hadn't been working.

Oh, what the hell, Annie thought.

It wouldn't hurt to try. She certainly didn't have a better idea. And she was definitely just as eager to get rid of Rico as Helena was to get him back.

"Okay," she said. "I'll help you. But under one condition. The project Rico and I are working on together is very important to me. Rico has to finish filming my video game. No interference from you in that respect. Agreed?"

"Agreed," Helena said. "And there is also one condition from me. No sex with my Rico. Or . . ." She made the scary motion across her throat again.

Annie shivered. "Got it."

"Because the sex is the second part of my plan," Helena said with a confident smile. "Rico will come to *me* for the sex."

Annie's mouth dropped open. "And that doesn't bother you? That Rico is romancing *me*, but he'll come to you only for the sex?"

"*Only* the sex? Ha!" Helena rolled her eyes. "You big career women, you worry too much about all the wrong things. It is the *passion* that is important." She pressed both hands zealously over her heart. "You must live it. Breathe it. Taste it. Without the passion? Pffffft," she said. "There is nothing."

Boom. Boom. Boom.

Bing. Bing. Bing.

"I will think on this," Helena said, standing up from her unglamorous seat on the toilet. "On the things you should do to make Rico not want you. We will meet later, sí? To discuss the plan."

Annie nodded, then walked back over to the sink vanity and rummaged through her purse. She found one of her business cards, scrounged around for a pen, and jotted her cell phone number on the back. When Helena walked up to stand beside her, Annie handed over the card.

Helena unzipped the small fanny pack strapped around her trim waist and slipped the card safely inside. Then she ran her fingers through her long black hair several times before giving herself a final look of approval in the bathroom mirror. "Now we go out," she said with authority. "I will tell Rico I give him my blessing. You and Rico will have dinner. Then he will take you home." She reached for the door handle, but then turned back to face Annie one last time before she opened the bathroom door. She held her finger up and shook it back and forth. "But no sex."

"No sex," Annie repeated.

She made the slashing motion herself this time, to save her passionate new friend the trouble.

Rico stopped pacing in the hallway and looked at the closed bathroom door. That Helena would do this to him was no big surprise. The woman loved him. With the passion of a thousand burning suns, she loved him. Though it saddened him to pretend he was turning away from such a phenomenal love, his own desire for a better life was fierce enough to win the battle with his guilty conscience.

There had been no need to tell Helena about his master plan. She would never have agreed anyway. Of that, he was certain. To Helena, it would not matter what type of future they had together. As long as she was his wife, Helena would be happy. And that's why there was no other way than to let her believe — at least for now — that he was interested in Annie.

He sighed deeply, wishing he could bring Helena into his confidence and spare her the pain. But he needed Annie. At least until she had served her purpose. Once she introduced him to the right people, he would tell Annie she was right. That they should only be friends.

A good friend she has been, so far.

And very beautiful. But Annie was not his type of woman. He would never want a woman too timid to let go of her emotions. Annie was guarded. Maybe because she had been hurt. Maybe not. But his blood ran hot. A hot-blooded woman was the only type of woman he wanted. A woman like Helena, who had proved just how hot-blooded she was by tossing her pride aside and coming to the restaurant tonight to fight for him.

When the bathroom door suddenly opened, Rico prepared himself for the worst. When the two women walked out into the hallway, he shook his head.

"Helena," he said with the disappointment of a parent scolding a naughty child. "Why do you do this? Have I not been truthful with you? And still you shame me? Try to make Annie think I am going behind your back, trying to hurt you?"

He expected her to fly at him and scratch his face with her long red fingernails, leave the mark of her desire on his face the way she did on his back when he made love to her. He wasn't prepared when Helena said, "You are right, Rico. I am sorry. You have been truthful from the day Annie stole your heart away from me. I will step aside. I give you my blessing."

That was the craziest thing he had ever heard.

Helena? Giving up? And giving him her blessing? Not in one million years would that happen.

He watched suspiciously as Helena turned to Annie. She kissed the air on each side of Annie's face. "Goodbye, Annie," she said with a dramatic sigh. "Be good to my Rico."

"Wait," Annie called out when Helena reached the

place where Rico was standing. Annie said, "It's getting late, Rico. Tomorrow is an important day for both of us."

Ah yes. The morning television program. Annie had told him about it when he first arrived at her apartment. After she had told him there could be no more flowers and no more private lunches. There was too much talk at her office, she'd said. It was important to keep their relationship professional in front of her peers.

But Annie was right. A promotion for the video game would also be a promotion for his own career. Tomorrow would be a very important day for both of them.

"Why don't you take Helena home?" Annie suggested. "I can take a taxi."

"No," Helena said, her nose in the air.

Rico looked in her direction. *No? Who is this woman? Not my Helena.*

"A taxi is how I got here," Helena said with a toss of her regal dark head. "And a taxi is how I am going home."

Rico looked from one beautiful woman to the other, his brow wrinkled in a deep frown. Annie did not want to stay and have dinner now. Helena did not want him to take her home. This did not sit well with his ego. Any of it. Not Annie, always trying to order him around. And especially not Helena saying she was giving up and giving him her blessing to be with Annie.

He would *not* let two women push him around.

"Annie is right, Helena. It is late and she has an important business appointment in the morning. I will take you home. Annie will take the taxi."

Rico dug into his pants pocket and handed Helena his car keys. "Wait for me in the car," he ordered. When Helena didn't argue, took the keys, and disappeared down the hallway, Rico knew he was back in charge.

He turned back to Annie.

With her, however, he would need a softer approach. Not that he expected anything he said to change the situation now. Helena had seen to that. Sadly, just when he was finally making a little progress. Now maybe Annie would even fire him.

Rico sent her an apologetic smile. "I am sorry, Annie. For everything. I am embarrassed more than you can know."

Wait. Was that a smile? That Annie would smile back at him was not what he expected.

"I'm sorry, too, Rico," she said. "There's no reason to be embarrassed. Helena seems like a wonderful person. I'm sorry us being together hurts her."

What? He took his time, turning Annie's words carefully over in his mind. "Can I be so fortunate?" he finally dared to ask. "You would possibly see me again? And not just as business associates?"

He was shocked when she said, "Yes."

Maravilloso!

"Diego," Rico called back over his shoulder. When his friend appeared, Rico said, "Diego, call a taxi for the lady, por favor." He turned back to Annie. "I will wait with you, of course, until the taxi arrives."

She walked up to him and placed a hand on his arm. Touching him was also something she had never done before. "Thank you, but that's not necessary. I'll be fine, Rico. You take Helena home. Just remember to watch *City Singles* at seven in the morning. I'll call you after the television interview."

Annie will call me?

Bravo! Another first. Maybe Helena showing up had been a blessing in disguise.

Rico was still marveling over the amazing change in Annie's attitude as he walked toward the parking lot. The irony of the situation amused him. But it also left a bittersweet taste on his tongue. Annie's sudden interest meant he would have to continue lying to both women. He would have to keep pretending he was interested in Annie. He would have to keep telling Helena that, at the moment, they could not be together.

Women.

That God Himself understood them, Rico knew, was questionable.

He opened the car door and slid behind the wheel.

"Santa Maria!" Rico exclaimed.

Helena was stark naked.

And she was sitting sideways in the passenger seat in one of her no-doubt-about-what-she-wanted poses.

Rico sent a hasty look around the dimly lit parking area, thankful he'd parked far away from other cars, as usual, to protect his treasured sports car.

"Do you think your Annie would ever do this?" Helena asked when he looked back in her direction. "That she would ever be so hot for you? That she would rip her clothes off and beg you to make love to her no matter who was watching?"

She ran her hands seductively over her full, luscious breasts, letting her fingers trail even lower to caress the dark triangle between her long, tanned legs. And when the unquestionable movement she was making with one finger in particular got faster and faster and faster, the blood in Rico's brain rushed to a more demanding part of his body.

"You like this?" she asked through pouty, parted lips. "You like that I am so hot for you? That when I take many lovers, it will still be *you* that I want?"

"Many lovers?" Rico shouted.

The thought of Helena taking even one lover other than himself filled Rico with a surge of jealousy he couldn't control. He grabbed her slender shoulders and pulled Helena forward, crushing his mouth against hers.

"For you, there will be no other lovers," he told her when their lips broke apart.

Helena's answer was to smile. She leaned backwards, slipping between the front seats into the small backseat area of the car. When she opened her legs wide, beckoning Rico to enter the gates of a heaven no sane man had ever been able to resist, he unzipped his pants and set the primeval green-eyed monster free.

"Sí!" Helena screamed triumphantly.

"Give it to me, Rico.

"Give it *all* to me!"

CHAPTER 9

It was still dark at 5:30 a.m. Friday morning when Annie drove up to the building that looked more like an old southern plantation than a television studio. She entered the building, amazed to find so many people scurrying around at such a ridiculous hour. She stopped the first person she could, explained who she was and why she was there, and was directed to her first stop — makeup.

She was not a happy camper when she walked into the room and found Matt already there, seated in a salon-type chair with his usual cocky grin on his freshly shaven face. She'd hoped to arrive first. Have time to sweep away the sleep-deprived cobwebs in her brain before she had to deal with him.

No such luck.

"How'd the big date go?" were the first words out of his mouth.

Annie was tempted to tell him the wild monkey sex was fabulous. Instead, she told him another lie. "I had a *wonderful* time. Thanks for asking."

She was relieved when a rather attractive brunette entered the room, pre-empting one of his famous wise-ass answers.

The young woman introduced herself as Jan and told them she was the makeup artist. Annie felt like giving her a great big hug. She knew Matt would postpone drilling her further about her date with someone else present. He proved her right when he remained silent as Jan started opening and closing drawers, taking out her magic potions that would make them presentable to Atlanta's viewing audience.

Annie glanced over at Matt again, noticing the paper in his hand for the first time. "Is that your foolproof game plan?" She decided she might as well go ahead and let him get it out of his system if he were going to lecture her about not going back to the office the day before.

He shook his head. "Nope. Just a few rules of manhood to boost my confidence. I figured I might need them since I'm going to be outnumbered by you and Claire Winslow when the cameras start rolling." He grinned. "Want to hear a few timeless rules we men live by?"

"I'll pass," Annie told him.

"Are you sure?" Matt urged. "Not even just a teeny-tiny bit curious?"

Jan laughed. "Okay, I'll bite. Since it's obvious you're dying to piss one of us off."

"That would be me," Annie said, raising her hand.

Matt ignored her. "Rule number one, and possibly the most important. It is acceptable for a man to cry only under the following circumstances: (a) when a heroic dog dies to save its master; (b) the moment Angelina Jolie starts unbuttoning her blouse; and (c) after wrecking his boss's car."

Jan laughed.

Annie said, "Thank you for not sharing further."

"Just one more," Matt insisted. "You know. To help us get the old man versus woman juices flowing, so to speak."

He held up two fingers. "Rule number two. It is permissible for a man to sip a fruity tropical drink only when he's sunning on a tropical beach — then only if the drink is delivered by a stunning topless supermodel — *and* only if the drink is free."

"You guys are going to do great on *City Singles*," Jan said, chuckling as she dusted Annie's face with light pink blush.

"Yeah," Annie said. "Matt's a real riot."

She reluctantly closed her eyes for what she hoped wouldn't be a ton of some horrible shade of eye shadow.

But she'd already decided she wasn't going to let Matt get her flustered. She'd remained relatively calm in the face of having her throat *sleeted*, hadn't she? Matching Matt word for word would be a piece of cake.

Unless, her foggy brain said as it stretched and yawned, *the shark Greg warned you about takes an immediate liking to Matt.*

Ick. She hadn't even thought of that very good possibility. She'd had her mother and her date with Rico on her mind yesterday. Then, after the unexpected Rico and Helena dog-and-pony show at the restaurant, she'd been so emotionally drained she'd practically gone to sleep the second her head hit her pillow.

But Claire Winslow was bound to be attracted to Matt. Why wouldn't she be? He even had on that damn Hugo Boss suit that made him look like a million bucks.

"Good morning, Paragon," the familiar-from-television voice called out.

Annie opened her eyes to Claire Winslow's reflection smiling at her in the salon mirror Annie was facing.

Claire was tall and slender and had the standard television personality look. She was a definite aeroplane blonde — no visible black-box roots showing, but you knew they were there. She was obviously the beneficiary of thousands of dollars' worth of dental work. Her color-enhanced contacts gave her Elizabeth Taylor's violet-colored eyes. In other words, Claire was a real live Barbie doll, complete with silicone and even her own microphone.

Matt immediately sent Claire what Annie had come to recognize as one of his well-hello-there smiles.

He said, "I didn't think it was possible you could be more beautiful in person than you are on television."

Matt, Annie thought, *a hard-on does not qualify as personal growth.*

Claire instantly thrust her too-big-to-be-real breasts forward. "Why, Matt. That type of flattery will get you anywhere you want to go with me."

Just his type. Inflatable.

Matt laughed. Claire laughed. Annie thought, *If bullshit had wings, this place would be a freaking airport.*

But hey? What did she care if La Femme Shark devoured the flirty red herring who had just offered himself up as sacrificial bait? Matt was a big boy. He could take care of himself.

Annie only wished Jan had an instant game face she could whip up so she could get out of there. If Matt and Claire kept grinning at each other like two idiots in heat, they were definitely going to make her hurl.

Matt knew he'd shimmied out on a limb and taken a big risk trying to flatter Claire Winslow. But from the appraising look she was giving him, the flattery seemed to be working. He might still be a long way from the hand-kissing stage, but he had secretly read Annie and Collin's sainted what-a-woman-wants Joe Video script.

Talk about knock-you-on-your-ass shocked.

To think women supposedly appreciated such fakey and flaky responses from men had totally boggled his brain.

Still, he couldn't imagine a better time to put their theory to the test than this one. Not that he had any personal interest in Claire, because he didn't. What had Greg called her? A shark in the water?

Yeah, Matt could tell from the way she was looking at him now that Greg probably wasn't too far off track. Her eyes asked, "What can *you* do for me?" Matt was willing to bet that attitude was carried over into the bedroom as well.

He could see Claire being one of those women who rated a man's sexual performance with a give-me-an-immediate-orgasm meter. And if a poor guy happened to want to take things nice and slow and do a little exploring on his own, she would either shout out specific orders or grab his hand and put a quick end to his little discovery mission.

"The first thing I tell all of my guests on *City Singles*," Claire said with a big smile directed only at him, "is that we're here to have fun. Our viewing audience is basically made up of singles in their twenties and thirties, all looking for new information about anything pertaining to single life in the new millennium." She paused and looked from Matt over to Annie, then straight back to Matt. "Our female viewers are going to love Joe Video."

"That certainly won't hurt our feelings," Matt told her, and smiled again for good measure.

Jan stepped between them. "What do your rules of manhood say about men wearing makeup?"

"Rule number three," Matt said, trying to pretend he wasn't nervous about the dreaded makeup process. "Go easy on the eye shadow."

Jan laughed. "Eyes closed, please."

Matt closed his eyes, listening while Claire spent the next ten minutes going over what she had in mind for the format of the show. *And* praying he wasn't going to look like a drag queen when Jan finished with him.

Claire discussed the online poll she would announce during the telecast, encouraging the viewing audience to either make or break the game. In addition to a simple yea or nay vote, the online ballot had been designed to provide Paragon with a wealth of statistical information: age, sex, level of education, and occupation of the voter.

Claire reminded them they only had the first fifteen minutes of the show, since she'd borrowed time from a previously scheduled guest. Which suited Matt just fine. Surely he and Annie could survive fifteen minutes in front of the camera without killing each other.

She also cautioned that their man versus woman debate should be witty and light, not hostile and argumentative. "Viewers are turned off by open confrontation between the guests," Claire insisted, making Matt wonder if she'd ever compared her *City Singles* ratings with *The Jerry Springer Show*.

Claire rambled on about how the easiest way to get over stage fright was to ignore the camera completely. She assured them she would always keep the dialogue flowing so there wouldn't be a ghastly lull in the conversation. And she promised she would never ask either of them a question they couldn't answer.

Finally, she summed up with, "Any questions?"

Matt forced himself to open his eyes. His tan looked a little darker, but at least he wasn't wearing blue eye shadow.

"Yes. I do have one question," he said, realizing it was a little late to ask. "This stuff Jan just put all over my face will wash off. Right?"

The set for the *City Singles* morning show looked exactly like anyone would expect, Annie decided. Raised platform, carpeted in bright blue. Three comfortable-looking chairs, the upholstery the same shade as the carpet. A modern-design coffee table holding a water pitcher and several glasses. The backdrop, a floor-to-ceiling poster of the Atlanta skyline, aerial view.

She felt her mouth go dry when the man standing beside the huge television camera aimed in their direction held up one, two, three fingers and pointed to Claire.

"Good Morning, city singles," Claire said in a voice way too cheerful for seven o'clock in the morning. "Our first guests this morning are video game designers Annie Long and Matt Abbington of Paragon Technology. Paragon is based here in Atlanta and is responsible for the development of many of the most popular video games on the market today."

Breathe in, breathe out, Annie kept reminding herself.

"But wait, ladies," Claire said, holding up a polished finger. "Don't tune us out because you heard the words 'video game.' We have some exciting news for our female viewing audience this morning. Paragon has designed a new video game for women only. And he isn't your average Joe, ladies. He's called Joe Video."

Get ready. Almost time.

"According to Annie, Joe Video is every woman's dream guy. And according to Matt, he'll be every man's best friend. But we want *you* to decide, city singles. Register your vote to make it or break it. You can do that by logging on to www-dot-city singles-dot-com for our make-it-or-break-it poll. Tell us what you think, Atlanta."

Ready or not, here — we — go.

"Annie," Claire said, turning toward her. "Another member of your design team who spoke with me on the telephone yesterday told me you got your idea for Joe Video after you were *dumped* on a videotape. How embarrassing for you. Is that *really* true?"

A crowbar couldn't have pried Annie's tongue from the roof of her mouth at that moment.

She leaned forward, took the water pitcher from the coffee table, and managed to fill a glass with a shaking hand. She drained the glass in one easy gulp.

When she sat back in her chair, she forced herself to smile at La Shark. "Yes, Claire, as embarrassing as it is to admit, I did get dumped on a videotape."

But then Annie ignored Claire's advice and looked directly at the camera, addressing the women who could hopefully identify with her pain instead of exploit it. "I felt a lot like Carrie on *Sex and the City* when she got dumped on a Post-it note. Except I had a huge advantage Carrie didn't. I had the jerk on the videotape he'd sent me. I hit pause and froze him right where he stood while I told him exactly what I thought of him."

"I see," Claire began, but Annie ignored her, never once taking her eyes off the camera.

"That's when it hit me that every woman deserved such an option," Annie told the viewers. "And I don't mean having a jerk on a videotape. Women run into enough jerks in real life. I'm talking about a video soul mate that a woman can control with a remote or the click of a mouse. Her very own hero, like in the romance novels we women love because we're always guaranteed a happy ending. Except with Joe Video, *you*," — she pointed directly at her viewers — "will play the role of the heroine yourself. And Joe Video will guarantee you a happy ending at the end of every day, until a man worthy of your love and devotion finally comes along."

"Well, thank you, Annie," Claire said quickly. "We can certainly see that your horrible luck with men has left you bitter — but also extremely impassioned about this game."

Screw you, Jaws, Annie almost yelled.

Claire immediately turned to Matt and gave him a glowing smile. "Matt. I understand that you also support this new female-focused video game, but from a male point of view. Annie insists Joe Video will be a woman's own personal hero. Tell us why you see Joe Video becoming a man's best friend."

Annie was relieved when Matt didn't look at the camera but instead directed his comments to the pretty blonde sitting next to him. Had she been one of those women watching the show, that would have instantly pissed her off. What woman hadn't been ignored at some time or another in favor of a snooty blonde like Claire Winslow?

Annie sat passively by while Matt rambled on about

his "let Joe Video do the dirty work" philosophy, which would supposedly liberate men from all of those validating responses that they never seemed to get right anyway. That is, Annie sat passively by until she noticed that every time Matt finished a sentence, the camera director pointed to camera number two.

Gotcha! she thought when she realized they were switching back to her for her reaction to what Matt was saying.

"I think every guy out there should purchase a copy of Joe Video for the lady in his life the second the game hits the market," Matt said. "He should encourage her to enjoy her own video game romance where she can be the heroine. Maybe then she'll understand the fascination her man has for *his* video games. And maybe she'll stop giving him so much grief because he'd rather spend a little quality time with his PlayStation 2, instead of watching Lifetime on the tube with her."

When the director pointed to camera two, Annie made a big production of rolling her eyes, the way she was sure every woman watching was also doing at that very moment.

"A valid point, Matt," Claire said, "but shouldn't you also warn men out there that Joe Video has"— she looked down at her notes —"a 'Pleasure Me' option for the ladies?"

Annie winked at camera two.

"I mean seriously, Matt," Claire continued. "What guy wouldn't be a little intimidated by his lady spending *intimate* time with some fantasy video game man?"

Poor Matt suddenly cleared his throat, possibly at the feel of sharp teeth quickly closing around his windpipe.

He finally said, "I don't think I need to *warn* men

about any aspect of this game, Claire. The 'Pleasure Me' option is a self-discovery exercise that is intended to help a woman get in touch with her *sensuous* side." Matt finally caught on and looked directly at the camera. "How about you guys out there? Would any of you complain if *you* benefited because your lady spent a little time getting in touch with her sensuous side?"

"Well, there you have it, city singles," Claire said. "We want to give you ladies a sneak peek at the video hunk who will be more than happy to help you get in touch with your sensuous side."

Annie watched as a photo of Rico appeared on one of the studio monitors. It was the shot of him leaning against the doorjamb, thumb hooked in the waistband of his faded jeans, hair across one eye, and that sexy please-come-and-play-with-me smile on his lips.

Annie smiled.

Sales are sales are sales.

Miraculously, she and Matt had both survived the fifteen-minute shark attack.

The second they cut to commercial, Annie stood up, unhooked her microphone, and tossed it onto her chair. Despite her personal feelings toward the woman who had just embarrassed her in front of thousands of television viewers, she did the professional thing and thanked Claire politely for having her on the program.

It didn't surprise Annie that her thank-you was barely acknowledged, or that Claire quickly turned back to Matt. "I hope you don't have to leave so quickly, Matt," she said. "If you'll stick around for the remainder of the show, we'll check the poll results together when I'm finished."

Annie didn't wait to hear Matt's answer.

Of course he would stick around. And not, Annie suspected, only because he was interested in the poll results. It would be a big surprise if Claire didn't already have her own booty-call Web site up and running. The witch would probably even be turned on by Matt's stupid rules of manhood.

Rule number four, Annie thought. *The only acceptable excuse for a man not sticking around for possible future sex with a bleached-blonde television talk-show host is if said man is six feet under and doesn't have a shovel in his cold, dead hands.*

To hell with both of them.

Annie headed to her car.

She'd no sooner pulled out of the parking lot than Collin rang her cell phone, literally bubbling with excitement. "You looked amazing on television," he said. "Although I would have gone for more color than your basic black and white."

He just had to throw that in, Annie knew, miffed that she didn't consult him before she dared risk what Collin called a "wardrobe malfunction."

Too bad.

She was miffed herself.

"If this is the member of the creative team who spoke with Claire Winslow on the telephone yesterday," Annie said, "please inform Mr. Chatting Up the Enemy I'm not talking to him at the moment."

That got his attention.

"*And*," Annie said, "ask him how *he* would feel if I told the entire city of Atlanta he had a gay police buddy do a complete background check on every man he met. Thanks to a brief encounter he'd once had with a to-die-for credit card thief from Miami."

She heard Collin gasp.

Annie grinned, snapped her cell phone shut, and tossed it on the passenger seat. It rang a second later, but Annie ignored it. Let Collin have a few minutes of angst. He deserved worse. If she'd been the type to pout and hold a grudge, telling Claire about her being dumped on a videotape would have been good for a week's worth of silent treatment.

Of course, Collin knew as well as she did that she'd never be able to make it through an entire day without talking to him. As much as his gossiping annoyed her, Annie also knew Collin's motormouth affliction had no malicious motivation whatsoever. He simply couldn't help his gotta-tell-it-all bad self. Collin was a hopeless blabaholic. Just as she, according to her mother, was a hopeless maleaholic.

Thinking about the first order of business in her soon-to-be maleaholic recovery program, Annie leaned over and retrieved her cell phone from the passenger seat. When she coasted to a stop in the snarl of early-morning traffic, she used her thumb to scroll down her phone book until she found the stored number she was looking for.

"Did you watch *City Singles*?" she asked Rico as she held her cell phone between her chin and her shoulder. She shifted gears and then rolled forward hardly far enough to bother with the effort.

"Yes, I think it went well, too." *Except for the part about having to admit on live TV that my ex dumped me on a videotape*. She pushed that thought aside and asked, "How did it feel to see yourself on TV?"

Annie laughed. "I think you mean 'the cat who swallowed the *canary*,' not the cranberry, Rico. But that's the reason we chose that photo. Your smile makes it appear you have a secret. We want women to buy the game and find out what that secret is."

Finally. The traffic was moving again.

"How did it go with Helena last night?" Annie couldn't resist asking. If Helena had been successful zapping him with her passion-is-everything plan, maybe Annie's worries were already over.

She should have known better. Rico mumbled something irrelevant about Helena, then immediately asked when he could see her again.

"Soon," Annie said, as disappointed as her answer was vague. Especially since she could kick herself for being suckered into Helena's the-man-who-got-lost-in-ten-days plan.

Annie made another stab at getting herself out of the situation. "If we get a good response from the *City Singles* viewing audience, billboards are going to go up all over Atlanta this weekend with that same picture of you, Rico. So be prepared. Once we leak to the press who you are, you're going to have so many women chasing after you, you won't even remember my name."

Annie groaned inwardly when Rico insisted that would never happen. "Well, have a good weekend, and be ready to start filming bright and early on Monday morning." Before he could press her about going out with him again, Annie muttered a quick "Bye now," and closed her cell phone.

Damn.

The one and only time she'd ever had the opportunity to play the role of the *dumper*, the damn dumpee wouldn't take her seriously.

Her irritation only increased when the traffic slowed

to a standstill again. Annie scrolled to another stored number on her cell phone. "Hey, June. Could I speak to my mother for a second?" She laughed. "You're not going to believe this, June, but I thought you said Bev wasn't coming into the office today."

Annie frowned. "Is she ill? No explanation at all? Thanks, June. I'll call her at home."

By the time Annie reached the Bank of America Plaza, she had left urgent messages on both her mother's home phone and her cell phone. She wasn't being dramatic. Bev taking a day off wasn't only unheard of, it was downright sacrilegious.

She tried to remember the last time her mother had even taken a vacation. She couldn't. Possibly all the way back to Annie's thirteenth birthday, when Bev had taken her to New York City and they'd spent two glorious weeks doing everything there was to do in the Big Apple. They'd even stayed at the Waldorf, a memory she would always cherish. In fact, the entire vacation was one Annie would always treasure and one she hadn't thought of in a long, long time.

By the time she reached the thirty-second floor, Annie had already decided if she didn't get a call back from her mother within the hour, she would head to Druid Hills and investigate the situation herself.

She made that decision, however, before she walked into the full-blown party going on at Paragon. The fact that it was only nine o'clock in the morning didn't seem to matter. The excited group of people gathered in the reception area gave her an enthusiastic round of applause the second she walked through the door.

*   *   *

"So? What would you say if I told you I didn't have any plans I couldn't break tonight? And that I'd like nothing better than to spend the night getting naked with you to celebrate your huge Joe Video success?"

Matt tensed when Claire leaned against him and boldly ran her hand not so gently across the front of his crotch. The effect was that of a turtle jerking its head inside its shell.

He let out what he hoped sounded like a disappointed sigh. "I'd say those words are going to make this grown man cry, Claire. When I called J.B. with the good news a few minutes ago, he told me to be prepared to pull an all-nighter. Now that we know what type of response we can expect for the game, we have to get ready to start filming on Monday."

If Claire suspected he was lying, she didn't show it. She stepped back and struck a pose that practically thrust the fully erect nipples poking against the sheer fabric of her blouse in his face. With her lips pursed in a pretend pout, she gave him a slow once-over before she said, "For you, I'll extend a rain check. But don't disappoint me again, Matt. I'm used to getting exactly what I want."

I don't doubt that for one second, sweetheart, Matt thought.

He lied again when he said, "Give me a few weeks to get this game up and running, and I'll call you to cash that rain check."

Then, Matt swam away as fast as he could, out of reach of the hungry shark, who still managed one more crotch-clutch in passing before he made it out of the green room.

"What a piece of work," he grumbled to himself as he headed across the studio parking lot toward his Jeep.

He'd run across bold, pushy women in the past, but Claire was definitely in a class all by herself. He was surprised she hadn't demanded that he take his bad boy out and let her measure it right there on the spot. Besides, that's what she'd been doing anyway. Feeling him up so she could size him up. Making sure he was well worth her time.

God, he hated to admit it, but being around Annie and Collin was starting to rub off on him. He was evidently getting in touch with his feminine side more than he realized — even if only through osmosis.

I actually feel violated.

When two guys started laughing a few cars away, however, Matt was reminded real quick what kind of response he would get if he told any of his buddies he'd felt violated when a hot chick like Claire Winslow, shark or not, practically rammed her hands down his pants and told him she wanted to get between-the-sheets naked with him.

I'd never live it down.

His buddies would laugh him right out of Atlanta.

Matt shook his head, trying to determine exactly what was responsible for the sudden shift in his outlook on life. It was beginning to scare him. He was secretly reading corny scripts about what a woman wants. He was backing off from brassy women willing to get naked. And most of all, he was letting the whole Rico business mess with his mettle.

He'd been shocked that in the short span of an hour, the *City Singles* Web site had received over 35,000 hits — the majority from women — and an unbelievable ninety-five percent in favor of Joe Video. Wasn't that enough to make any guy worry that he didn't know jack shit about his role as a man in the female scheme of things?

Worse yet, that he probably never had?

As he drove out of the studio parking lot, he knew he should be shouting to the rafters over their success with Joe Video. His promotion was practically a guaranteed shoo-in now. Yet here he was, actually dreading going back to the office for the first time since he'd started working at Paragon Technology.

He was used to being the resident hunk, so to speak, dammit. He was used to strolling into Paragon, doing a bit of innocent flirting here and there, and walking back to his office with the satisfaction that he still had what it took to turn a pretty head.

But lately, if there did happen to be the usual chick cluster at Kathy's desk, the women barely even looked in his direction.

Hell no.

His once faithful admirers were too busy trying to pry information out of Kathy as to when Rico might show up for what had become his daily take-Annie-to-lunch routine.

Annie.

Another big sore spot where Matt was concerned.

Like now. When he returned to Paragon, he'd have to laugh and smile and pretend he was excited about Joe Video while he accepted everyone's congratulations. And all the while, he'd be silently seething over Annie's *wonderful* comment about her date with the man whose picture would soon be up on billboards all over Atlanta.

The little liar.

He didn't care what Annie said, there was no way she could really be serious about Rico. She knew it. He knew it. And when he got back to the office, he was going to make her listen while he finished the conversation they were trying to have when Greg Wilson had barged in and interrupted them.

He'd apologize.

Annie would put an end to her pretend affair.

Then he wouldn't have it on his conscience that Annie had gotten involved with jerk Rico just to spite him.

End of freaking story.

CHAPTER 10

A stalled eighteen-wheeler had kept Annie from being in the office when Matt called from the television studio to report the good news. But it didn't take long for Collin to fill her in on all of the details.

J.B. had declared an all-day TGIF party in honor of their big success. And to make it a real TGIF party, he'd not only ordered a champagne breakfast for the entire office, he'd promised a fully catered lunch as well.

Collin ushered Annie into the boardroom, where the long mahogany table had been covered with thick white tablecloths. According to Collin, the steaming silver serving pans held everything from eggs Benedict to good old southern homestyle grits. Standing behind the table in crisp white jackets were hired servers with big smiles on their ready-to-please faces.

Even J.B. Duncan couldn't have made such elaborate arrangements on such short notice. He'd obviously been sure of their success from the very beginning.

"I know you're not talking to me, lovey, but that's okay. I deserve it," Collin said, grabbing an already filled champagne flute and handing it to her. "Still, I also deserve to be your first clinky-dink, whether you're pissed at me or not. I've been behind you on Joe Video from the very beginning."

When he clinked his bubbling glass against hers, Annie said, "Are you trying to make me feel guilty, Collin?"

Sheepish best defined the faint smile Collin sent her. "No. I feel guilty. I'm sorry I told that horrible woman about the videotape. I would willingly curl up and die if I thought you were never going to speak to me again."

Annie took an unhurried sip from her glass before she said, "You know, Collin, groveling with a dash of deep remorse looks extremely good on you."

They both burst out laughing.

Annie had just finished telling Collin what a witch Claire really was when the room suddenly grew quiet.

Collin looked past her and said, "Who on earth is that?"

Annie turned around and quickly handed Collin her champagne glass. The "who" that had everyone's attention was Helena standing in the boardroom doorway. She was wearing another hoochie-mama outfit and four-inch spiked heels. Yet her nose was in the air with such complete confidence she might as well have been swathed in Versace or Prada.

"She's a friend of mine," Annie said and hurried off before Collin could quiz her any further.

"You said you were going to *call* me," Annie said, grabbing Helena by the arm and pulling her toward the nearest place of refuge.

"I am calling," Helena said. "In person. Now."

"Well, you might have noticed that *now* is not a good time."

Annie practically pushed Helena through the door and

into the women's restroom. The moment they were inside, Helena turned around, her hands on her slim, spandex-clad hips.

"Again we are meeting in the toilet?" she said. "You have no big fancy office on this thirty-second floor?"

"I have an office that I share with other people," Annie said. "People who don't need to know *our* business."

The explanation seemed to pacify her.

"I'm sorry you came without calling, Helena. I doubt I'm going to be much help with Rico after today anyway. The party going on outside is because Rico is a big success. His picture is going to be plastered on billboards all over the city. Women who *will* be interested in him personally are going to be all over him everywhere he goes."

Helena's shoulder came up in a shrug. "I do not fear those women." Annie expected the throat-slitting motion, but Helena said, "It is you who makes me worry."

Annie let out a long sigh. "Look. I told you before. I have no personal interest in Rico whatsoever. Period."

She tossed her long black curls over one shoulder, her look still suspicious. "Rico, he can be very good at changing minds. You might change yours. That is why I come. There is something you do not know."

"And that would be?"

Helena took a deep breath and said, "Rico did not break our engagement because it is you he loves, like I am thinking. He will not honor our engagement because his oldest brother, Ernesto, ordered him to postpone our wedding plans. Ernesto is greedy. He wants big money. He was afraid your company would not want Rico if he was engaged."

"And Rico agreed to break your engagement? Just because his oldest brother told him to postpone it?"

Helena said, "Of course. Ernesto, he is the head of the family."

Annie shook her head, trying to clear it. "Then I guess we don't have a problem, do we? As soon as we finish filming, you and Rico can go ahead with your wedding plans."

Helena shook her head. "No, no, no. Rico's middle brother, Manny, he is the one who told me everything. Ernesto did not order Rico to send the flowers. Ernesto did not order Rico to buy you the lunches. Manny knew this and he was worried. Manny has been watching Rico closely. He listen when Rico say to someone he is winning you over because you can make him a mucho mucho mucho big star."

It took Annie a second to realize what Helena was trying to tell her. "Me? You mean Rico thinks I can make him a star other than just the video game?"

Helena nodded. "Sí. A big star out in Hollywood."

Annie couldn't believe what she was hearing. So that was it. She'd been flattered by the attention in the beginning, but she'd always known something wasn't quite right about the whole situation. Rico was pursuing her because he thought she could further his acting career?

Well, damn. Rico was just another typical self-centered male, after all.

"You are getting angry. I can see it," Helena said, a worried look on her face.

"Yes," Annie said. "I am getting angry. Rico has done a rotten thing to both of us. Especially to you."

Helena nodded. "Rico is the wolf hiding under the cover of the sheep's wool."

Annie stared at her. "I don't understand, Helena. How

can you still love him, when you know Rico is being so deceitful?"

Helena stared back at Annie as if she were nuts. "What? You think you cannot love a man unless he is perfect?" She shook her head. "I do not understand how you think up here." She tapped a finger to her forehead. "You love who you love. You take the good with the bad. Each day it is your duty to make the bad not so bad, and the good a little better. That is what I will do. Rico will think coming back to me is his idea. Then I will put a collar around his wolf's neck and tame him. A little each day. One day at a time."

If I'm not careful, Helena is going to start making sense. "Or," Annie said, refusing to accept such simplistic logic, "we could face Rico together and put an end to his game playing right now."

Helena stamped a four-inch spiked-heel foot. "Are you loco? We tell Rico now and he would be angry. I would not get him back and Rico would not do your filming."

Good point. "So?" Annie said. "What do you suggest?"

Helena smiled. "Let Rico think he is winning you over. We will play the game better. Just like we agreed." She unzipped her fanny pack and took out a folded piece of paper. "These are two things Rico hates women to do. You try these. Rico will not be pleased with you. He will not want you helping him to be a big star."

Helena pointed to "smoking." "Rico, he hates to see the women smoke. In the bar, all the time they are smoking. The smell in their hair and on their clothes, he hates it. It makes him sick to the stomach."

"I can understand that," Annie said.

Helena pointed to "gambling." "Too many of our people are slaves to the lottery. All the time they are buying the scratch-off tickets. Wasting their money on false hopes when they can barely put the food on their tables. To Rico, gambling is a mortal sin. You buy some of these lottery tickets. You show him you are foolish and wasteful. Rico will not want you helping him to be a star if he thinks you are hooked on the gambling."

Helena handed the list to Annie. "You try the smoking. You try the gambling. If they do not work, we will talk again."

Annie stuffed the paper in the pocket of her DKNY suit jacket. "Well, at least I won't feel so guilty about tricking Rico now," she said more to herself than to Helena.

Helena laughed. "This is what I was hoping by coming to tell you what I just found out from Manny. Rico is playing a big trick on you already. Now I am sure you will not want my Rico for yourself."

"I've never wanted Rico for myself, Helena," Annie said. "But I'm glad you told me the truth."

Helena paused for a second, a puzzled look on her pretty face. "If you never wanted my Rico, why not? Because there is someone else that you love?"

Annie hesitated. "No. Not at the moment."

Helena shook a finger at her. "You are not a good liar, Annie. That is something we must work on if you are going to trick my big bad wolf."

By the time Annie finally got rid of Helena and sent the Hispanic bombshell on her way, her head was reeling. Helena was definitely a tell-every-graphic-detail kind of gal. Helena had stripped off naked? For urgent sex right there in Rico's car? In the restaurant parking lot where anyone could have seen them?

Please.

Or maybe Annie just felt that way because her own sex-in-the-car career had ended after her humiliating punch-chuck episode when she was only sixteen years old. She still had occasional nightmares about that coming-of-age experience.

Still shaking her head, Annie was trying to erase Helena's ever so graphic thrust-by-thrust details from her mind when she walked back into the boardroom. Just as she knew he would, Collin made a beeline in her direction.

With eyebrows raised, he said, "So? What game are you planning to launch next? A "Ho" video game?"

"She isn't a ho," Annie said. "I met her at the restaurant last night with Rico." Annie said this with a straight face, determined to prove Helena wrong about her lying ability.

Collin motioned with his hand to continue. "And?"

"*And*," Annie said, "she wants me to help her find a secretarial job."

There.

How was that for telling a big fat fool-any-wolf whopper?

Collin seemed convinced. "Did you tell her the first order of business would be to get her bad fashion fatality self a new look?"

Fortunately, Annie didn't have to think up another lie in answer to Collin's question. The room burst into applause again when Matt walked through the boardroom door.

So this is why J.B. stressed I should hurry back to the office. He should have known the old man had something up his sleeve.

Matt put on his fake smile as he accepted pats on the

back and congratulations, trying to work his way across the room to where Annie and Collin were standing. He'd almost made it when J.B. walked into the boardroom and stopped him in a booming voice that always got everyone's attention.

"Now that both of our rising stars are back, I think a toast is in order," J.B. said. "Matt. Annie. Grab yourselves a glass of champagne and come stand beside me where everyone can see you."

They both obeyed the boss's order.

J.B. directed Matt to his right side and Annie to his left. Then the big man regaled everyone with the amazing responses they were still getting for Joe Video on the *City Singles* Web site.

Matt chanced a glance at Annie.

She didn't look happy.

Maybe he should get her alone for a quick pep talk as well as an apology, Matt decided. Boost her morale a little. Remind her what was at stake. Encourage her to stick with the game plan now that they practically had the promise of their promotions locked down tight.

But hell. *Who am I kidding?* How was he going to boost Annie's morale when his own promotion was becoming less important every day? Thanks to the overall turmoil the Joe Video project was causing in his life, if anyone needed a morale boost, it was him.

Sometimes life is just one big pain in the ass, Matt thought. The things you thought you wanted most ended up being inconsequential. And the things you told yourself you never wanted kept annoying you like a damn toy poodle humping your ankle.

When J.B. finally finished his center-stage performance, Matt decided taking Annie aside for a private discussion was a necessity. He would give her the pep talk. Right after he apologized for their argument over Rico.

He was just about to ask Annie if she could talk to him for a second in private when J.B. turned to him and said, "We have some strategizing to do, Matt. This project is picking up momentum faster than we anticipated. Staying ahead of the game is our first priority."

With his arm firmly around Matt's shoulder, J.B. led him out of the boardroom and down the hall to his private executive office suite.

As soon as Matt and J.B. left the boardroom, Annie walked over to the chair where she'd dumped her purse earlier. She dug out her cell phone. *Drat*. Still no message from her mother — and it would soon be noon.

She didn't realize she was frowning until Collin walked up beside her. "Would you stop frowning and at least *act* like you're having a good time. This party *is* being thrown in your honor. Remember?"

"I'm worried about my mother," Annie told him. "I called her earlier and her secretary said she'd taken the day off."

"So?"

"So, Bev never takes the day off. Never."

"Maybe your mother is scoping out another great case like LOOTA," Collin said.

Annie groaned. "Don't remind me."

LOOTA stood for Lesbians Outraged Over Theater Advertising. It was a class action lawsuit Bev had taken on the previous year, challenging the practice of making moviegoers sit through not only upcoming feature film trailers, but also advertising commercials that the outraged lesbians claimed were prejudice because they were tailored strictly for a heterosexual audience. The local media had made so much fun of the lawsuit that many theaters profited by selling T-shirts at their concession stands that read: *LOOTA — The Real Reason Lesbians Are Suing Our Theater.*

"Maybe you're right," Annie said. "Maybe Bev's just caught up in another one of her outrageous causes."

But that thought didn't keep her from trying both numbers again. When she still only got her mother's voice mail, she looked at Collin and said, "How bad do you think it would look if I ducked out of here for a little while?"

Collin made a face. "Honestly? I don't think J.B. would like it."

But Annie didn't have to make that risky decision.

Matt suddenly appeared beside her. "J.B. has a few things he wants to go over, Annie, and he wants you to be in on them."

Crud.

Annie shoved her cell phone back into her purse, hooked the purse strap over her shoulder, and headed for J.B.'s office when Matt motioned for her to follow.

To say this particular TGIF had been one of the most exhausting days of her life didn't even put a dent in the fatigue Annie felt. She'd passed the exhaustion stage several hours earlier.

Other than a short break for lunch and a quick bathroom break, she'd spent the entire day in J.B.'s office.

Still no message from her mother.

She'd even called Bev's office again at lunch. Same story from Bev's secretary. Not a word from Bev all day.

When J.B. finally gave them the go-ahead-and-leave

nod at 5 p.m., Annie bolted out of her chair before Matt could say something stupid like they were willing to stay as long as J.B. needed. She quickly thanked J.B. for the party. She thanked him for the incredible support he had given Joe Video from the beginning. Then she excused herself, fumbling for her cell phone before the door to his office even had time to close behind her.

Dammit.

Where in the hell was her mother?

She hurried down the hallway and found Kathy placing the cover over her computer. "Finally," Kathy said when she looked up. "I was afraid J.B. was going to hold you and Matt hostage all weekend."

"That makes two of us," Annie said. "My mother didn't happen to call, did she, Kathy?" Bev always used Annie's cell phone number to contact her, but it didn't hurt to ask.

Kathy shook her head. "No. Sorry."

But before Annie could escape, Collin called her name and waved for Annie to wait. "A bunch of us are going to the Cabaña Club," he said, all excited. He grinned and did his signature "jazz-hands" dance. "I just love a group bar party, don't you? Lars is back from his weeklong coast-to-coast jaunt. He's going to join us there. He's so dying to meet you, Annie."

Annie groaned inwardly. The last thing she was up for was a group bar party. Before she could tell Collin exactly that, he waved to Matt, now sauntering up the hallway in their direction.

"Group bar party at Rico's Cabaña Club," Collin announced again. "Paragon's ready to party hearty, so get your salsa shoes on, big guy."

Matt never cracked a smile. His answer was a simple "I made other plans."

"Oh, I almost forgot," Kathy said, handing Matt his messages. "Claire Winslow called you all afternoon."

Collin frowned. "Is *she* your other plans?"

Matt neither confirmed nor denied Collin's suspicion.

Collin stuck his nose in the air. "I can't believe you'd rather spend the evening with a backstabbing bitch like Claire Asslow instead of hanging out with us."

Matt only grinned. "Be careful, Collin, someone might think you're jealous for all the wrong reasons."

Collin rolled his eyes. "Like I'd waste my time on a player like you, even if you *were* gay."

Matt blew him a fake kiss, tossed his hand in the air, and started for the door.

Collin looked over at Annie. "Can you believe him?"

At the moment, Annie was too tired to care. "Don't go ballistic, Mr. Party Hearty, but I've been up and running since four a.m. I'm not up for a group bar party, either."

"Puh-leeze," Collin scoffed. "It's Friday night and you'll slide into your second-wind zone as soon as you get out of this office. So stop whining. You can ride with me."

When Collin was in party mode Annie knew there was no point in arguing. But there was something she had to do first. "Okay, I'll go. But I'll catch up with you guys at the Cabaña Club later. The first thing I need to do is find my suddenly missing mother."

CHAPTER 11

B y the time Annie reached Ponce de Leon Avenue, she found that second-wind zone Collin had mentioned, where your energy snaps back and you decide you aren't as tired as you thought you were. Or maybe her sudden burst of energy stemmed from the fact that she was quickly going from concerned to flat-out angry.

It was obvious she was being ignored by her mother.

And Annie didn't like it.

She didn't necessarily talk to her mother every day. On occasion they'd even gone several weeks without talking to each other. But Bev was a faithful every-other-second message checker. Annie knew Bev was fully aware she'd been trying to reach her all day. For some reason her mother was *not* interested in returning Annie's call.

Which took Annie right back to being concerned.

After all, Bev would soon turn fifty. And she smoked. Although Annie had finally stopped nagging her about it. Bev's insolent outlook was: eat right, stay fit, die anyway.

"You have your vice, I have mine," Bev always reminded her, referring to Annie's "dipshit addiction," as Bev not-so-politely phrased it.

Thinking about dipshits pushed the dipshit who was

idiotic enough to date Claire Winslow right back to the front of Annie's mind.

Maybe she *would* head for the Cabaña Club after she gave Bev a good lecture, Annie decided. Hook up with Collin and the rest of the group. Even if it meant putting up with the other dipshit who had been causing her grief. Having to pretend she knew nothing about Rico's big Hollywood dreams wouldn't be easy, but it would certainly beat going home to an empty apartment where all she had to think about was what acrobatic position Matt and Claire were trying at the moment.

Yes, she would definitely go to the Cabaña Club.

She'd probably need a stiff drink after she had it out with Bev for ignoring her all day.

Annie made a right turn into Druid Hills, one of Atlanta's first planned suburban communities. The city sprawl had the area completely surrounded now, but wise Druid Hills residents had fought hard to preserve their space, protect their parks, and keep the hungry city from gobbling up the charm and the seclusion of the place they called home.

She had grown up in this subdivision. In the very house her mother was living in now, as had Bev. A charming old brick colonial that was slightly larger than some of the other residences, but not nearly as large as most. Her grandfather Long had purchased the house shortly after he returned home from Korea a decorated war hero.

Annie had always found it both tragic and ironic that her grandfather had survived a war, only to be killed a few years later in a freak on-the-job accident at the Southern Railway. His military pension and the generous railroad settlement had provided an adequate living for

her widowed grandmother to raise her baby daughter
alone. At least in the financial realm of things.

That both she and her mother had grown up without a
father, however, was a fact Annie had pondered often.
Was not having a father the main reason Bev had gravi-
tated toward a much older man like esteemed Professor
Thaddeus Dick? Also, was Collin's theory correct — that
Annie kept hoping to fill the father-void by searching for
her own Mr. Right who could provide her with the family life she'd never had the pleasure of knowing?

The parallel in her and Bev's lives didn't end there.

Annie's deceased genteel Southern grandmother had
been just as disappointed with a radical feminist daughter
like Bev as Bev had been with a Cinderellaesque daughter like Annie who was constantly looking for a Prince
Charming to make her life complete.

Annie often wondered what her own daughter would
be like — if she were ever lucky enough to have a daughter of her own. Conventional like her? Or radical like
Bev? The radical possibility made her shudder as she
pulled into her mother's driveway.

She turned off the engine and hopped out of the car,
briefly considering walking to the back of the house to
see if her mother's Volvo was parked in the garage. *Until*
she heard the stereo blaring from inside the house.

At last, the mystery was solved.

Her mother was lost in one of her crusading briefs
again, oblivious to the fact that Pavarotti was belting out
some aria loud enough to threaten a disturbing-the-peace
call from one of the neighbors.

Marching up the cobblestone path, Annie skirted the
three steps leading up to the brick front porch stoop. She
used her own key to open the door, knowing Bev would

never hear the bell above the ridiculously loud music. Once inside the house, she intended to make a left turn straight into the library that served as Bev's office, but she caught a glimpse of something reddish gold from the corner of her eye.

Annie stopped dead still and looked to the right, peering into her grandmother's never-used parlor. Her grandmother's Queen Anne sofa was positioned with its back to Annie, facing the parlor's brick fireplace. That's when fear reached out and grabbed Annie's heart with an ice-cold fist.

Her mother's head was thrown back against the sofa. Lifeless.

Her reddish gold hair cascading almost to the floor.

"Mother!" Annie screamed.

Sheer terror propelled her forward.

And sheer terror stopped Annie short when a head suddenly popped out from beneath Bev's long tie-dyed billowing gauze skirt.

This startled opera star was *not* Pavarotti!

Annie's hand flew to her mouth in horror.

She started slowly backing up as Bev and her interrupted guest both jumped to their feet, obviously as surprised and embarrassed as Annie was herself.

Oh. God. Oh. God. Oh. God.

Annie turned and ran.

By the time she reached her car, Bev was hurrying down the path behind her. "Annie! You wait right there."

Bev's angry tone caused Annie to whirl around, ready for battle. "Don't you *dare* act like you're the one who has the reason to be angry, Mother."

Bev crossed her arms stubbornly. "I have every reason

to be angry," she fumed. "Do you think I would ever invade *your* privacy like that?"

Annie threw her hands up in the air. "Well ex-cuse me! Tell me, Mother. When in my twenty-nine years of life have I ever had a reason to think my all-men-are-scum feminist mother needed *that* kind of privacy?"

When Bev didn't answer, Annie said, "If you'd bothered to call me back and confess you'd dropped out of the Feminist Majority and started seeing a man half your age, I wouldn't have freaked out and rushed over to see if you were lying dead from a heart attack or stroke."

Bev's eyes narrowed. "Umberto is *not* half my age. He's thirty-seven. And I resent you implying that I have anything to *confess*. Even to you."

When Annie didn't answer, Bev said, "I'm sorry I didn't call you back the exact minute you thought I should. I've been out of town all day. Umberto asked me to take a day trip with him to Valdosta to pick up a truckload of rose bushes. The white teacup is a new hybrid breed Umberto's really excited about."

"Just not the 'bush' Umberto was really excited about when I showed up!"

Oh God. Did I really say that out loud?

Bev's beet red face gave Annie her answer.

"I think you'd better leave, Annie. Before this gets ugly."

Annie lifted her chin indignantly. "It got ugly about three minutes ago, Mother."

She opened her car door, slammed it, turned on the ignition, and roared backwards out of the driveway. She left Bev there with an angry scowl on her still flushed face. But Annie only made it a few blocks away before she pulled over to the curb and stopped the car.

Dammit. Dammit. Dammit.

She pounded on the steering wheel with both fists.

Was her life turning into some kind of sadistic test? Were the let's-turn-Annie-into-a-raving-lunatic gods determined to rip everything she thought was true into nothing but shreds of her own self-fabricated lies?

Was there any truth in the world?

It was bad enough having to admit being adored, even if it had only been pretend adoration, had literally bored her to tears. But now she was going to have to swallow another bitter lie from a woman who had shamed her all her life for being a hopeless maleaholic?

Annie was beginning to think even gravity was a myth. Maybe what kept her sucked facedown in the dirt was only Mother Earth herself, doing so for nothing more than pure idle amusement.

God, she just couldn't believe it.

Her mother? Now an ex-feminist? Getting it on with a man thirteen years her junior and known around Atlanta as the freaking singing gardener?

Has Bev lost her mind?

First she'd picked a man with one foot in the grave. Now she'd decided to rob the freaking cradle!

Annie's hands were shaking as she reached for her cell phone. Going to the Cabaña Club was definitely out of the question now. Face Rico? Casually mention she needed a double shot of straight whiskey because she'd walked in and found his uncle's head beneath . . . *Oh God.* She couldn't even go there.

Maybe she could persuade Collin to leave his group bar party and meet her at his house. He always had the ability to help her make at least marginal sense of life as she knew it. She would tell him it wasn't a life-

threatening emergency, just a life-as-she-knew-it-
threatening emergency.

Annie found herself laughing hysterically as his cell
number started ringing. She was losing it. Life as she
knew it really was going up in flames right before her
ready-to-burst-into-tears, squeezed-tightly-shut eyes.

When Collin answered, she could barely hear him
over the din from the bar when he yelled, "Annie? I hope
you can hear me. I was just about to call you. Lars is getting frisky, so we're leaving early and heading to my
house. He's been gone all week, you know. Don't feel
bad that you couldn't make it. Most of the gang only
stayed for happy hour anyway. Annie? Annie? Can you
hear me?"

Annie disconnected the call without saying a word.

Then she burst into tears.

The fact that an elderly couple walking their pudgy
Boston terrier on the opposite side of the street looked in
her direction didn't matter. In fact, it only made matters
worse. Annie suspected even Mr. and Mrs. Somewhere-
in-their-eighties were probably hurrying to walk old
tubby so they could cuddle on the sofa for the rest of the
evening.

Crap!

Am I the only one on the planet completely alone?

Lars was getting frisky. Helena was probably stripped
off naked beneath the bar, letting Rico cop a feel between
his drink-mixing duties. Matt probably had Claire teth-
ered to his workout bench. Umberto and her mother . . .

No.

I'll never be able to go there.

Her sobs were becoming so loud the old couple had
now crossed the street and were walking in her direction,

concerned looks on their kind but wrinkled faces. At least she didn't recognize them as anyone she knew in the neighborhood. That's all she needed. Some neighbor to tell Bev her crazy daughter had a nervous breakdown sitting in her ridiculous bright purple car at the side of the road.

"Are you okay, dear?" the old woman asked, her arm still linked through her husband's.

Annie wiped at her eyes with her fingertips, trying to ignore that tubby was now happily pissing on her left rear tire. "Sorry, just an attack of nostalgia," Annie said, offering what she hoped was a believable excuse. "I grew up here in Druid Hills. Back when I was an innocent kid and life was wonderful."

The old couple exchanged knowing looks for a moment.

"Go make up with your young man, dear," the old woman said. "Makeup sex always makes life wonderful again." She turned to her husband. "Makeup sex still works for us, doesn't it, Morty?"

Morty winked and gave Annie an enthusiastic thumbs-up.

Okay, that does it!

Even eighty-something-year-old strangers were now telling her that what life really boiled down to was nothing but sex, sex, sex.

Annie bid the old couple a hurried good-bye and pulled away from the curb. With tears still stinging her eyes and her hands on the steering wheel in a white-knuckle grip, she made a decision that was going to change her life.

To hell with relationships, she decided.

If sex was the answer, then sex and nothing but sex was going to become her new mission in life.

It was time to live, breathe, and taste the passion. Badda-bing herself silly. And have makeup sex until life was wonderful again.

But with whom?

Her foolish heart told Annie she already knew the answer to that question.

But her much wiser brain yelled, "Not on my shift. No F-wording way!"

Matt crumpled the microwave popcorn bag in his fist and tossed it backwards over his head, then returned to his lethargic reclining position on his plush leather sofa. He aimed the remote at his big-screen TV, thinking that being home alone at midnight on a Friday night didn't bother him half as much as imagining what was going on at the group bar party at big man Rico's Cabaña Club.

Dirty traitors.

He'd intended to invite Collin and Annie for a group bar party of his own. Just the three of them. To celebrate privately. To make good on his idea to spend some creative team camaraderie time together. He'd intended to extend the invitation to Annie first, right after he apologized for the misunderstanding they'd had over Rico. He'd been sure Collin would agree to stopping off for a few beers. But during their break for lunch, Annie had spent her time with her back to the world and her cell phone to her ear.

Talking to Rico?

Probably.

And making Matt wonder exactly what Annie's "wonderful" time with the jerk really meant.

Surely she hadn't let Rico hand-kiss her out of her panties on the first date. Nah, that wasn't possible. Annie was smarter than that. He wasn't going to compare the one night they'd spent together with some meaningless dinner date she'd had with Rico. Not only had they spent two full months leading up to that mind-blowing experience, but the night never would have happened as soon as it did had they not accidentally bumped into each other when no one else was watching.

Nope.

Annie was *not* sleeping with Rico.

He'd bet his priceless Corvette on it.

Still, she'd sure jumped up and bolted out of J.B.'s office with her cell phone to her ear when five o'clock rolled around. Making him again miss his chance to pull her aside, apologize, and extend his invitation for a few beers.

Calling Rico again?

Probably.

To tell Rico all about the big group party heading his way. And making sure the night was going to be all about Rico, just as the day had pretty much been all about Rico and the off-the-chart responses Paragon had gotten to his stupid beefcake televised photo.

Well, screw Rico.

And to hell with Collin and Annie.

There was no way this dawg was going to roll over and beg for anyone's attention. Annie and Collin could salsa themselves into oblivion for all he cared. He was just glad Collin had assumed Claire Winslow was involved in his "other" plans. He sure as hell had no intention of ever admitting he'd had Collin and Annie in mind for the "other" plans he'd mentioned.

Both of them could politely kiss his royal —

Matt bolted upright.

The urgency of the finger on his doorbell propelled him over the back of the sofa without the slightest concern that he was wearing nothing but his boxer shorts.

It had to be Mike and Steve, he decided, chuckling to himself. He'd halfway promised to meet them at Sweeny's and tag along for the big bar crawl they'd planned through Midtown later on. Yup, they'd just be getting right and tight about now. If the big boys had come to get him, he *would* go along. Those two idiots would see to it.

"Ease off the bell, you drunken bozos," he yelled.

But his big grin disappeared when he opened his front door and found Annie standing in the hallway.

"Not the drunken bozos you were expecting, I gather?"

Matt was speechless. He finally said, "I wouldn't be this shocked if I found Catherine Zeta-Jones standing in my doorway." And he meant it.

Annie peeped around him. "Did I interrupt something? Or are you alone?"

Matt opened his front door wide as proof. "Care to come in?"

Annie shook her head. "Not yet. Not until I make myself crystal clear about why I'm here."

"The fact that I'm standing here in nothing but my underwear couldn't persuade you to at least step inside the door?"

Her eyes dropped to his boxers, then back to his face. "No. Not until we understand each other."

Matt frowned. He'd already decided if Annie had

come to give him a hard time over that prick Rico, she'd
picked the wrong damn night to do it.

"I want you to bing me," she said.

For the second time Matt was speechless. "Huh?"

"You heard me. Badda-bing, Matt. Your definition.
But that's all I want. No relationship bullshit. No idle
chitchat. I'm offering you a no-strings bingfest. Are you
up for the challenge or not?"

*Up for it? Matt Jr. was up for it the second you said
"bing."*

But when he noticed that Matt Jr. now had Annie's attention, Matt positioned himself slightly behind the door.
"Very funny, Annie. As much as this is one *fab* concept of
yours I actually could go for, something else is going on.
So spill. What's wrong?"

Her chin came up. "I said no idle chitchat. To bing? Or
not to bing? *That* is the only question I'm interested in."

She's bluffing.

The look she was giving him said she wasn't.

Matt decided to call her on it.

"Hell yes, I'm up for it," he said, taking Annie by the
arm and pulling her inside his apartment. He sent her a
covert grin as he made a big production of locking his
front door with a loud *click*.

"You want a bingfest?" He grinned again. "You've
come to the right man."

Then he reached down, slipped off his boxers, and let
Matt Jr. back up his bold statement.

This is the part where Matt expected her to toss some
obscenity in his direction and march out the door. Tell
him that's exactly what she expected from an insensitive
macho ass like him. Caution him that she never wanted to

hear him say another word against her adoring, precious, and sensitive Rico again.

Instead, what Annie tossed at him was something she took from the front pocket of her incredibly *short* short-shorts. It hit Matt in the chest with a thwack, but he caught it before it fell to the floor.

He looked down.

Holy shit!

A four-pack of condoms.

Annie was *serious*.

All Matt could do was stand there and stare.

Whoosh. Off came her top. *God, no bra*. Just breasts. Just two amazingly wonderful smother-your-face-in-me breasts.

Zip and Slip. Down came the shorts. No panties, either. *No panties. God, no panties*. Did he mention *no panties? Wow*. He definitely needed to start sending daily thank-you notes to the person who came up with that bikini wax idea.

He was fading in and out of sheer slap-happy delirium now, yet Matt was still fully aware there had never been a more perfect pair of mile-long legs than the ones walking toward him now.

Tug. Off came the ponytail thing. Now he really was a goner. Annie's long silky hair always knocked him on-his-ass silly.

He gulped when Annie took the pack from his hand and ripped one of the squares open with her bare teeth. He shivered when she helped Matt Jr. into his play suit.

"God, Annie," Matt whispered, but she clamped a hand over his mouth.

"No idle chitchat," she warned.

Before Matt knew what hit him, Annie had him on his

back on the sofa, with her on top. She positioned herself
so he slid deeply inside her and Matt moaned one long,
loud guttural plea.

Oh hell.

Was moaning allowed?

He couldn't remember.

But it didn't matter. His hands slid from her wonderfully hardened nipples to her tiny waist, trying to slow
her down. If he didn't slow Annie down right *now*, all
they'd be having tonight was a two-seconds-and-we're-
done fest.

Bing. Bing. Bing.

The warning bell sounded loud and clear again and
Matt quickly changed their positions. *Yes.* Much better
now. Now he was back in control. He could take things
slow and easy with him on top. Pleasure her just as much
as she was pleasuring him. Man oh man, how much
pleasure could one man stand?

Yeah, he could keep the old bing at bay all night in this
position. But then she pulled another dirty trick and
reached up and pulled his head down for a kiss like there
was no tomorrow.

Urgency grabbed Matt like the need to make a three-
pointer from half-court with only one second left on the
clock. *Go for it.* Those little bites on his neck were
driving him crazy. Driving him harder and faster and
harder and faster. *No. No. No.* Not the earlobe. He'd
never survive her sucking on his earlobe.

Oh, baby!

Matt finally managed to pull away from her, but the
second he did, Annie pulled another whopper of a sucker
punch. She flipped over on her stomach, arched her back,
and pushed temptation right up into his po'-boy face.

At that moment, Matt lost all sense of reason.

Annie — ever so tempting in that position — was the last thing Matt clearly remembered when he opened one eye several hours later to find her slipping out of his bed where they'd finally ended up during round four of their no-strings-attached and no-idle-chitchat bingfest.

He squinted at the illuminated dial on his bedside clock. "Annie. It's four in the morning. Come back to bed."

He cursed when she kept walking and closed his bedroom door behind her. *Damn.* He flipped on his bedside light and hurried to his dresser drawer for another pair of boxers. When he walked into the living room Annie had turned on a light herself, had on her shorts, and was pulling her top back over her head.

"Annie. This is crazy. You don't have any business wandering around Atlanta by yourself at four in the morning."

She sent him a defiant look when her head popped through the neck of her top. "I thought we made an agreement, Matt. No talking *during* or *after* sex. And don't worry about my safety. This isn't a relationship."

Matt shook his head and ran a hand through his bed-head hair. "You think I wouldn't have been worried about your safety yesterday, Annie? Or the day before? Even last week? Christ. There's nothing relationship-oriented about me being concerned that you're driving around Atlanta by yourself at four o'clock in the morning."

She slipped on her sandals. "I'll be perfectly safe. My cell phone's in the car. I can call 911 all by my big-girl self."

Matt frowned. "Well, I'm walking your big-girl self to

your car, whether you like it or not. So wait right there. And that's not idle chitchat. That's an order."

She shrugged. "Okay. As long as you promise no more chitchat on the way to my car. Chitchat after sex would make this seem like a real relationship."

"We can't have that."

"You bet we can't," she said, her nose in the air. "Relationships are your worst nightmare, and I've decided they're going to become mine. That makes us perfect bing buddies. At work we can go right back to business as usual. Just like we did after the first time we had sex. Only this time we can be mature about it. I know where you stand. You know where I stand. End of story."

"Yeah, end of story," Matt said with a sigh. He still hadn't figured out exactly what was going on with Annie, but at the moment he was too whipped to care.

Of course, then she smiled, throwing him completely off guard again.

"But I do hope you're willing to continue our bing arrangement, Matt," she said brightly. "This could really work out well for both of us. Just straight sex. No strings attached."

I get it, dammit. All you want from me is sex.

But if Annie was trying to pull some type of reverse psychology crap on him, she wasn't getting away with it. Matt purposely grinned and winked. "You're finally talking like a woman of my own heart, Annie. Anytime you need a bing, just give old Matt a ring."

Take that.

He could be as nonchalant as she was being.

If Annie wanted straight no-strings sex, that's exactly what she'd get from him. She could bet her cute little ass she'd never hear him complain about it.

Matt headed back to his bedroom to get dressed. When he returned, he played strictly by the rules. Neither of them spoke a single word as they left his apartment and headed for the visitor parking area. Matt didn't even say good-bye when Annie unlocked her car, slid behind the wheel, and turned on the ignition.

Hell no.

That might have fallen into the "too relationshippy" category and he would have been rapped on the knuckles by his new disapproving, rule-making bing teacher.

But what was really going on here?

Annie had spent the last four hours binging his brains out. Right now they should be upstairs in bed, basking in the afterglow of being completely sexually satiated. But what was he doing? He was standing outside his apartment. At four o'clock in the morning. Watching the woman he *wasn't* having a relationship with drive off in a bright purple Volkswagen.

What did a guy say to that?

One word sprang to mind.

Un-binging-believable.

CHAPTER 12

Annie had read somewhere that you spent one-seventh of your life dreading Mondays. She faced this particular Monday morning, however, with a huge smile she didn't have to fake. Reality had stolen the rose-colored glasses right off her snooty, I'm-holding-out-for-love nose. All she had to say about that was — *good riddance*.

For the first time in her life, she felt she was finally seeing life clearly. She'd been hopelessly chasing the elusive L-word for as long as she could remember. Now she realized that love basically equaled two vowels, two consonants and two *idiots*, temporarily addled by the *real* L-word — lust.

Well hell-o, lust!

Meet Annie Long, your new best friend.

At least lust was honest. Lust didn't have you dreaming about long-term commitments and wedding bells and baby booties. Lust didn't have you yearning for flower bouquets, cozy candlelit dinners, or romantic moonlight walks on tropical beaches. Lust was straight and to the point.

That's exactly how she'd approached her bingfest with Matt. Straight and to the point. She'd erased all other thoughts completely from her mind. She'd simply allowed herself to live, breathe, and taste the passion.

She felt liberated.

She felt reckless.

Yet she also felt amazingly in control.

She was going to forget searching for some nonexistent perfect man to make her happy. She was going to live for the moment. She was going to enjoy her success. She was going to revel in her big upcoming promotion. And never, ever, was she going to get hung up on the *phony* L-word again.

Amen.

Annie's own conscience, however, wouldn't let her get away without at least considering that her sudden jump to the down-with-love side of the fence had something to do with her ex-feminist mother's sudden mutiny. But what woman didn't do her best to make sure she was nothing like her own mother?

Once cynical Bev was now I've-found-my-true-soulmate Bev, according to the long and way-too-much-information message she'd left on Annie's voice mail over the weekend. And once looking-for-her-soul-mate but now cynical Annie had left a follow-up message for her mother, one that said Bev might want to start looking around for a good support group before she became a hopeless gardener-holic.

Childish?

Yup.

But Annie wasn't ready to talk to her mother about the big May–December affair Bev was having. At least not until she was comfortable with her own new outlook on life.

Her new outlook was so simple it had blown her away

when she finally realized what she'd been failing to understand all these years. Basically: happiness is pretty much a do-it-yourself kind of thing.

That lightning-bolt moment had hit her while she was standing under a hot shower, after she'd gone straight home from her embarrassing encounter with Bev and Umberto. All her life she'd been waiting for some man to rescue her and make her happy. To finally admit that no one could be responsible for her happiness but herself had been a life-altering experience.

But it hadn't been until later, after the next few hours she'd spent trying to figure out exactly what it would take to make herself happy, that lightning-bolt number two had zapped her silly.

She'd switched on *News Live at Eleven* to catch the latest report on Joe Video. And the face she'd found staring back at her from the television screen had been the same face she'd assumed was still playing whatever with I-made-other-plans Matt.

Everything that happened next was so surreal, Annie wasn't sure if she could ever explain it. It was as if she instantly developed a new personality. A new free-spirit Annie had jumped up from the sofa and dressed, leaving the old earthbound Annie slumped on the sofa munching woefully from her emergency stash of chocolate.

It had been the new free-spirit Annie who had shown up on Matt's doorstep shortly thereafter — to live, breathe, and taste the passion. God, how delicious that passion had tasted. She could possibly be on her way to becoming a bingaholic now, but there was no looking back.

Annie adored her new free spirit.

She liked the new her much better than she'd ever

liked her old earthbound self. She hadn't even been offended by Matt's "ring me for a bing" comment, which would have propelled the old earthbound Annie into a full-blown hissy fit. In fact, knowing she could ring Matt for a bing anytime she wanted was a huge relief now that the big relationship hunt had been crossed off her gotta-have-it list.

Matt had been a safe bing choice for many reasons. Sure, sex with him was sizzling, but that was merely an added bonus. She trusted him. He'd been honest with her from the beginning about his view on relationships, eliminating any danger of her ever backsliding. Plus she already knew he was healthy and had always practiced safe sex. They'd had what Collin called the "no glove, no love" discussion during general conversation way before they'd even had sex the first time.

She could also count on Matt to keep their arrangement a secret and keep it separate from the workplace. In other words, thanks to Matt being a willing bing buddy, the man-in-her-life-when-she-wanted-one worries were pretty much over.

No more bar scenes.

No more blind dates.

Just let her fingers do the walking and occasionally ring Matt up for a bing.

Annie was still smiling over her new outlook on life as she raced along the I-285 loop, heading for the first day of filming for Joe Video. After she'd explained to Gretchen what she had in mind for the setting of each Joe Video option, Gretchen had come up with the idea of filming the game at one of Atlanta's premier furniture stores.

Groveman's was famous for its individual showrooms

set up to showcase the store's expensive furniture. The store manager had been delighted to close its doors to the public and lease Paragon the facility for a full week of filming. Particularly since Groveman's would also be getting free publicity from the morning *City Singles* program, and from the four-page feature story that had appeared in the entertainment section of Sunday's edition of the *Atlanta Journal-Constitution*.

Marketing's huge buzz article had the full Joe Video scoop. The game was explained in detail. Rico and his Cabaña Club were featured. Anyone interested was encouraged to come get an up-close-and-personal look at the rising star of Paragon's new made-for-women video game during filming all week at Groveman's.

The "y'all come" idea had been J.B.'s. "Everybody loves a local celebrity, people, never doubt it," he had insisted.

Annie had never known the big man to be wrong yet.

She made her way into the far right lane for the upcoming exit, and she let out a loud "woo-hoo!" when she saw the huge billboard she was quickly approaching. Greg Wilson was a genius. The last thing you saw before taking the Groveman's exit was Rico's now famous photo. The caption under the photo was Paragon's own marketing slogan that Claire Winslow had used on *City Singles*: *Joe Video — Every Woman's Dream Guy. Every Man's Best Friend.*

Priceless.

When she reached the store, Annie had expected the TV crew and Claire to be at Groveman's. Exclusive coverage of the Joe Video filming had been part of the advertising deal Greg Wilson had negotiated with *City Singles*. What she hadn't expected was not being able to find a parking place in the store's huge parking lot. Especially when she'd made it a point to arrive early.

Sheesh.

It was only 8:30 a.m.

She finally found a space in the back parking lot at the rear of the store. But when she reached the front of the building, she got her next big surprise. The crowd of women gathered in front of Groveman's was enormous. So large that the security guards Paragon had hired for the weeklong event were already holding them back.

And standing in front of the store was Rico.

Looking completely overwhelmed.

Claire Winslow at his side, microphone in hand.

Dammit!

Annie started running.

She should have realized a bitch like Claire wouldn't think twice about jumping ahead and interviewing Rico alone, instead of honoring the scheduled 9 a.m. live interview they'd agreed on. She also should have made it a point to warn poor Rico about Claire. She'd just assumed she and Matt would be there to run interference when shark Claire started circling Rico, those thousand-dollar capped teeth of hers ready to rip him to shreds.

"Claire," Annie called out. She was too angry to take any satisfaction over the perturbed scowl the TV personality immediately sent in her direction.

The second she reached them, Annie said, "I'm afraid I'm going to have to steal Rico until our scheduled *nine o'clock* interview." She linked her arm through Rico's and quickly pulled him away from Claire and toward the waiting crowd.

"Ladies," Annie called out loud enough for everyone to hear. "Paragon is thrilled all of you are here this morning. Please don't leave early. We have a wonderful promotional gift for all of you that Joe Video himself will personally autograph after his nine o'clock live interview with *City Singles'* own Claire Winslow."

The crowd applauded with enthusiasm and Annie leaned toward Rico and whispered, "Blow these ladies a kiss. Smile that sexy smile of yours. And wave. Now."

Just as she knew they would, the women went wild.

"Boy, that was close," Annie said, practically pushing Rico through Groveman's front doors to safety. "I should have warned you about Claire, Rico. That woman can't be trusted. How long have you been here, anyway?"

"A few minutes only," Rico said, glancing nervously through the glass doors at the large crowd of women pushing and jostling for a better position in line. "The women. I was not prepared. They come running the minute the guards had me to park at the front of the store. Then the TV woman, she had the guards to push them back so I could get through the crowd."

"You mean Claire didn't have time to quiz you on live TV before I got here?"

Rico shook his head. "No."

Annie let out a sigh of relief. "Good. When we do the interview with Claire, you just be your gorgeous self. You look straight into the camera. You let me or Matt do all of the talking. Understand?"

Rico nodded absently, but his eyes were still fixed on the unruly crowd of admiring women, some waving to him now, trying to get his attention.

Annie looked him over slowly. It certainly didn't surprise her that Rico had almost been mobbed on sight. He was dressed casually, just as Gretchen had instructed, in his tight photo-fame jeans and a simple white shirt with the sleeves rolled up to his elbows. The stark white showed off his dark skin and his dark hair that was loose this morning and threatening to fall into his eyes, just like in the photo. To say he looked even better in person than he did on the billboard would be an understatement.

Gorgeous, Annie decided, simply didn't do Rico justice.

"Don't be nervous about your new adoring fans," she said, trying to encourage him. "These women already love you. All you need to do is be your charming to-die-for self."

He turned his head to look at her. When his sexy, come-on smile appeared, Annie noticed his teeth were just as white as the shirt he was wearing. "And you, Annie? Will you ever be adoring me?"

Annie automatically glanced through the window at Claire Winslow, who was now interviewing random women from the crowd. If Claire had even the slightest inkling that there was anything personal going on between her and Rico, the bitch would pounce on it in a heartbeat. Annie looked back at Rico. "Rico. Today has to be all about business, okay? Today you aren't Rico Romero. Today you're Joe Video. There's no room here for any personal agenda between me and you."

"I understand," he said, but he looked disappointed.

Annie smiled warmly, hoping to appease him. "I'm glad you understand. Because when we get in front of those cameras, the last thing we need to do is give those women out there" — she pointed to the crowd — "or those women watching TV at home any reason to believe you are interested in anyone but them. Okay?"

"Yes," he said. "Today, I am Joe Video. Every woman's dream man."

"Dream *guy*," Annie corrected. "Always use the marketing slogan. Your job today is to sell yourself to these women. You look them in the eye. You smile, just the way you smiled at me a second ago. You give them their own special dream to remember."

"A dream to remember," he repeated.

"Yes," Annie said, nodding happily. "Marketing had these incredible pink satin sleep masks made up for you to give to each of your adoring fans. You'll autograph them personally. Try to work the marketing slogan into each message. Write something like, 'Giving you a dream to remember — love, Joe Video.' Or, 'Let me be your dream guy.' Or just sign the masks, 'Your dream guy, Joe Video.' Any or all of those will work."

He glanced at the crowd again. "This signing. It will take place after the interview?"

"Yes," Annie said. "Immediately following the interview."

Rico sighed. "I am thinking this will be a long day."

Annie looked out at the still growing crowd and smiled. "Sales are sales are sales, Rico. That's why we're here. But don't worry. You're going to be fantastic."

Rico wasn't pleased when Annie led him deeper into the furniture store. She ushered him into a room decorated as a library. Then she pointed to a large leather chair and told him to sit. *And* to wait for her.

Like a sniveling pet dog, I am to sit here?

Sit, Rico, sit.

Mierda.

He stared after Annie as she hurried off to find her gay friend, Collin, and the man who Rico knew would never be a friend of his, Matt. He had picked up on the hostil-

ity the second he met Annie's boss. But it was Collin who
had confirmed that Matt did not care for him during their
conversation at the Cabaña Club on Friday night.

Joe Video had not been Matt's idea, Collin had said,
and Matt was not pleased about the game. But Rico knew
there was more. Annie was the reason Matt did not care
for him. Rico could see it in Matt's eyes. Though, according to Collin, there had never been anything personal
between Matt and Annie, Rico sensed that was a lie.

Annie.

She was still a mystery he could not figure out.

He had said nothing while she lectured him about
today being all business. He had held his tongue when
she talked to him like a child, reminding him how to act
to attract the women to him. Did she think he was estúpido? He needed Annie to further his career, maybe, but
he did *not* need Annie telling him how to attract the
women.

*She is the stupid one if she thinks I know nothing about
attracting women.*

He'd been attracting women, plenty of them, since he
was old enough to understand what went on between a
man and a woman. And he was not speaking of thirteen-
year-old girls who had been his own age. Grown women
who had eagerly opened their legs to a mere boy when no
one was looking.

Annie did not know this, of course. But he would
show her later she had nothing to worry about where Rico
Romero and women were concerned. He would have the
women waiting outside eating out of his hand within minutes. Maybe then she would treat him with the respect he
deserved.

But Annie's remark about the sales worried him.

It made him think of Helena's warning after they had finished making love the night before. "It is not you Annie wants, it is the sale of her game," she had told him with a smug smile. "And when the filming is done, she will toss you aside. Then, *maybe* I will take you back and marry you."

Maybe *Helena will take me back?*

Rico almost laughed. Helena had never let him go. She was still holding on. Still offering him her love and her amazing body on a daily basis. Silly woman. Helena would always be willing to marry him. Of that, he was certain.

Still, he couldn't keep Helena's poisonous doubts from creeping into his mind. What if Helena was right? What if Annie did toss him aside as soon as the filming was over? The filming would only take a week, and then his part in Annie's game would be over. If he could not think of something to draw her to him quick, his entire acting career could be over before it even got started.

Hijo de puta.

Son of a bitch.

He cursed himself, as he had done many other times, for signing the Paragon contract that had given him only a modest fee for his acting services. He should have held out for more. A percentage of the game, maybe. That would have given him his own money that was not tied to the family. Money he could use to further his career himself.

Sí. I was estúpido in that respect.

But he had also been afraid Annie would find someone else for her Joe Video game if he asked for too much. And then Ernesto and Manuel would have been furious. Their only interest had always been in the publicity for the club. "You will do what this fancy lady says," Ernesto had ordered. Never once concerned about his acting career. Only the family. Always the family.

Rico stood up and began pacing back and forth.

He could not allow Annie to throw him over as soon as the filming was done. He needed her. She was important. She could help him mingle with the power people. He could not do it alone.

Him?

A bartender from his section of the city?

Never.

Maybe he could come up with some marketing ideas of his own. Talk to the marketing man himself. Make sure he and Annie remained in the spotlight long enough to be introduced to people in Atlanta who could point him in the right direction and further his career.

For that reason, he would endure Annie treating him like her pet dog a little longer. He would endure Annie acting as if he were stupid. It would be a hard thing for any man to do, sí. But when things got too difficult for most men, they were just right for Rico Romero.

He was in the game to stay.

He was every woman's dream guy.

Joe Video.

The positive attitude Matt promised himself he was going to maintain on Monday jumped ship after the first five minutes he spent trying to find a parking space at Groveman's. Ten minutes later, he finally gave up and made a space himself. He shifted his Jeep into four-wheel drive, jumped the curb, and parked on the grass.

He was late.

He was pissed because he was late.

He was also still confused over what had really brought Annie to his door at midnight last Friday night.

He'd almost called her several times over the weekend, but he'd stopped himself. He'd thought of calling Collin to see if he knew what was going on with Annie, but he hadn't done that, either. Collin was the human equivalent of a revolving door when it came to information. The last thing Matt wanted was Annie calling Collin and finding out he'd tried to pump Collin for any kind of information about her.

So he'd spent the remainder of his weekend doing guy stuff like he always did. Watching sports. Drinking beer. Playing golf. Drinking more beer. All the while, he had kept reminding himself that the only way to handle the latest screwed-up situation with Annie was — as usual — to play along according to her rules.

Now it was Monday all over again.

Back to work as usual.

Not a problem for her. Not a problem for him. And *not* the end of the story. He'd bet his cherished autographed pictures of Babe Ruth, Mickey Mantle, and Lou Gehrig on it.

"Matt. Wait up."

Matt stopped walking toward Groveman's and turned to find Collin hurrying across the parking lot in his direction. The fact that Collin was grinning from ear to ear didn't exactly improve Matt's already bad mood.

"Isn't this fabulous?" Collin asked when he fell into step beside Matt. "I would have been thrilled if even a handful of women showed up this morning. Who knew we'd have a Joe Video mobamania on our hands?"

"Yeah, who knew," Matt grumbled.

"Well excuse me," Collin huffed. "Suffering from IMS

this morning, are we? Or are you just pissed because the gorgeous himbo is still grabbing all the zazz?"

Matt groaned. "Would you lay off the gaybonics and speak English if you're going to ask me a question?"

"Take notes," Collin chirped, never missing a beat. "IMS — irritable male syndrome. Himbo — the male version of a bimbo. Grabbing all the zazz — getting all of the attention."

"I'll be sure and run straight home and jot those down in my sacred gay phrase book," Matt told him.

Collin reached out and swatted him on the shoulder. "Oh, for Christ's sake, Matt. You've been acting like an old tomcat with his nuts in a knot for weeks now. What the hell's wrong with you?"

Matt sent a guilty look at his best friend. "You know I've been concerned about his whole woman-focused game from the beginning, Collin. My reputation is at stake here, dammit."

The eye roll told Matt Collin wasn't buying it.

"Don't make me call you a liar, Matt. You know as well as I do Joe Video is going to be a bigger hit with women than S&M&M."

"Than what?"

Collin grinned. "S&M&M — kinky sex with chocolate."

Matt said, "Spare me any more gay humor this early in the morning. Please?"

Collin said, "It's a deal. *If* you'll tell me what's really bugging you." When Matt refused to answer, Collin said, "Are you getting nervous about the big promotion? Because if you are, that's ridiculous. You always aim out of the ballpark, Matt. You'll be the best executive vice president in Paragon history."

"You nailed it. I'm worried about the promotion." Matt didn't even feel guilty about the lie. Collin loved being right. *All* of the time. Besides, there wasn't anything wrong with him. Nothing that reincarnation couldn't cure. The only way he'd ever understand Annie is if he came back as one of her frickin' brain cells.

"Talk about sucking the sunshine right out of a good mood," Collin snipped as they rounded the corner of the building. "I forgot *she* was going to be here."

Claire Winslow waved the second she saw them.

"I still can't believe you're attracted to that woman," Collin grumbled. "Claire Winslow's only flair is in her plastic surgerized nostrils. And then only when she picks up the scent of her next victim's fresh spurting blood."

Matt laughed. "What are you suffering from this morning, Mr. Adair? BHS?"

Collin sent him a sideways glance. "And that would be?"

"Bitchy homo syndrome?"

"That is *so* embarrassingly lame, Matt."

Matt grinned. "Only because you didn't come up with it first."

When they reached Claire, she leaned forward and gave Matt a quick kiss on the cheek. Then she openly appraised Collin from head to toe. "I think Paragon's been holding out on me," she said, sending Collin a brilliant smile. "Introduce me to your exceptionally handsome friend, Matt."

"His exceptionally handsome *gay* friend," Collin spoke up before Matt could make the introduction. "Collin Adair." He offered Claire the type of handshake you would extend to a leper. "Remember? We spoke on the telephone? Before I knew better than to tell you anything I didn't want repeated on live TV?"

Claire's smile disappeared and her right eyebrow arched slightly. "Oh grow up. Do I look like a freaking people person to you?"

Collin looked her up and down, his smile lethal. "Sorry. I can't get past that hideous so-yesterday suit you're wearing."

Claire's eyes narrowed.

"But you're absolutely right," Collin said. "After the thirty minutes you spent me-deep in conversation on the phone, I should have realized you were way too self-centered to be a freaking people person."

Holy hell.

The claws were out and the hair pulling was going to start if Matt didn't do something fast. He glanced nervously at the front row of women waiting in line, already moving closer at the sound of raised voices. Wouldn't that be something? TV cameras rolling. J.B. watching, smiling over the huge crowd of screaming women. Only to realize the women weren't cheering for Joe Video, but for a catfight taking place between Paragon's queen and a talk-show host princess.

Shit.

Matt quickly stepped between them. He took Claire by the elbow and led her away from Collin and through Groveman's double glass doors. A smart thing to do, he realized, since he could feel Claire literally shaking with anger as he held on to her arm.

"How *dare* he talk to me like that," she said, and Matt tightened his grip on her arm when Collin entered the store right behind them.

Collin swished past without so much as a glance, his

nose held indignantly in the air like some prima donna dropped off by mistake at a championship mud wrestling competition.

"Who *is* that little prick, anyway?" Claire fumed. She glared after Collin a second longer, then turned her pinched face toward Matt.

"Collin's my assistant," Matt said.

"Then fire the rude bastard." Claire stared Matt down. "I'm serious, Matt. If you won't fire him, I'll go straight to the top and see that he's fired myself."

Matt shook his head in disagreement. "Not a smart thing to do, Claire. Ever hear of Adair Carpet Mills? Collin's the sole heir. His position at Paragon is merely his hobby. I wouldn't cross a man with seventy-five million at his disposal, if I were you. Especially not a gay man who has no interest whatsoever in your feminine charms. Ignore him. Collin's just bitchy enough to buy the television station and have *you* fired."

That got her attention.

While Claire was still mulling over Collin's financial power to take away her microphone, Matt said, "Look. I know you have a rep for the slice-and-dice job you do on the guests who appear on *City Singles*. Your viewing audience probably even finds it amusing that you make your guests squirm. But my CEO isn't amused, Claire. In fact, unless you want Paragon to start courting your competition, this interview today needs to be one hundred percent client-friendly."

Up came the eyebrow again.

Matt could tell Claire suspected he was lying, but after her run-in with a man she couldn't screw her way around, he was counting on the fact that she wouldn't take that chance. He knew his hunch was correct when she stepped much too close for comfort, a fake smile spreading across her cherry red lips.

"Oh, I can be extremely client-friendly, Matt," she said, running a polished finger down the full length of his tie. "The question is, how friendly is the client — namely you — willing to be if I cut you some slack during this interview today?"

Matt smiled. But his little victory turned sour when he glanced over the top of Claire's bleached-blonde head and saw Annie walking in their direction.

God, she was breathtaking.

Her short white linen skirt showcased her amazing long legs. Her sky blue top was the same color as her eyes. If he'd realized all it took to get Annie in short skirts every day was the promise of a promotion, he'd have insisted that J.B. promote her ages ago.

But damn.

Annie stopped walking when she saw them. She took one look at the compromising position Claire had him in at the moment. Then she turned on her heel and marched off in the opposite direction.

Damn. Damn. Triple flipping damn.

He wasn't exactly sure why he felt guilty, but he did. He certainly had no reason to feel guilty. What had Annie called him? Her bing buddy? Bing buddies had no reason to feel guilty about talking to other women. Did they?

He'd worry about it later.

He forced himself to look back down at Claire, who was still standing so close the scent of her overused hairspray had his nose twitching. "Let's see how the interview goes first," he told her. "Then I'll let you know how friendly I can be."

"Oh, I have no intention of *disappointing* you today,

Matt," Claire assured him. "Just remember. When we finally do make it between the sheets, you damn well better extend me the same courtesy. *Or* you won't live to regret it."

What am I? Matt thought. *Flypaper for demanding women?*

Annie suddenly wanted nothing but no-strings sex. Now Claire was threatening to do what, pay some thug to kill him if he disappointed her in bed? *Damn.* Were women turning into nothing but bottomless pits of sexual demands? Or was his problem having a PBS mind in today's MTV world?

Exactly when did women get so damn pushy?

Better yet, when did he start caring that they were?

Finally, Claire backed out of his space.

Home free, Matt thought, until she slid her purse strap off her shoulder and pulled out a daily planner.

"So?" she said, taking a pen from the center crease in the planner. "What's good for you? Let's nail down a night for our date between the sheets."

How about never, Claire?

Is never good for you?

But Matt said instead, "Why don't I call you after I have this video game nailed down?"

She ignored him, pen still poised above her planner. "Why don't I just go ahead and put you down for Friday night. Eight o'clock. My place. You bring the condoms. I'll furnish the wine. And the *dessert*." She ran her tongue suggestively around her lips after she mentioned the "dessert" part.

Matt cringed. "And if I have to cancel?"

Claire snapped the planner closed. "Do you want this interview to be client-friendly today, Matt?"

Matt said, "I thought I'd already made myself clear about that, Claire."

"Just as I'm making myself clear now. You get what you want today. I get what I want Friday night. Canceling *isn't* an option. Got it?"

Oh, he got it, all right.

He was the *Titanic*.

Claire was the iceberg.

Sunk. Sealed. Delivered. I'm yours.

CHAPTER 13

He was sitting astride an exercise machine, his back to the camera, wearing nothing but a pair of skimpy red briefs. His bronze skin glistened under the bright sunlight flooding across the outdoor patio. With each movement, rock-hard muscles rippled across his broad shoulders, pulsating to the steady rhythm of the exercise bars he was pumping up and down.

He paused for a moment and looked back over his left shoulder, his ink black hair tumbling across one eye just enough to make any woman want to reach out and push it away from his too-handsome face. Then he smiled a megawatt smile powerful enough to make any woman's breath catch in her throat.

"Hello, gorgeous," he said, his thick Cuban accent sexy as hell. "It is good to have you home."

"Cut," Gretchen yelled. "That was perfect, Rico."

Annie nodded in agreement. "Absolutely perfect, Rico. You're doing a fantastic job."

"For the second frame," Gretchen told Rico, "I want you to do exactly what we rehearsed. Turn slowly around on the bench so we can get a full frontal view, and then bend down to pick up the towel. Then I want you to take your time toweling yourself off, Rico. Try to imagine what the camera is seeing. We want to give the player of this game her money's worth. When you're through, you look right here at Annie." Gretchen grabbed Annie's arm and pulled her closer to stand beside the camera. "That's when you say your next line. Then the camera will follow you walking to the patio doors before you go inside. Any questions?"

Rico shook his head — a bit sullenly, Annie noticed.

But when the camera started rolling again, Rico followed Gretchen's instructions to the letter. The full frontal view Gretchen had requested left nothing to the imagination. Everything Rico had to offer was clearly defined beneath the stretchy fabric of his tight-fitting red briefs.

And Rico had *plenty* to offer.

He bent down, picked up the towel, and as he began toweling himself off Annie tried to imagine what the camera was seeing. Her gaze slid over well-defined six-pack abs. As she watched Rico toweling himself off in such a sensuous and inviting manner, she actually felt a mini heat wave creeping up her neck. *Yum.* Whether she had any interest in Rico personally or not, she wasn't blind.

Rico was one hot hunk.

Hot. Hot. Hot.

He casually tossed the towel aside, looked directly at Annie, and flashed another heart-stopping smile. "Come with me. Inside," he said. "I will pour the wine while you tell me about your day."

Annie moved aside, giving the camera room to pan across Groveman's outdoor patio area as Rico, in all his muscled splendor, walked toward the patio doors that would take them inside for the next frame of the game.

Frame three would be shot in one of Groveman's designer kitchen showrooms, where Rico would take a chilled bottle of wine from an ice bucket, pour both himself and his game player a drink, push the player's glass toward the camera, and seat himself at a designer bar.

The next few frames would capture Rico's thoughtful expressions as they filmed him listening and responding appropriately to Joe Video Option Number One entitled "After Work Chat." Under "After Work Chat" the player had two options: Good Day or Bad Day. Once the player chose the option, she had complete control over when she wanted a response from Joe Video. All she had to do was push the "enter" key on her keyboard or the "A" button on her video game player. The script Annie and Collin had devised for either scenario was generic enough to fit any situation.

For a bad day, Joe Video had several responses, such as, "Poor baby, you didn't deserve that." For a good day, a response would be, "You are amazing. Did you know that?"

In fact, Annie was proud of the entire script she and Collin had worked on so diligently. She was also secretly pleased that for once Collin had been the one who kept Matt in check. Other than an occasional eye roll or a disgusted grunt, Matt had contributed very little to the script.

When it came to binging, Matt ruled.

But as Collin had said himself during one of their brainstorming sessions, "*Matt.* Listen to me carefully. 'Get me a beer, babe' and 'Could you toss me the remote' are *not* terms of endearment."

In addition to "After Work Chat" there was also a "Sounding Board" option, where the player could vent about the top five subjects on most women's vent list: her mother, father, significant other, friends, and boss. Joe Video's responses were always both encouraging and sympathetic.

The "Striptease Aerobics" option was what Collin called "a thirty-minute workout with eye candy"—namely Rico, clad in the skimpy briefs he was wearing now, leading the player through the striptease moves Annie and Collin had learned from the male stripper. *And* (upon Collin's insistence) with a lot of encouragement from Joe Video for the player to release her inhibitions and take it all off for his eyes only.

As a final advertising gimmick, marketing had insisted they save the steamiest segment, the "Pleasure Me" option, for Friday's last day of filming. In hope of drawing a large crowd throughout the entire week, marketing was running a "behind the scenes with Joe Video" contest.

On Friday morning, ten lucky Joe Video fans would be selected via a random drawing to watch behind the scenes while the camera filmed the last segment of Joe Video. Groveman's had gone all-out and set up a special lavish Roman-theme bedroom for the shoot. If bitch-of-the-century Claire did her job and played up the contest on *City Singles*, every woman in Atlanta would be dying to come watch Joe Video sprawled across a king-size Roman-column canopy bed, scantily covered by a satin sheet, and delivering sexy-voiced instructions on how to discover each and every one of a woman's erogenous zones.

Claire.

For once, thinking about Claire didn't bother Annie at all. In fact, the new Annie hadn't batted so much as an eye when she'd caught Claire and Matt in a clutch earlier that morning. Truthfully, all Annie had felt was relief.

She'd been a little worried over Matt's protective attitude when she'd left his apartment in the wee hours of Saturday morning. But seeing him with Claire had put those concerns to rest. Matt hadn't let her down. He was still good 'ol one hundred percent player Matt. Her absolute perfect choice for a no-strings-attached bing buddy.

"Hey," Matt said and Annie jumped.

She'd been so busy congratulating herself on her new attitude, she hadn't realized Mr. Bing himself had walked up behind her.

"Hey yourself," she said, flashing him a friendly smile. "Are you as pleased as I am over how well everything is going today?"

"The day isn't over yet," he warned.

"No. But the *worst* is over," Annie said. "I don't know what you promised Claire this morning, Matt, and I don't want to know. Just promise *me* you'll continue keeping Claire happy. At least until we can finish filming."

What?

Not exactly the words Matt had expected to hear from Annie on the subject of Claire Winslow.

"About Claire," Matt said.

But Annie cut him off. "Yeah, I know. I was completely shocked. Claire? Playing the role of Miss Suzy Sunshine? I still can't believe it."

Just like I can't believe your new Suzy Sunshine role, either, Matt wanted to say.

"What about Rico?" Annie asked, beaming even more. "You have to give him credit for the way he handled that crowd this morning. He had those women practically doing cartwheels across the parking lot. I hate to say I told you so, Matt, but if there's ever been a true dream guy every woman can identify with, Rico is that guy."

She started to follow after the others who were going inside for the next phase of filming, but Matt reached out and took her arm. He led Annie to the far side of the patio.

She frowned. "What?"

Matt searched her face. "Just one question, Annie. If you really think Rico is every woman's dream guy, then why isn't Rico your bing buddy instead of me?"

She blinked. "I thought I explained that Friday night, Matt. I told you. I've adopted your views on relationships now. That's why I chose you. Rico wants more than I'm willing to give him."

"Do you mind explaining *why* you've suddenly adopted my relationship philosophy? Since you've never made it any secret that your main goal in life was finding and settling down with the perfect Mr. Right?"

"It *was* my goal, Matt," Annie said. "*Was* is the key word in that sentence."

Before Annie could continue, Collin rushed over to join them. "Goals? Did I just hear someone mention goals?" He looked at Annie, then Matt. "My main goal in life is to stay as thin as an earthworm with the shit slung out of it."

When neither of them laughed at his witticism, Collin frowned and put his hands on his hips. "Well excuse me. If this discussion is *that* serious, please tell me what I've missed."

Matt looked at Annie.

Annie said, "I was just telling Matt I need to adopt his philosophy about relationships. Once I take over the creative department, I can't have any outside interferences.

I'll need to focus on my new promotion and the enormous responsibility that goes along with the job."

Collin sent her a thoughtful look. "You're right, Annie. Relationships do take up a considerable amount of time. Time you can't afford to lose when you're climbing your way to the top."

The look he sent Matt was challenging. "But what about you, Matt? Now that you've 'made it'," he said, emphasizing "made it" with his fingers to indicate quotation marks, "shouldn't you *stop* avoiding relationships? I mean, what's the point of having arrived career-wise and salary-wise if you don't have anyone to share it with?"

Where in the hell did that come from?

Matt didn't have a clue.

When Collin and Annie both kept staring at him for his answer, Matt forced a wise-ass grin he didn't exactly feel at the moment. "Share? I'm not sure 'share' is on my single-guy vocabulary list, Collin."

Collin laughed and slapped him on the back. "That's what I love about you, Matt. You'll be walking the walk and talking the single-guy talk right up to the bitter end."

Bitter end?

Dammit, I'm only thirty-five years old!

"Guys, get a move on," Gretchen announced from the patio doorway. "We're ready to start filming."

"Aren't you coming?" Collin called over his shoulder as he and Annie hurried off.

Matt waved them on. "I'll catch up."

Maybe.

The last thing he wanted to do was sit through another one of Rico's nauseating pretend acting performances. And after Collin hitting him below the belt with the remark about him not having anyone to share his success, Matt needed a little breathing room.

He waited until the last straggler entered the furniture store, then surveyed Groveman's outdoor patio display area. Opting for one of the expensive patio tables with the largest supersize umbrella, he dropped down onto a chair and reached up to loosen his tie.

August in Atlanta was always a bitch, but the summer heat wasn't nearly as uncomfortable as the hot seat Collin had put him in a few minutes ago. What the hell was wrong with Collin, anyway? It wasn't like Collin to put him on the spot like that.

Plus, he still didn't know what was going on with Annie. Had she really been telling the truth? Had her big relationship hunt ended because she'd decided to focus entirely on her upcoming promotion?

Matt leaned back against the thick chair cushion, mulling over Collin's disturbing question and trying to decide for himself if there was any point in making it to the top if you had no one to share your success. He'd always assumed he would be content with a solitary life.

But until the bitter end?

Jeez.

Collin's brief glimpse into the future had left him slightly rattled.

Deciding all he needed was a quick shot in the arm to remind him how terrific his single life really was, Matt unclipped his cell phone from his belt. The speed-dial button he pushed was his oldest brother's office number.

Matt's father liked to tell the story that on their wedding night Matt's mother promised to give him four strong sons if he'd agree to name them after the first four books of the New Testament. His father agreed, but only if they named the boys in reverse order so the kids wouldn't pick on his sons at school. Whether he and his brothers had ended up being John, Luke, Mark, and Matthew by coincidence or on purpose, Matt wasn't sure. But as his father always said, it made for one hell of a great story.

Matt's oldest brother John was the lawyer in the family, and the person Matt always turned to when he needed sound advice. John was also the brother who cheered him on the loudest from their small hometown in southern Georgia, encouraging Matt to hold on to his carefree single life as long as possible.

"Big John," Matt said when the secretary put him through.

"Haz-Matt. Haven't heard from you lately, buddy. What's up?"

Matt flinched at his old nickname, though he wasn't sure why. "Can you talk a minute?"

"Sure," John said.

Matt grinned when he heard John take a slurp from the coffee cup he constantly kept close at hand. He imagined his big brother leaning back in his leather chair and propping his long legs up on his always cluttered desk.

"This is a hypothetical question, John. But I want you to be completely honest with me. Okay?"

"Hit me with it."

"If you could trade places with me right now, would you do it?"

"I'm not sure I know what you mean, Matt."

"Switch lives," Matt said. "Trade being a small-town lawyer with a wife, a mortgage, and two kids for a carefree single life with a great job and a great bachelor pad like I have here in the big city?"

"In a heartbeat," John said, and Matt grinned until John added, "since this is only a hypothetical question."

Matt frowned. "Meaning what? That you don't have any regrets? That if you had it to do all over again, you'd still marry your high school sweetheart right out of law school without ever having the opportunity to figure out what you really wanted out of life?"

"Okay," John said. "Who is she?"

"What?"

"Sounds to me like some lady's messing with your head, little brother. Am I right?"

Matt sighed.

"What's she pushing for? A ring on her finger?"

Matt laughed. "Not even close. She showed up at my apartment last Friday night and announced that all she wanted from me was sex with no strings attached."

It took John a second to recover from choking on his last slurp of coffee. "And you're upset because all this woman wants from you is sex with no strings attached? Are you nuts, Matt?"

"No, I'm not nuts. Or upset. I'm confused," Matt admitted. "This is completely out of character for her, John. She's been a walking testimonial for happily-ever-after from the moment I met her. Until now. I just don't get it."

"Maybe she's trying to trick you," John suggested. "Women do that, Matt. Be very careful. Or the next time you call me up, you'll be inviting me to your wedding."

"Marriage isn't something you recommend?"

"Do you love her, Matt?"

Matt paused. "Help me out here, John. I don't know. How did you know you were in love with Sherry?"

"You just know," John said. "And since you're not

sure, you either (a) don't love her ... or (b) you're just too stubborn to give in to the idea of love yet."

"Aw, come on, John," Matt grumbled. "Saying you just know when you're in love with someone isn't a good enough answer. Isn't there some kind of test you can take or something?"

"Okay. Let me put it this way. If she married someone else, or she moved away and you never saw her again, would it matter to you?"

A mental picture instantly flashed through Matt's mind. Annie riding off with Rico in his stupid silver Lotus, throwing her long white wedding veil out the window and never looking back.

"Since you didn't answer, I guess I can take that as a yes," John said.

"Maybe this is where you need to give me your usual lecture about holding on to my incredible single-guy life as long as possible."

John laughed. "Hey, you've fought the good fight, buddy. A lot longer than most. And you aren't getting any younger, you know."

"Dammit, John," Matt grumbled. "You could have gone all day without saying that."

"The truth hurts sometimes, little brother," John said. "But if you really want my advice, I'd do this. I'd take it slow with this lady. I'd enjoy the sex with no strings attached as long as possible. And I'd wait and see how things shake out."

"Yeah. I guess you're right," Matt said.

But after he spent the next fifteen minutes listening to John give him a detailed account of ten-year-old Brent's latest baseball game, and eight-year-old Betsy's winning soccer team, Matt realized his big brother had answered his hypothetical question about switching lives whether John knew it or not.

The thought of life without Annie bothered Matt far more than the thought of handing over his single-guy membership card.

"You were right, Rico," Annie said when they finally finished filming at seven o'clock Monday evening. "This has been one long day."

Rico nodded. "Yes. A very long day."

Annie said a polite goodnight to Groveman's security guard as they walked past. He promptly locked the large front doors behind them the second they stepped outside the store. Then she waved good-bye to Gretchen, who was driving away as she and Rico walked out onto the sidewalk.

Everyone else had left earlier. Annie had been the one who volunteered to stay behind with Gretchen, making sure Rico understood exactly what they wanted when they resumed filming on Tuesday morning.

"I hate to say it," Annie added, "but tomorrow will be a carbon copy of today."

She was hoping that if she stressed what a busy day they had planned for Tuesday, Rico would take the hint and leave before he got any bright ideas about them being left alone. From the way he was staring at her with that gleam in his eye, Annie feared she wasn't going to be that lucky.

"We'll have another brief interview with Claire tomorrow," Annie rattled on. "You'll spend the first two hours meeting and greeting your fans again. Then it's back in front of the camera."

"And tonight," Rico said with a sigh, "it will be just as busy at the club."

Annie was surprised. "Surely your brothers don't expect you to tend bar tonight."

"Tend bar, no," Rico said. "But pay attention to the ladies all evening, yes."

Annie shrugged. "What can I say, Rico? Sales are sales are sales."

This time, Rico frowned. "All this sales talk," he said. "I am tired of that most."

He stepped much closer than Annie preferred. She tried to back away but he took another step forward, closing the distance between them.

"All day I have been thinking of nothing but you, Annie." He sent her a smoldering look that Annie might have fallen for had she not known the true reason behind his actions. "I have been patient waiting. Come have a drink with me now. Before I have to go to the club. A new quiet place. One Helena does not know about."

Helena.

Crap!

Annie hadn't thought about Helena in days. Or about the promise she'd made to Rico's ex-fiancée. The old Annie might have gone along with Helena's ridiculous lose-a-guy-in-ten-days movie script plan. But the new Annie?

No how. No way.

The new Annie had no interest whatsoever in playing silly head games with Rico, with Helena, or anyone else.

Rico reached out and took her hand. "If Helena is putting the worried look on your face, you have no reason to worry."

"But I am worried about Helena," Annie said, which

wasn't exactly a lie. Since she'd never thought to ask how she could get in touch with Helena herself, she said, "I need Helena's phone number, Rico. I'd like to talk to her before I go out with you again."

Rico shook his head adamantly. "Not a good idea."

Annie sent him a pleading look. "Please? It's a girl thing, Rico. I'd really like to talk to Helena first."

He paused for a moment, thinking it over. "If I give you the number," he said, "then *you* have to give me the time alone with you. That is my answer."

"Friday night," Annie told him. "After we wrap up the final day of filming. Dinner. Just you and me. My treat. You have my promise." She crossed her fingers over her heart as proof of her statement.

Rico finally smiled and let go of her hand. Annie took a slip of paper and a pen from her purse. After Rico handed over the number, he glanced around the parking lot. Annie did the same. The only car in sight was Rico's silver Lotus, sitting directly in front of the store.

"If not a drink, then at least let me take you home."

"I'm parked in the back of the store," Annie was quick to tell him.

"Then let me give you a ride to the back of the store."

Annie shook her head. "I'd truthfully just like to be by myself. You know, unwind a little. The short walk around back will be just what I need."

"If you are sure," he said with a disappointed sigh.

Annie smiled as proof. "I'm sure. And thanks again for doing such a great job today. You were fabulous."

Thank God, Annie thought when Rico and his Lotus finally roared out of the parking lot. She slipped Helena's number into her purse.

What she hadn't told Rico was that, in addition to

treating him to dinner on Friday night, she would also be treating him to the big news that she knew exactly why he had been so interested in pursing her from the beginning. But she'd meet with Helena first.

Annie's hand found its way to her throat.

It would be just like Helena to start up with that throat-*sleeting* business again.

But maybe there *was* a way she could help Helena get Rico back.

Regardless of what Rico thought he wanted, Annie could tell he didn't like being ordered around one little bit. He'd been polite, but his body language had told a different story. And this had only been the first day of filming.

Rico had been used to having his days to himself to do as he pleased, and without people pulling him in fifty different directions at once. Maybe that would be the key to solving Helena's problem. Maybe if she turned up the pressure and became a little more demanding each day, Rico might not be as excited about his new acting career as he imagined.

Annie was still pondering the Helena and Rico dilemma as she made her way down the sidewalk in front of Groveman's, heading for the parking lot at the rear of the building. When she turned the corner, the last thing she needed after a long, hard day was exactly what she found.

Matt.

Looking like a model straight out of *GQ*.

Propped against the driver's side door of her VW bug, his navy blazer slung casually over one shoulder, he had a sexy come-hither smile on his wickedly handsome face.

Since he'd had no success in getting Annie alone all day, Matt had decided to wait patiently while Annie wrapped things up with every woman's dream guy. But he wasn't taking any chances. He'd propped himself against her driver's side door on purpose, just in case Miss To-Hell-With-Relationships got any bright ideas about driving off before he had his say.

But when Matt saw Annie start walking toward him with that prissy little swish to her hips and the warm evening breeze blowing her gorgeous reddish gold hair back away from her beautiful face, something amazing happened. And it hit him as forcefully as Mike Tyson's famous knockout punch to Leon Spinks's jaw.

I love her.

He loved everything about Annie, from the top of her too-stubborn head to the tip of her hidden-heart-tattooed toe.

Perhaps it had been Collin's glimpse into the future. Or perhaps it had been John's question about how it would feel if he never saw Annie again. Whatever had propelled him to this point in his life, it left Matt with no doubts whatsoever.

Annie's the one.

The problem was, what was he going to do about it now that Annie had decided the last thing she wanted in her life was any kind of relationship?

"I thought you were gone," she said when she walked up and stopped in front of him.

"I thought you would be driving off with your dream guy to celebrate today's success," Matt said. "That is, until I saw him drive out of the parking lot without you."

Annie said, "So you decided to do what? Stick around and make sure I got *safely* to my car again?"

Matt shrugged. "The jerk could have at least walked you to your car, Annie."

Which, of course, was the wrong thing to say.

"Move, Matt," she ordered. "I'm dead tired and I'm in no mood to argue with you."

She tried to push him out of the way, but Matt grabbed both of her arms. "Hey. I'm sorry. I'm the jerk, okay?" He released her. "That's the reason I waited for you. I wanted to apologize for the silly argument we had last week. I was an arrogant ass to assume you were just going out with Rico to keep me from saying I told you so about my stupid adored and bored theory. It's obvious you really like the guy. So, I'm sorry, Annie. I mean it."

She looked at him for a moment.

Then she tossed her head, slinging her hair back over one shoulder. "I agree, Matt. You are definitely an arrogant ass. But you were also right. Being adored has bored me to tears."

Matt's heart lurched with excitement.

Really?

Rico had bored her to tears? He felt like telling Annie everything he'd just figured out for himself. They belonged together. It was just that simple. But he knew Annie too well to spill his guts before she was ready to hear what he had to say.

He'd have to show Annie he loved her first.

And there was no better time to start than now.

"Maybe being adored didn't bore you," Matt said. "Maybe it's just being adored by the wrong guy. Ever think of that?"

She stamped her foot. "Dammit, Matt, don't try to confuse me. Not when I finally have my head on straight." She threw her head back and sighed. "All my life all I wanted was a great guy who loved me, a house in the suburbs with the golden retriever in the yard, and the soccer-mom minivan with three or four kids hanging out every window."

"Who said there was anything wrong with that?" Matt broke in. Now that he'd finally admitted the only happily-ever-after he'd ever have was if Annie shared it with him, he could go for that scenario, too. All of it. The dog. The kids. Even (*gulp*) the minivan.

"Me," Annie said, poking her chest with her finger. "I'm saying there's something wrong with that fantasy. I finally realized I've only been kidding myself to think I'd ever have that kind of life. And that's why I'm going to stop living with my head in the clouds and focus on my new promotion. So don't try to confuse me with any of that 'wrong guy' crap. Every guy's the wrong guy for me at this point in my life. Any more questions?"

Matt held his hands up, signaling he was done. "Nope. No more questions. I got the message loud and clear."

"Good," she said, and tossed her hair again.

"Wait a minute," Matt said, sending her a playful grin. "Maybe I do have just one more question."

She rolled her eyes.

"You haven't changed your mind about our bing buddy arrangement, have you?"

She stared him down. Matt noticed whatever she was thinking at the moment was doing crazy things to the deep blue of her eyes.

"Why don't you try me and find out?" she said with a flirty little smile.

Matt laughed. "You mean why don't *I* ring *you* up for a bing in a day or two?"

She shook her head. "I mean right now."

Matt gulped. "Right now? Seriously? Your place or mine?"

She shook her head again. "I mean right now. Right here."

Right here?

Matt looked slowly around the vacant parking lot. But when he turned to look back at Annie, she was already walking toward the back door of his Jeep.

Holy hell.

She was actually opening the back door of his Jeep and climbing inside.

Is Annie crazy?

Was she really proposing that they get it on in the backseat of his Jeep? Right in the middle of Groveman's back parking lot?

Shaking his head, Matt walked over to his Jeep and opened the back door. "Very funny, Annie."

He wasn't prepared when she snatched his blazer out of his hand and tossed it over her head. She grabbed his tie and, rather than be choked to death, Matt followed his stretched neck right into the backseat with his determined bing buddy.

"Close the door," she ordered.

Matt did as she said, more confused than ever.

She pulled her blouse out of the waistband of her skirt and appeared ready to pull it up and over her head. That's when Matt came to his senses and reached out and grabbed her hand.

"Stop it, Annie. There's no way I'm going to make love to you in the backseat of a car."

She stared at him with complete surprise. "Make love? Who said anything about making love? I was under the impression all you and I were having was sex with no stings attached."

Matt ran a hand through his hair, stalling for time. He knew he had to choose his words wisely or risk Annie putting a quick end to the sex that he hoped to convert into happily-ever-after.

"Sorry," he said. "Making love was the wrong choice of words." Then he sent Annie a slightly embarrassed look. "Will you promise not to laugh if I tell you something deeply personal?"

She leaned back against the car seat for a second, thinking it over. "Okay. I promise."

Matt took a deep breath. "I have this car-sex phobia kinda thing, okay? I was sixteen. Parked at a popular make-out spot. She had her panties off. My pants were down around my ankles. Neither of us realized her older brother had just pulled in beside us. Before I knew what was happening, her brother jerked the back door open, grabbed me by the ankles, and pulled me out of the car with my pants still down around my ankles."

Matt paused for a moment. "So. What I'm trying to say. With as little embarrassment as possible. Is that even the thought of having sex in a car pretty much takes the lead right out of my pencil, if you know what I mean."

Annie couldn't help herself, she burst out laughing.

Matt frowned. "Hey. You promised you wouldn't laugh."

Annie grinned. "At least you didn't throw up all over the poor girl. That's what I did to my date during my first almost car-sex experience."

Matt cocked his handsome head to the side. "You really threw up on some guy?"

Annie nodded. "I was also sixteen. We were in his father's brand-new Cadillac. He couldn't talk me out of my panties. And then I lost it. Bright red punch. White leather seats. The guy never spoke to me again. I heard his father had to have the seats reupholstered."

When they both stopped laughing, Matt kept looking at her for one of those longer-than-necessary moments. A few butterflies immediately took flight in her stomach.

He finally broke eye contact and looked down at his watch. "Hey," he said, "since car sex has been vetoed, why don't you have dinner with me instead?"

More butterflies fluttered, this time startled by her better judgment screaming she should run for her life.

"I don't mean a *date* type of dinner," Matt said quickly. "We both know where we stand on that subject. But we do have to eat. And I'm starving. How about you?"

Whew!

Matt seemed as eager as she was about sticking to her nonrelationship rules. She politely shoved her better judgment out of the way.

"I could eat," she admitted.

She kept telling herself the new Annie could handle sitting there laughing and sharing deep secrets with Matt — even having dinner with him — without spiraling into a tailspin that would take her right back to her old dreaming-dreams-that-never-would-come-true kind of life.

"Where?" Matt said. "I'm up for anything. Italian. Chinese. You name it."

Annie shrugged. "I really don't know this part of town. Anything close, I guess. Even a burger would be fine with me." But just to be safe, it was on the tip of her tongue to remind Matt that she would be driving herself wherever they went.

He saved her the trouble when he grinned and said, "Follow me. One of my favorite sports bars is barely a mile from here. The burgers are delicious. The beer's cold. And if you behave yourself, I might even let you beat me at a few games of pool."

You're dancing with the devil, her better judgment kept warning as Annie followed closely behind Matt's black Jeep Cherokee. This time, she gave her better judgment a sound punch in the nose.

Dammit, she was looking forward to stopping off for a burger and a few beers. Maybe even a few games of pool. It had been weeks since she'd done anything fun.

Besides, other than Collin, who could be a safer person to hang out with than Matt?

Matt had always been relationship-proof to the core.

She was sure she had nothing whatsoever to worry about.

CHAPTER 14

"H urry," Annie moaned after she and Matt half fell and half stumbled into her darkened apartment.

They didn't even stop to turn on the lights. The second Matt had the condom in place, he pushed Annie back against her closed front door, pushed her skirt up, slipped off her thong, and lifted her up so she could wrap her legs tightly around his waist.

"Matt," Annie gasped when he plunged deeply inside her.

"No idle chitchat," Matt whispered. "Your rules."

He covered her mouth with a searing kiss so demanding that Annie feared she might pass out. And when his mouth finally slipped away from her lips and slid down to her neck, Annie sank her fingers into Matt's short dark hair and held on.

Oh yeah!

She really liked it this way.

Quick and hurried.

Hard and fast.

No time for thinking about now. No time for worrying about later. Just live the bing. Breathe the bing. And taste the bing.

Mercy!

How could any man possibly move like that?

Her hands slid from Matt's hair down to his broad shoulders. He didn't even flinch when her fingernails dug into the rock-hard flesh beneath his dress shirt, trying to slow him down.

Please. Please. Please.

She had to slow Matt down.

With every pounding thrust he was already bringing her closer. And closer. And, oh. Man. Closer and closer.

Yes! Yes! Yes!

Her hands left his shoulders and Annie reached up and pulled his head forward. She shivered at the feel of his hot mouth against the sensitive hollow of her neck.

Matt. Oh, Matt. Oh. Matt. Oooooooh, Matt!

"Ahhhhhhhh," she moaned, unable to wait even one second longer. She smiled into the darkness when she felt Matt shudder only a short second later.

He whispered her name against her hair and her hands searched for his face. She drew his head forward for one long, fabulous kiss. And then Annie let out one loud completely satisfied sigh.

But wait.

Oh. Wow. Oh. Wow. Oh. Wow.

Matt wasn't even close to stopping.

Annie's breath caught in her throat.

He was moving again.

Faster. Harder.

Harder. Faster.

The room was starting to spin now.

Oooh. Ahhh. Oh. My.

There.

Right there!

Yes. Definitely there. Yes.

Annie could feel the warm tingle starting up again.

Fan-binging-tastic.

Faster. Faster. Oh, yeah. There it was.

She arched her body and threw her head back against the door — ready — willing — waiting to feel another amazing scrape-you-off-the-ceiling bing.

And just when she swore nothing else had ever felt that wonderful, Matt removed her legs from around his waist, slid down on his knees, and made a complete liar of her.

Annie stretched leisurely when her alarm sounded at 7 a.m. on Tuesday morning. But she remained lying in bed, thinking that her life had never been more perfect.

She'd finally pushed Matt out the door at 1 a.m. Now she was slightly disappointed that she hadn't let him stay. A little somethin'-somethin' first thing in the morning could have been exactly what she needed to help her get through another long, exhausting day of filming Joe Video.

No.

Don't go there.

The last thing she needed was to let her mind wander down that slippery slope. Things between her and Matt were perfect just the way they were.

She couldn't explain it, but it was liberating not being caught up in all the stress of a relationship. The spontaneity suited her. In fact, she wished she'd had the good sense to adopt her new philosophy ages ago.

There was no pressure. No worry. No angst over where things were going. Because things weren't going anywhere. That gave her the freedom to embrace nothing but the excitement and the anticipation of their next wonderful no-strings-attached adventure.

She didn't even feel guilty about still promoting Joe Video to her fellow sisterhood. Every woman deserved at least a *fantasy* dream guy she could depend on. Joe Video filled that void perfectly.

When she thought about it, maybe her mother had been right after all. The entire concept of Joe Video did have a strong feminist ring to it. With Joe Video, a woman always had complete control.

Control was one of the things she liked best about her new philosophy. She liked being in the driver's seat and directing and calling the shots. No all-over-the-place emotions. No worrying that life was passing her by. No pressure because she would soon be thirty and her biological clock was ticking like a time bomb waiting to explode.

Guys never worried about those things.

Especially not guys like Matt. Matt lived strictly for the moment. And now, so did she. Just like Matt, she intended to seize each and every opportunity, grab life by the horns, and have a freaking blast.

Good-time Annie.

That was going to be her new nickname.

She lifted her arms above her head and stretched, thinking that they did have such fun yesterday. Sitting in Matt's Jeep laughing at each other's embarrassing teenage stories. Talking nonstop about nothing in particular over burgers and beer. Playing pool at the sports bar. Which is how they'd eventually ended up back at her apartment. Matt had insisted the winner of each game got the privilege of naming both the time and the place of their next big bing.

Annie smiled happily to herself.

The big dummy didn't have a clue she'd purposely let him win all four games.

Her bedside phone ringing at such an early hour surprised her. The name on caller ID didn't.

"This call better be work-related," Annie said when she answered. "You know the rules."

She heard him chuckle before he said, "Don't panic. This call is definitely work-related. I wanted to make sure you could do without me if I skipped today's filming."

"Is the golf course calling your name?" Annie teased.

"Just a few personal things I need to take care of if you can spare me," Matt said.

"I don't see why that would be a problem," Annie said. "Gretchen has everything under control."

There was a slight pause before he added, "One other thing, bing-related. Do I need to remind you that I won all four games of pool last night?"

Annie laughed. "Since you reminded me of that fact about every five minutes last night? No, Matt. I'm well aware you won all four games."

"Good," he said. "Because I'm calling in my marker for bing number two. Tonight. Park at the back of the building where you did yesterday. I'll be waiting when you finish filming. No excuses."

"It could be another late night," Annie warned.

"No excuses," Matt said.

Annie laughed when Matt hung up before she could argue.

Matt tossed the phone aside, swung his legs over the side of his bed, and headed for the shower. He couldn't help but be pleased at his own ingenuity. He had three more guaranteed chances to prove to Annie that *he* could be her dream guy. The fact that she hadn't tried to renege on their pool-playing bet gave him hope he'd be able to complete his new mission with success.

Annie wanted car sex. He'd see she got it. Tonight. But on his terms. And with a lot more class than in the backseat of his Jeep Cherokee.

Then on Wednesday night, his plans for bing number three would only take a quick phone call to his old golfing buddy, Bart. The successful stockbroker had a downtown penthouse apartment that was the envy of every single guy in the city. Rooftop Jacuzzi. Total privacy. Breathtaking view of Atlanta at night. Annie was bound to be impressed.

He'd wait until Thursday night for bing number four, however, before he proposed to Annie that they should negotiate a new deal. He'd make that suggestion in the privacy of his own apartment that — after today — would be the perfect setting.

Matt actually laughed as he stepped under the hot shower spray. Had anyone told him he'd ever be taking a day off from work to "feminize" his apartment, he would have blown a gasket. Yet that's what the personal business he'd mentioned to Annie was all about. He was going to get in touch with his (*gulp*) feminine side.

He'd need help, of course, which wouldn't be a problem. The wife of one of his racquetball buddies was the manager at a nearby Pier 1. Wasn't that one of the most popular female-focused stores? At least according to Collin's sainted *Queer Eye* boys.

Out of curiosity, he'd watched the program a time or two. Enough to get the message that if a guy had any hopes of the lady in his life hanging out at his apartment, he needed to make it more female-friendly. Matt hoped Annie would agree to spending *all* of her time at his place.

As he gave his hair a good scrubbing, Matt assured himself he wasn't going to let the thought of (*grimace*) a gazillion scented candles and a bunch of poofy cuddly pillows strewn across his manly leather sofa give him a heart attack. He assured himself he didn't mind shelling out extra bucks for some suitable wineglasses, tableware, and even some (*groan*) matching placemats and napkins. He might even consider some of those (*be strong here*) pleated fabric lampshades if it would further his cause.

An overhaul in the bedroom wouldn't be a bad idea either. Satin sheets would be a nice touch. *Yes, definitely satin sheets.* He mentally added those to his list.

He'd been forced to sit through enough of Collin's damn menu planning that he could probably open a catering service himself. He wasn't totally clueless when it came to the culinary side of his plans for Thursday night. What was the name of Collin's favorite to-die-for caterer downtown? Ganache? *Yes, that's it.* Someone there could easily help him choose something more appropriate to dazzle Annie than last night's burgers and beer. According to Collin, Ganache not only delivered, they also arranged and displayed their catered meals to perfection, so he couldn't go wrong there.

As far as the music for Thursday night's big finale, he would take the sounds from his own collection.

R&B all the way.

Barry White. Al Green. Michael McDonald's entire *Motown* album. Maybe even a little Luther Vandross thrown in for good measure. Soulful and sexy was bound to be perfect.

Whatever it took, that's what Matt was willing to do.

Besides, he had the entire day to make all of the arrangements. Surely he could become at least one woman's dream guy if he had the entire day to get in touch with his (*double gulp*) feminine side.

Bring it on, Matt thought with confidence.

He could handle it.

Annie's first five minutes after the interview with Claire on Tuesday morning were spent outside on the sidewalk in front of the store. She wanted to make sure the marketing department had everything under control while Rico spent another morning with his excited and adoring fans.

Just like clockwork, everything seemed to be moving along right on schedule. The autographing table had already been set up. An ample supply of marketing's clever pink satin sleep masks was stacked, ready and waiting. Though Rico had tried to get her alone the second she arrived, she'd managed to sidestep that situation with ease. Now she finally had Rico sitting at the place of honor, pen in hand, a sexy smile on his face, wowing his adoring fans.

It didn't seem possible, but the crowd was larger than it had been on Monday. She smiled. J.B. Duncan had to be pleased with the way things were going. The only thing that worried Annie was Rico. He'd seemed disturbed before the autograph signing began.

But when she thought about it, who could really blame him for being a little overwhelmed? The endless line of doting admirers was already snaking down the sidewalk and disappearing around the side of the building.

Annie leaned down and whispered into Rico's ear,

"I'll be back in a minute," before she left her post behind his chair and walked into Groveman's, hopefully in search of some hot black coffee.

"Annie!" Collin called out, hurrying in her direction.

Since it was Collin, his worried look didn't concern Annie one bit. Something as simple as a piece of lint on his pants could make him hyperventilate. But when he grabbed her arm and pushed her behind one of the towering elephant-ear ferns in Groveman's lobby, Annie realized something was wrong.

"Why didn't you tell me Miss Spandex was Rico's fiancée?" Collin demanded.

"Why do you think I didn't tell you, Mr. Blabbermouth?" Annie said right back. "But your information is wrong. Helena is Rico's *ex*-fiancée."

"*Ex* or not, she's here."

Annie blanched. *Here?* "Where?"

Collin pushed down a fern leaf. He peered around the lobby before he said, "I hid her upstairs in the Roman bedroom showroom. No one will find her there."

"This is so not what I need this morning," Annie said. "How did she get in here?"

Collin threw his hands up in the air. "I don't know how she got past the security guards. But she really caused a scene. She's demanding to see you, Annie."

Annie tried to push Collin out of her way, but he grabbed her arm. "It gets worse. Claire Winslow walked into the lobby during Helena's tirade about you avoiding her. I managed to push Helena into the elevator. I don't think Claire had time to put two and two together, but that bleached-blonde bitch is still circling around here somewhere. You need to get her out of here, Annie. Fast."

The second Collin let go of her arm, they both sprinted for Groveman's first-floor elevator.

"Can you imagine what Claire would do with the information if she found out Rico dumped his poor fiancée so he could play the role of every woman's dream guy? Claire would crucify him."

Annie kept pounding on the elevator button with her fist. She gave up and ran around the side of the elevator, heading for the stairway. Collin burst through the stairway door right behind her. He stayed on her heels as Annie took the steps two at a time.

"I'm telling you, Annie, everything we've worked for could go right down the drain."

Annie ignored him. They were almost to Groveman's second floor.

"We can kiss our promotions good-bye. And Rico will go from being every woman's dream guy to the biggest jerk of the century. We won't even be able to sell any of his sexy pictures. Unless women use them for a dartboard."

It was pointless to argue. Collin had only been saying out loud everything she'd already been thinking herself. She opened the second-floor stairwell door and hurried through it, Collin still right behind her.

They finally reached the showroom.

There was Helena, lying leisurely on the king-size Roman-column canopy bed, her head propped in one hand, striking a most befitting Cleopatra pose.

"What are you doing?" Collin shrieked. "You're going to soil that thousand-dollar comforter, missy. You get up from there. Right now!"

Helena's answer was to send Collin a bored screw-you look. She remained exactly where she was.

Annie pushed Collin behind her and started walking toward the bed. "Helena. I was going to call you."

Helena sat up in the middle of the bed. Annie didn't miss the displeasure radiating on her pretty face. "But you did not call. Did you, Annie?"

"I'm sorry," Annie began.

Helena shook a finger in her direction. "I am tired of your excuses." Her black eyes flashed. "You said you would help me get my Rico back."

"Get Rico back?" Collin echoed.

"We'll discuss it later," Annie said, sending Collin a don't-ask look.

Helena unbuckled the fanny pack from around her waist and unzipped it. "These I brought for you," she said, and tossed two packs of cigarettes onto the bed.

Collin gasped and looked at Annie in horror. "When did you start smoking?"

Annie sent him another pointed look. "I *said* we'd discuss it later."

"And these," Helena said, digging a handful of scratch-off lottery tickets out of her fanny pack. She tossed them onto the bed as well.

"Oooh, scratch-offs." Collin grinned, apparently less offended by Helena's second gift.

He reached out, but Helena smacked Collin's hand. "Those are for Annie," she warned. "My Rico hates the smoking. My Rico hates the gambling. When Annie does both of these things, Rico will stop wanting to be with Annie and come back to me."

Collin looked at Helena. Then back at Annie. "Is she for real?"

Annie punched Collin with her elbow. "Think Kate Hudson. Matthew McConaughey. Big box-office hit."

"Hell-o. That was a *movie*," Collin said in a singsong voice.

Helena's eyes narrowed. "What do you know about any of it?"

Collin put his hands on his hips, striking his best diva pose. "The first thing you do when you get dumped, girlfriend, is develop an attitude real quick. You tell Rico you wait for no one. You tell him you'll find yourself a new man who *wants* to marry someone as beautiful as you are."

Annie rolled her eyes. "And do you care to share with Helena how many times that approach has worked after you've been dumped, *girlfriend*?"

Collin stuck his nose in the air. "We're not talking about me. We're talking about Helena."

Annie looked at Helena and said, "I was going to call you, Helena, because I have come up with a new plan. A plan that Collin is going to help us carry out."

Collin jerked his head in her direction. "I am?"

Annie whacked him on the arm.

Collin frowned and rubbed his arm. "I mean, yes. I *am* going to help you." He nodded at Helena in agreement with Annie's statement.

Helena didn't look convinced. "This new plan? What is it?"

Annie walked over and sat down on the bed beside Helena. "You're going to have to trust me, Helena."

"I can tell I am not going to like it," Helena said. She crossed her arms stubbornly over her ample bosom.

Annie said, "Regardless of what Rico thinks he wants, I can already tell he doesn't like being bossed around. He was irritated most of the day yesterday when we kept telling him exactly what to do during filming."

Helena nodded. "You are right. All the time Rico's brothers, they are bossing him around. That is why Rico wants his new career. He wants to be his own boss."

"And that's what Rico doesn't understand," Annie said. "If his acting career did take off, every second of his time would be accounted for. He'd have a publicist pushing him in front of the spotlight for promotional purposes. He'd have a director dictating his every move when he was in front of the camera. Even his private life wouldn't be his own. Rico wouldn't be in control of any aspect of his life if he became a big Hollywood star."

Helena said, "Rico would not like this."

"Exactly," Annie said. "And that's why I think my new plan will work. We're going to let Rico find out for himself that being a big star comes with a big price tag. But to prove this to Rico, I'll have to introduce him to another woman."

Helena frowned. "I knew I was not going to like this plan of yours."

Annie said, "I promise, Helena, this woman is so obnoxious and so controlling she'll have Rico on his knees and begging you to take him back."

Collin grinned. "Have I heard you call this woman La Femme Shark a time or two?"

Annie grinned back. "You have."

Helena shook her head. "No. No. *No.* I am not liking the sound of Rico and the other woman plan. I am liking the sound of the me with the new man plan better."

Collin sent Helena a sly smile. "Why not try both?"

Annie glanced at Collin, then back at Helena. "That isn't a bad idea, Helena. Do you think you can convince Rico you've found someone else? You told me yourself he got extremely jealous the night you mentioned you were going to take other lovers."

Helena shook her head. "Rico, he knows everyone in Little Five Points. No man will talk to me. Rico has made it certain if they do . . ." and she made the slicing motion Annie hated across her throat.

"Some nerve," Collin snorted. "No wonder Rico doesn't see anything wrong with breaking your engagement. He still has you all to himself." He paused for a moment. "You need to spend a few days hidden away. So Rico can't be sure of what you're doing."

"But I have nowhere to go," Helena protested.

Collin smiled. "You do now. You can stay at my place." He got a sudden gleam in his eye. "And while you're staying with me, we're going to find you a new look. We'll go on a shopping spree to end all shopping sprees. My treat. I insist."

Helena's look was suspicious. "You would do this for me? Why?"

Annie answered that question. "Because Collin has more money than he knows what to do with, Helena. *And* he considers himself a fashion expert."

"I *am* a fashion expert," Collin insisted.

Helena still didn't look convinced. "My uncle. He would not agree with me going away."

"Tell him you need some time alone because you're heartbroken about Rico breaking your engagement," Collin said. "Tell him you're staying with a new friend. You can pretend it's Annie you're staying with, and you can give him my number where he can reach you anytime he wants. But make your uncle promise not to give the number to Rico."

Helena threw her head back and laughed. "With Rico

my uncle is furious. To Rico he would never give the number."

"Good," Collin said. "You go home and pack a few things right now. Do you have a cell phone?"

Helena took her cell phone from her fanny pack and held it up. Collin wiggled his fingers for her to hand it over. He programmed in his cell phone number and handed it back.

"When you're through packing, call me," he said. "I'll come get you and take you to my house. And do it now, Helena, while Rico is tied up here all day. We can't risk him finding out where you are."

Helena scooted off the bed. The second she did, fuss-budget Collin immediately picked up the cigarettes and scratch-off tickets and started rearranging and smoothing out the thousand-dollar comforter.

"This plan is going to work, Helena," Annie said, wishing she was sure of that statement.

Helena looked at her for a moment. "Make sure of it." Then she prissed out of the showroom, never looking back.

Annie let out a long sigh. "I hope you know what you're doing, Collin. You're going to have your hands full with that one."

Collin walked up and held out Helena's loot. "Here."

Annie frowned. "What am I supposed to do with those?" Collin walked over to a trash can and dumped the cigarettes. But he handed the scratch-off tickets back to Annie as they headed for the showroom door. "These you keep," he said. "Today could be your lucky day."

"Not likely," Annie said, but she stuffed the tickets into her purse anyway. "I'd say this being my lucky day is about as likely as you getting Helena out of her spandex."

"Oh, I'll get her out of that spandex," Collin said with confidence as they reached the elevator. "How am I supposed to help with *your* portion of the plan?"

"By doing what you do best," Annie said. "Start a little gossip on the set today that you've heard Hollywood has its eye on Rico. Elaborate if you feel like it." Which Annie knew Collin wouldn't be able to resist doing. "Just make sure Claire is within hearing distance when you tell your big yarn. Twenty bucks says Rico will become the new man in Claire's life. There's no way she's going to pass up getting her fifteen minutes of fame."

Collin rubbed his hands together as they stepped into the elevator. "Oooh, this is going to be such fun. What big Hollywood director should I say is interested in Rico? Quentin Tarantino, maybe?"

"That's up to you," Annie said as she reached over and pushed the button. "Just make it believable."

"Don't insult me," Collin said. "I'm an expert when it comes to making any type of gossip believable."

"And you say that like it's a good thing," Annie mumbled under her breath.

This time, it was Collin who whacked Annie on the arm.

Rico held back a sharp remark when Gretchen scolded him for not paying attention.

"You have to focus, Rico," Gretchen said. "Look at Annie. Your expression needs to be thoughtful and sympathetic. Try it again."

Focus?

How was he supposed to focus when his mind was

cluttered with questions about what had gone on between Helena and Annie earlier that morning? He had tried to stop Helena when she showed up unexpectedly, but she'd pushed him away and hurried inside the store in search of Annie. He had tried to warn Annie that Helena was there, but Annie had pushed him into his chair, saying he needed to pay attention to his fans.

Fans.

The women. They wore him out. All of them. Looking at him as if he were some piece of tasty meat ready to be carved up and served for supper. The old ones. The young ones. The pretty ones. The not-so-pretty ones. They looked him over the way they would a new toy. A possession. A thing to be devoured for their own greedy pleasure.

Mierda.

He had no interest in any of them, or in their fantasy about him being their dream guy. What true man could endure such scrutiny day after day, afraid that one move or one look would be the wrong one?

The women of his culture would never do this. They appreciated strong men. Men who would take charge and be the boss. These American career women being *his* boss was not right.

None of it.

My lovely Helena.

He was worried about her. She had left the store never once looking in his direction.

He had to talk to Annie. But Annie had been avoiding his questions all day. Just the way Annie was always avoiding his questions.

"I'll tell you everything later at lunch," she'd said.

But it is already past the time for lunch, Rico thought disgustedly, which was another sore spot with him.

What did these women think he was? Some robot? Some mechanical man who did not get hungry? He had never been able to think well on an empty stomach. He was tired of trying to look thoughtful and sympathetic when no one had any sympathy for him.

Enough!

I am through with these women pushing me around.

"I am hungry," he complained to Gretchen. "That is why my look is not sympathetic and thoughtful. My look is that of a hungry man." And he added with pride, "I will not continue this filming. Not until I get something to eat."

That Gretchen and Annie both frowned in his direction made Rico smile inside.

Gretchen shook her head. "Okay, let's break for lunch," she said with a sigh, but only after she sent him another mean look. "One hour only, guys. The buffet is set up outside on the patio where it was yesterday."

Rico ignored Gretchen and marched over to Annie. "First, you and I will talk," he told her instead of asking her. "Alone. Then we will eat."

He could tell she did not like his firm tone.

"Is there a problem, Rico?"

"That is my question to you," Rico said. "About the problem with Helena."

"Follow me," she said.

"No. *You* come with me." He would not be ordered around by this woman. He placed his hand firmly at Annie's back and escorted her off the set and away from the others. She looked annoyed, but he did not care. "You tell me now. Why did Helena come to see you this morning?"

She reached out and placed her hand on his arm. "I want you to brace yourself, Rico. I'm afraid you're going to be upset about Helena's news."

"News?" He had no idea what Annie was talking about.

"Just remember you can't think about Helena now, Rico. You have to focus on your new career. And I hate to say it, but personally, I think it's better for you that Helena has found someone else to marry."

Someone else to marry?

Was Annie crazy?

"Helena told you this?" He couldn't believe it.

Annie nodded. "I can understand why you'd be upset. Even if you didn't want to marry Helena, she was still your intended fiancée. It's only natural you'd feel a little hurt that she's found someone else so quickly."

Rico ran a shaky hand through his hair, pushing it out of his eyes. Helena had told him none of this. But he had not been able to see her the night before. Ernesto had kept him busy playing up to all the women who had swarmed into the bar until the place was overflowing.

He had to know. "This new man? Did Helena tell you his name?"

"No, I don't remember a name," Annie said, a sad expression on her face still. "Just someone her uncle has arranged for her to marry. That's all she told me."

Damn Ernesto.

He would cut out Ernesto's heart. He never should have trusted his brother. Ernesto had said he would make things right with Helena's uncle. He should have gone to see the man himself. But that was forbidden. Arrangements were made only by the head of each family. Ernesto had let him down. And Ernesto would pay dearly.

Annie squeezed his arm. "If it makes you feel any better, Rico, I don't think you have to worry about Helena. She said the man was handsome, very wealthy, and that she thought she could eventually learn to love him."

Make me feel better?

He would never understand how the brains of these crazy Caucasians worked. Why would it make him feel better to know Helena could learn to love another man? That reasoning made no sense. Helena was meant to love *him*. Only him.

"Rico? Are you okay?"

Rico grabbed on to his pride and pulled himself back together. "Yes. I am fine."

"Great," Annie said. "Then let's go get you something to eat. We can't have our superstar dying of starvation."

Superstar.

That is what he wanted. The life of a big star. The fame. The fortune. It was his dream. He'd just never expected not to have Helena sharing it with him. She would never care that he was not perfect.

My Helena?

Becoming another man's wife?

Could he really allow that to happen?

When Annie motioned for him to follow, Rico did not protest. Like the sniveling pet dog he'd become, he followed meekly behind her as if Annie were holding the chain to the collar around his neck.

But was he hungry still?

No.

Just as he'd lost his Helena, Rico had also lost his appetite.

CHAPTER 15

"Did you see how fast Rico charged out of here when we finished filming that last scene?" Collin asked Annie with a delighted chuckle.

Not as fast as I wish you'd charge out of here, Annie felt like screaming.

"How I'd love to be a little fly on the wall when Rico rushes home to Little Five Points and can't find Helena anywhere."

Do they ever shut up on your planet? But the second she thought it, Annie was ashamed of herself. She sighed. Of all the nights for Collin to want to hang around and chat, he had to pick this one.

Everyone else had been gone for at least thirty minutes. But not Collin. He kept sitting in the library showroom where they'd been filming all day, as if he didn't have a care in the world. And so did Annie. Waiting Collin out. Willing him to leave first, so there wouldn't be any chance of him following her to her car and discovering who just happened to be waiting for her in Groveman's back parking lot.

Annie looked down at her watch again.

It was already 6:45 p.m.

"I'm not trying to brag, but you should have seen

Claire while I was telling the cameraman my big Hollywood producer lie. She practically fell over, she was leaning forward so far trying to hear what I was saying." He chuckled again. "The only thing that saved poor Rico from Claire pouncing on him today was Gretchen, keeping him in front of the camera." He grinned. "But there's always tomorrow."

Annie nodded absently. *Forget tomorrow, dammit. I'm concerned about tonight.*

"Speaking of Helena," she said. "Do you think she'll be able to hold out for a couple of days? I mean, she is just sitting there at your house. All *alone.*"

"She isn't alone. Lars is with her," Collin chirped. "I talked to them a few minutes ago. Lars thinks Helena is a real hoot. The two of them are getting along famously. Helena's even teaching Lars to make authentic Cuban carne mechada. It's a Cuban pot roast of sorts. To-die-for ingredients. First you take . . ."

Annie tuned him out, watching instead the second hand tick, tick, tick around the face of her watch.

"Doesn't that sound yummy?" Collin finally said.

"Definitely yummy," Annie repeated, fighting the urge to grab him by the hair and drag him to the front door.

"Hey," Collin said brightly. "Come home with me and sample it yourself. The more the merrier."

"Thanks, but I'm going straight home," Annie lied. "Rain check, though?"

"Any time, lovey." Collin finally stood up from the expensive wing chair he'd been sitting in.

Annie stood up from her chair as well. "You go ahead," Annie told him. "I have a few quick things to check on, then I'm right behind you."

Collin nodded. "See you in the morning, then. But

don't stay here all night, Annie. Everything is running so smoothly, I can't imagine anything going wrong now."

Annie waited until she was sure Collin had time to leave the store before she followed after him. The second she saw his Mercedes drive past the front entrance, she sprinted for the first-floor women's restroom.

She hurried up to the bathroom vanity and plowed through her purse, jerking out her brush.

Brush. Brush. Brush.

Scrunch. Scrunch. Scrunch.

Okay, so she was preening a little. Matt hadn't been at work all day as she had. He was bound to be fresh and rested. She couldn't stroll out to the back parking lot looking all drained and frazzled, could she?

But she'd already made up her mind that she wasn't going to agree to anything date-like tonight. Hanging out with Matt could get too comfortable too quickly. She'd just follow him to his apartment and then . . .

Oh God. I hope he intends to go to his apartment.

Her place was a wreck. She hadn't even made her bed this morning.

Annie leaned close to the mirror, studying her teeth, then popped a breath mint into her mouth. After pursing her lips, she applied a little lip gloss, pinched both cheeks for a little color, then sprayed a cloud of perfume into the air and walked through it on her way back out the bathroom door.

As she headed for the back parking lot, the only thing that worried her more than the fact that she'd kept Matt waiting for two hours was the fear that he wouldn't still be waiting at all. That fear became a reality when she reached the back of the building and found her VW bug sitting in the rear parking lot all by itself.

Idiot.

That's what she was. A first-class idiot. She'd thought about meeting Matt on and off all day. Oh hell. Who was she kidding? Meeting Matt was *all* she'd thought about all day. That's what happened when no-strings-attached spontaneity turned into relationship-like plans.

Someone ended up disappointed.

Oh well, Annie told herself. What did she expect? It was just like Matt to get all pissy and leave mad because she hadn't come charging around the side of the building at five o'clock sharp, tearing her clothes off as she raced across the parking lot.

Well, she had news for him. She wasn't just some little peon flunky in his creative department now. Joe Video had been her idea. She had a job to do. And J.B. Duncan himself had said Joe Video had the potential to make Paragon more money than any video game developed in the company's history.

But she wasn't stupid, either.

The sex was way too good to give up.

Tomorrow morning when she saw Matt, she would simply apologize for not being able to get away sooner. Then she'd point out that maybe they should stick to the rules if they wanted their current arrangement to work out.

No more sharing deep secrets. No more hanging out together. No more cryptic early-morning phone calls. Just occasional great sex.

Here a bing.

There a bing.

Everywhere a . . . .

Annie stopped walking when a sleek white limousine turned into the back parking lot and headed straight in her direction. The limo pulled up and stopped in front of her. When the passenger-side window slid down, Annie couldn't keep the silly grin off her face.

Matt extended his arm out the window and handed her a beautiful long-stemmed red rose. "I decided we needed a new bing buggy."

Annie laughed. "You can't be serious." But she couldn't resist pulling the blossom to her nose to sniff the fragrant petals.

He hopped out of the limo and bowed low as he held the door open wide. "Get in," he said, wiggling his eyebrows up and down. "And I'll show you how serious I am."

"How did it go today?" Matt asked when the limo eased out of the parking lot for what would be an uninterrupted two-hour drive around the city.

Not that either of them would be paying any attention to where they were going, if he had any say in the matter. He took a bottle of chilled champagne from the ice bucket sitting on the limo's bar, poured both of them a glass of champagne, and handed one to Annie.

She did look amazing leaned back against the plush leather seat relaxing, her long legs crossed at the knee, sipping from the fancy champagne flute like a supermodel in a magazine ad.

He could see them starting every evening like this one. Relaxing after a long day at work with a drink before dinner. Later, making love all night long.

"Today went well," she said, breaking his train of thought. They looked at each other for a moment and she said, "But I think we need to stick to the rules, don't you? Didn't we agree there'd be no idle chitchat?"

Matt grinned. "If I remember correctly, the rules were no idle chitchat during or after sex. We're not having sex at the moment, so our chitchatting isn't during. And since we haven't had sex yet, we aren't chitchatting after."

"A minor technicality," she said, but he could see the mirth in her deep blue eyes. She smiled. "Maybe we should stop whatever type of chitchat we're having, and start concentrating on the during sex instead."

He smiled back. "Excellent idea."

Matt reached over and slid the privacy cover into place over the small window separating them from the driver. He placed his glass on the bar and took the glass from Annie's hand and did the same with it.

"Why don't you move over there, lie down, and make yourself comfortable," he said, pointing to the long seat stretching along one side of the limo.

She smiled again. "I thought you'd never ask."

Next stop, Wonderland, Matt thought smugly when Annie stretched out seductively on the seat. He reached into the jacket pocket of his suit and handed over his next surprise gift.

"Here," he said. "This goes along with tonight's agenda."

"No way," Annie said and laughed when Matt placed the pink satin sleep mask into her hand.

"Put it on," Matt urged. "It will make it easier to keep your eyes closed."

Annie sat back up. "Now you're scaring me. Why do I need to keep my eyes closed?"

"Just following your own instructions, Annie. Lie back. Close your eyes. Relax so you can discover the sensuous areas of your body. Sound familiar?"

"Not funny," Annie told him.

"Not meant to be," Matt said and he sent her a smoldering look that made her pulse race.

She didn't try to stop him when he took the mask from her hand. Or when he slipped the band over her head and settled the sleep mask securely into place.

"Tonight's bing is all about you," he whispered and kissed her gently on the lips.

The sensation of Matt's warm lips brushing against hers when she couldn't see a thing was so erotic that Annie shivered. It was as if the minute she was sightless every inch of her body came alive to compensate for what she couldn't see.

She felt his fingers unfastening the buttons on her blouse and grabbed his hand. "*Matt . . .*"

His finger pressed against her lips. "This is *during*, Annie. No chitchat."

By the time he'd peeled away every stitch she was wearing, Annie's head was reeling. His hands seemed to be touching her everywhere at once. And the more he caressed her face, her neck, and her bare shoulders, the better she liked it. She allowed him to guide her nude body back against the soft leather seat. Her pulse kicked up another notch when his fingers trailed down her neck to the sensitive hollow between her breasts.

She gasped when his hand didn't stop there.

"Your body is like a beautiful flower waiting to be discovered," he said, his voice low and sexy as he recited a line straight from her own Joe Video script.

His finger slid into deep recesses and between soft petals, confirming her flower analogy. Annie bit down hard on her lower lip.

But she cried out Matt's name when his amazing hot

mouth took the place of his finger, giving Annie a whole new appreciation for the phrase *in full bloom*.

All day on Wednesday, Annie couldn't even look in Matt's direction without blushing. If he noticed, she couldn't tell. But her embarrassment over the things she'd eagerly allowed him to do to her in the privacy of that limo was the least of her worries.

Although Rico had been attentive enough to his fans that morning, he'd become more sullen than ever once he got back in front of the camera. He seemed distracted, and Gretchen was quickly losing patience with him. To make matters worse, Claire kept running over to him every time they took a break to whisper who-knew-what into his ear.

Damn Helena. Annie had been so eager to keep her away from Claire, it never crossed her mind they should have waited until *after* they finished filming to implement Helena's get-Rico-back plan.

"You need to have a talk with Rico, Annie," Gretchen said, hurrying over to where she was standing. "We're running way behind schedule. We can't afford that."

"I'll take care of it," Annie said.

But Gretchen had no sooner walked away than Matt strolled across the room in her direction. Annie felt the heat start at her feet and zoom to the top of her head. *Maintain eye contact*, she kept telling herself. If she let herself look at that marvelous mouth of his even once, she'd melt into a puddle right where she was standing.

"Is there a problem?" Matt asked in his strictly business voice. "Gretchen seems upset."

"Nothing I can't handle," Annie said, her cheeks still ablaze.

He started to say something else, but Claire swished her way over to both of them. "Just the two people I needed to see," she said, a conniving grin on her face. "I'm afraid I have some disappointing news for both of you."

Claire found out about Helena was Annie's first thought. She held her breath.

Claire looked at Matt first. "Sorry, Matt, but I'm going to have to cancel our between-the-sheets date on Friday night."

Annie's head jerked in Matt's direction. The only thing that kept her from decking him was the extremely relieved look on his face.

"And sorry, Annie," Claire said, turning back to her, "but Rico isn't going to be available for the intimate date you'd planned for him on Friday night, either. He's going with me to a cocktail party some of Ted Turner's people are having on Friday night."

When Claire prissed off, Annie turned to Matt, eyebrow raised. "Between the sheets?"

"Intimate?" Matt said right back. But he pressed a folded piece of paper into the palm of her hand before he walked away.

Annie unfolded the paper and read the note: *Bing Number Three. Tonight. Sevenish?* The address wasn't his, but Annie knew the building — some of the highest-priced real estate in downtown Atlanta. He'd drawn a smiley face at the bottom of the note. Except this smiley face had a distinctly Mick Jagger–type tongue.

Annie blushed again from head to toe.

"Annie!" Collin wailed, wringing his hands as he ran across the set. "Rico hates the music for the 'Striptease Aerobics' segment. He's insisting on using salsa music.

No one could strip to salsa music, Annie. No one. Who does Rico think he is all of a sudden? Ricky fucking Martin?"

What is this? Hell with fluorescent lighting?

"We hate the F-word, remember?" Annie reminded him calmly. Then she said the same thing she'd been saying all morning long: "I'll take care of it."

Annie stepped off the elevator on the top floor of the Regency Building at exactly 7:02 p.m. that evening. She found herself standing in an impressive wall-to-wall marble foyer, with exotic plants aplenty. But she laughed when she saw the life-size poster of Betty Boop sitting in front of the massive double doors that Annie assumed led into whomever's penthouse apartment.

Hooked onto one of Miss Betty's cardboard arms was a quilted pink hanger with a black string bikini so tiny there wasn't any reason to bother putting it on. And taped to Miss Betty's other arm was a note that said: *The door's unlocked. The bathroom's to the left. Follow the trail for bing number three.*

Annie took the hanger with her, opened the door, and stepped into an apartment worthy of an entire issue of *Architectural Digest.* Expensive wood. Glass brick. More marble than anyone should be able to pay for. The place was posh, contemporary, and definitely all male.

She found the guest bath, which turned out to be larger than her entire loft apartment. Against her better judgment, she even put on the skimpy string bikini.

She told the new-Annie reflection staring back at her in the bathroom's floor-to-ceiling mirror that there was absolutely no reason to be nervous. That she wasn't reading anything but sex into Matt's elaborate efforts. And that she could handle the situation completely.

But still, she couldn't keep her idealistic heart from sighing as she followed the terribly romantic trail of rose petals through the lavish apartment and out onto a breathtaking rooftop garden.

And that's where she found Matt.

Sitting in a bubbling Jacuzzi. A glass of wine in his hand. And a welcoming come-and-get-me look on his incredibly handsome face.

As she walked toward him, something told Annie the dynamic between them was changing — becoming way too serious.

She was having too much fun to listen.

She flashed Matt a here-I-come-to-get-you smile and kept walking in his direction.

"Wow," was all Matt could think to say as his gaze traveled over Annie's amazing body. After seeing her in that bikini, if he died at that moment, he could truthfully say he died a happy man.

She put her hands on her shapely hips, drawing his attention to her tiny waist and flat stomach. He swallowed, hard. He'd thought of nothing but her the entire day. And now that he finally had her here all to himself, he was overwhelmed at how much he wanted her.

"I didn't realize Betty Boop lived here in Atlanta," she teased.

Matt laughed. "Go figure. Who would believe a guy who could afford a place like this would collect posters of cartoon characters for a hobby?"

She looked around, taking in the 360-degree view of

the city at night. "Nice view," she said. "Trying out a
place like this to see if it fits with your big promotion?"

"Nah," Matt said. "Trying to impress you with ex-
traordinary bing places."

"It's working," she said.

"Prove it," he told her.

Matt put his wineglass down and held out his hand.
After he'd helped Annie into the Jacuzzi and had her settled beside him, he leaned in for a long, slow kiss. It
wasn't enough. He pulled her close and kissed her again.
Harder this time, and with much more urgency than before.

She kissed him back. Her arms slid around his neck
and she maneuvered her body so she was sitting astride
him. Matt moaned. He could feel the delicious pressure
of exactly what he wanted — pressing firmly against exactly what he couldn't wait to give her.

When their lips broke apart, she whispered, "Maybe
we should slow down. Enjoy the spectacular view first."

"I'm already enjoying the spectacular view," Matt said
and sank his fingers into her long, sexy hair and pulled
her head forward for another kiss.

She was the one to break the kiss a few seconds later,
slowly, and tease his lower lip between her teeth as she
pulled her head back. "Nice touch," she said, reaching for
one of the plump strawberries he'd arranged on a silver
tray and placed on the side of the Jacuzzi. "You even
thought of chocolate." She dipped the berry into the
melted chocolate, then brought it to his lips to taste.

To hell with berries and chocolate, Matt Jr. yelled.

Matt reluctantly took a quick bite and swallowed. "I
hate to bring this up," he said when Annie put the berry

to her own lips for a leisurely nibble. "But aren't you the one who is always concerned about the chitchat rules?"

You tell her, big guy! came another cry from down under.

She shrugged and reached for another berry. More dipping. "I was concerned until you pointed out that as long as the chatting didn't occur during or after sex, we weren't really breaking the rules."

Way to go, big mouth!

Matt pulled Annie closer, nuzzled her neck, and whispered into her hair, "I vote for us getting back to the during sex part."

She snuggled closer to him, her firm, wet breasts pressing against his chest and pushing his desire quickly to the boiling point. Their eyes met for a moment. And just when Matt thought he had Annie's attention exactly where he wanted it, she smiled and said, "Remember when we were sharing silly teenage stories the other night?"

See where getting in touch with your feminine side gets you, dumbass? Nothing but talk, talk, talk.

Okay. It was obvious Annie was in the mood for one of those needing-to-be-validated-with-a-supportive-answer chats. He could do this. It wouldn't kill him.

"Of course I remember," he said. Trying his best to feel all feminine, he threw in for good measure, "I enjoyed sharing my past with you." It was even true.

She smiled sweetly and offered him another bite of strawberry. Matt bit into the berry. But when Annie leaned forward and licked the chocolate from the corner of his mouth with her hot, pink tongue, Matt kicked his damn feminine side to the curb.

"Come here, you," he said and kissed her again.

Again she pulled away after what barely passed for a playful kiss. *Hell, I might as well be bobbing for apples here*, Matt thought sadly.

"I just thought of another bit of trivia from my childhood past that might amuse you," she said, smiling at him so innocently that he felt ashamed of himself.

He tried the truth again. "I'd love to hear it."

She grinned. "Eighth-grade swim team. I was the only kid on the team who could hold my breath underwater for four full minutes."

Matt gulped. "Really?"

Her eyebrow came up in a provocative arch.

When Annie's head slid beneath the water to back up her statement, Matt held on tightly to each side of the Jacuzzi to keep from floating blissfully up to heaven and the stairway of brilliant stars twinkling above them.

CHAPTER 16

M ind-blowing evenings with Matt and hair-raising
days keeping the peace between Gretchen and
Rico were beginning to wear Annie out. *Just two more
days*, she kept telling herself, and filming Joe Video
would be over.

As for Matt, he'd called in his last bing marker before
she left the penthouse the night before. She'd be meeting
him at his apartment tonight. The anticipation of another
beyond-belief evening had her tingling with excitement,
sighing in awe, and congratulating herself for finally realizing the only way to survive in this life was to maintain a no-strings-attached existence.

She'd feel guilty about it later.

When the magic between them ended.

Then she'd do what she'd been doing from the moment she'd met him. She'd lie to her broken heart and say
she wasn't hopelessly in love with Matt and never had
been.

But for now, she was going to enjoy being happy.

When Collin hurried over with his usual concerned
look, Annie said, "Don't bother me, Collin. I'm living
happily ever after at the moment."

Her request didn't stop Collin from saying, "Well,

you're the only one who's happy around here. Rico is getting more impossible by the minute. And Gretchen is threatening to strangle him."

"I'll have a talk with him," Annie said, but she and Collin exchanged spare-me-please looks as Rico's new shadow swished past them.

Claire hurried across the set and eagerly handed Rico the glass of water he'd demanded before he would finish the last part of the aerobics segment.

"How many times do you think we'd have to flush before Claire goes away?" Collin said.

"Two more flushes," Annie told him. "Today and tomorrow. Then we'll be rid of her."

"*And* Rico, thank God," Collin said. "I just hope your idea to sic Claire on him works soon. Helena is starting to second-guess her decision to go along with your plan. Which is why I'm leaving in a minute, if that's okay with you. Maybe shopping will keep Helena pacified."

"Sure, go ahead," Annie said. "Just be here bright and early in the morning. It's going to be a madhouse around here tomorrow. You'll need to help me keep the winning fans in line while they watch tomorrow's filming."

"God, don't remind me," Collin said with a sigh. "See you in the morning."

He had no sooner walked away than Matt sidled up beside her. "It looks like your dream guy is turning out to be your worst nightmare."

Annie eased her hand behind his back and pinched him on the butt for making that smart remark.

"Be careful," he said, still looking straight ahead. "There's a fine line between pain and pleasure."

"Then you're about to have an orgasm, because I'm going to deck you if you keep ragging me about Rico."

She kept looking straight ahead herself. "I need your team support today, Matt. Not your ridicule."

He leaned sideways. "I am thinking that is not all you are needing from me, Ah-nee," he said, mimicking Rico's accent and manner of speaking to perfection.

"Cute," Annie said.

Matt winked at her and walked away.

The music started up again. The camera started rolling. And Rico, clad in nothing but his skimpy red briefs, did a few extremely seductive gyrations. But then he threw his hands up in the air and exclaimed, "Stop everything! I cannot do this."

Oh yes, by God, you can!

Annie marched onto the set where Rico was standing. "We need to talk," she told him. She pointed in the direction of the outside patio.

Rico nodded curtly. Claire started to follow until one look from Annie stopped her in her tracks.

Once they were outside and alone, Rico started pacing back and forth. "You are angry," he said. "And I am sorry. But I cannot do this any longer."

Hands on her hips, Annie said, "I don't want this to get ugly, Rico. But you did sign a contract. Paragon has invested a lot of money in this game. And J.B. Duncan *will* sue you if you don't fulfill your contract."

He stopped pacing and glared at her. "You think I care about that? I do not. I do not want to be every woman's dream guy. I do not want to be a big star. I want my old life back. My friends and my family, they make fun of me. Rico, the pretty boy, they call me. To them, I am nothing but a big joke. But I am no big joke." He pounded his bare, muscled chest with his fist. "I am a man. A man who will not continue to let women boss me around!"

You arrogant jerk! Annie thought, until Rico slumped onto one of the outdoor patio chairs and buried his head in his hands.

"Helena is all I care about," he said. "She has gone away with this other man. I cannot find her."

Annie couldn't help it. She felt sorry for him. Even if Rico *had* brought the whole situation on himself, she could only hope someone would love her that much one day.

"Maybe I can find Helena for you."

His head came up. "Find her? How could you do this?"

You twerp. You thought I could make you a big Hollywood star? But you doubt I could find your girlfriend?

"I have connections," she told him. It wasn't even a lie.

A look of relief washed across his handsome face. "Please. I beg of you, Annie. Call up your connections. Find my Helena. Find her before she marries this other man and it is too late for me."

"Under one condition," Annie said.

Rico nodded without her having to say it. "I will finish the filming. All of it. You have my word."

Annie smiled. "Good. You have my word, too, Rico. When we finish filming tomorrow, I'll do everything in my power to see that Helena will be waiting for you."

Thanks to Rico's cooperation the remainder of Thursday afternoon, Annie had time to go home and take a long, relaxing bubble bath before she headed off to Matt's apartment. She'd dressed casually, wearing a short and sexy white eyelet sundress with spaghetti straps, and her favorite sandals — a much-welcomed relief after dress clothes and heels all day.

Underneath the sundress, the only thing she was wearing was a lacy white thong. She blushed slightly, realizing how eager she was for Matt to get her out of that thong. Then she took a deep breath, reached out, and rang Matt's doorbell.

The first thing she thought when he opened the door was that she should have given more thought to her attire. Matt was dressed fit to kill. Dress shirt. Dress slacks. Even dress shoes. She panicked for a moment. *Surely he isn't planning on us going out first. He knows I'd never agree to that.*

"You look gorgeous," he said and pulled her close for a long delicious kiss as the deep voice of Barry White coming from inside the apartment kept insisting, "Give it up . . . ain't no use . . . can't help myself if I wanted to."

However.

When Annie stepped into Matt's apartment, she was so shocked that she walked back to the front door and peeped around it to look at the number. "Just checking," she said, getting a little nervous. "I thought I was in the wrong apartment."

"Cute," he said.

He took her purse and placed it on the new rattan bench-style table that was so-not-him sitting by his front door. And that's when Annie took her first long look around. The place looked like a Pier 1 display ad. She wasn't sure she had ever seen that many candles in one room, but the candles were the least of it. Abstract floral paintings had taken the place of Matt's cherished black-and-white framed autographed photos of famous baseball players. A giant urn sat in one corner of the living room, stuffed with multicolored feathery ferns. There were even pleated paisley fabric lampshades on the lamps on his end tables.

Decorating for Dummies. I'll find him a copy.

Matt ushered her over to his leather sectional sofa — the one thing she did recognize, for a number of delicious reasons — where an ice bucket, a chilled bottle of champagne, and a spectacular array of hors d'oeuvres were waiting on his coffee table. When Annie glanced into his adjoining dining room, she saw that the table was set to perfection, complete with matching placemats and napkins.

He followed her gaze. "I wanted us to celebrate privately tonight." He took her hand. "Brace yourself, Annie. PlayStar is going to buy Joe Video. J.B. told me today. We did it, Annie. Paragon is going to make a bundle. And J.B. is going to announce our promotions tomorrow when we finish filming."

Matt could have knocked her over with one of his new feathery ferns.

PlayStar? That would mean worldwide distribution of her idea. Annie lowered herself onto the sofa. They really had pulled it off. After tomorrow, Matt would be an executive vice president. And she would be Paragon's new creative director.

Matt moved a plush beaded pillow out of his way and sat down beside her. "Take a minute," he said. "I was speechless myself after J.B. told me."

Wait a minute.

Plush. Beaded. Pillow.

Annie felt the hair stand up on the back of her neck.

Matt reached over and took the champagne bottle from

the ice bucket. He filled two champagne flutes and handed one to her. "To success," he said and clinked his glass against hers.

"To success," Annie repeated, still slightly addled.

When Matt took a fancy petit four from the tray and lifted the small tea cake to her mouth for her to taste, the fog began to lift and Annie's mind screamed *Tea cake? Are you freaking kidding me?*

She swallowed the bite in one unladylike gulp.

"Okay, Matt. What's going on?"

He smiled. Facetiously. And they both knew it. "What do you mean?"

"All of this so-not-you stuff," Annie said, waving her arm around the room. She picked up the pillow and held it up in front of his face. "This." She put it back down and pointed to the urn in the corner. "That." She shook her head. "And where are your baseball pictures? You treasure those pictures."

Matt shrugged. "Is there some new law that says a guy can't feminize his apartment?"

Feminize? Annie stared at him for a moment. "Who are you?"

Stay calm, Matt told himself. It made perfect sense that Annie would be a little overwhelmed. Hell, he was overwhelmed himself. About all of it. PlayStar. His promotion. His new feminized outlook. Being in love for the first time in his life.

"Who am I?" He took her hand. "I —"

She cut him off. "You're scaring me, Matt."

She wasn't kidding. Her palms were sweaty. Her breath was becoming short and raspy. Hyperventilation could be just around the corner. He put his finger under her chin, forcing her to look at him.

"Why am I scaring you?"

She stared him down. "Because . . . I can feel it. You're going to ruin everything. Don't do this, Matt. It wasn't part of our deal."

You little dummy. Don't you realize I love you?

Matt leaned forward and kissed her lightly on the lips. "Don't do what, Annie? Don't tell you that I'm in love with you?" *There, I said it.* He leaned in and kissed her again. "That I want a new deal? The real deal. You. Me. Together."

Annie tried to get up, but Matt held on to both of her hands, forcing her to stay seated. Now he was getting scared. "I'm not trying to ruin anything, Annie. I'm trying to tell you how I feel. I want it all. Just like you said. The house. The dog. The kids. Even the minivan. All of it."

She wrestled away from him and stood up. "Please don't do this, Matt. We've been getting along great just the way things are."

What? He'd just bared his soul to her? Told her he loved her? And all she could say was, "Don't do this"?

Anger rolled over Matt like a two-ton steamroller. He stood up and faced her. "Didn't you hear a word I just said? I all but handed you my heart on a silver platter, Annie. What are you holding out for, the goddamn ear in the mail?"

Her eyes narrowed. "Welcome back," she said. "*That's* the Matt I know."

She stomped across the room.

Matt stomped across the room right behind her. "Well, excuse me. I've evidently fallen short of your dream guy expectations. Which I find pretty damn funny, since it was *your* made-to-order outline I was following."

She whirled around to face him. "Whose made-to-order outline did you think *I* was following when I came up with the idea for sex with no strings attached?"

Matt glared at Annie.

Annie glared back.

She jerked her purse strap across her shoulder. "Can I leave now? Or do you have any other insults you want to hurl in my direction?"

Fine!

She wanted insults. He'd see what he could do.

"I guess that means tonight's bing is out of the question then."

She paled. Then she sent him a screw-you glare that made him step back just in case she decided to slap him. Which he certainly deserved for that comment. But that was beside the point.

She opened the door, marched through it, and headed down the hallway, never looking back.

Matt slammed his front door with a bang and stood there for a moment, seething. *What in the hell have I been thinking?* To hell with love and everything that went along with it. He was through trying to be everything he wasn't. And for what? To have all of his efforts thrown back in his face? *You're ruining everything.* Proving exactly what he'd known all along, dammit. No matter what a woman said she wanted, she'd change her damn mind when tomorrow rolled around.

You did blindside her, you know, his conscience yelled out. *Annie had no idea you were going to drop the big L-word bomb on her tonight.*

Matt thought it over and decided it was too damn bad.

Annie had done her fair share of blindsiding, too. Like the first night she showed up at his apartment while he was minding his own damn business. She was the one who had started what had turned into this full-blown disaster, not him.

He headed back across the living room. He picked up the tray filled with hors d'oeuvres and walked into the kitchen. He also picked up the new serving platter he'd purchased especially for the occasion, the one holding the grilled-to-perfection salmon steaks he'd had especially catered. Then he walked over to the waste can and dumped the whole mess, platters and all, into the trash.

With the same determined resolve, Matt walked back into the living room. Once he had the beaded pillows stacked under his chin, he walked back to the kitchen, slid open the glass sliding door and walked up to the iron railing surrounding his patio deck. He was still feeling like the village idiot Annie had turned him into when he sailed the first pillow off his fourth-floor balcony. By the time he'd finished pitching all six pillows as far as he could throw them, he felt pretty damn good.

Forget Annie.

She wanted no part of what he was willing to give her, so forget her. He had a new promotion. And he had a long list of new goals to reach when he became Paragon's youngest executive vice president ever.

He was going to be just fine.

At least, that's what Matt kept telling himself when he walked back inside to blow out the friggin' candles and to proudly put Babe, Mickey, and Lou right back on his soon-to-be *defeminized* single-guy wall where — by God — they belonged!

CHAPTER 17

By the time Annie made it to her car, she was crying so hard she could barely fit the key into the lock on her car door. She finally got the door open, dropped onto the seat, and threw herself against the steering wheel, sobbing even harder.

Of all the times for Matt to decide he wanted to try his hand at a serious relationship, he had to pick now. Just when their careers were coming together for both of them. Just when they were having so much fun together. And just when Annie had finally decided she liked her life exactly the way it was.

But it's my fault. Not Matt's.

She never should have shown up on his doorstep. She should have left things between them exactly as they were — nothing personal.

Annie leaned her head against the steering wheel and sobbed a little more. Matt was right. He'd practically handed her his heart on a freaking silver platter — something she'd never let herself even hope for from him. She hadn't meant to sound like she was making light of his telling her he loved her. Her response had just been a knee-jerk reaction when she felt her no-strings-attached unraveling to put a noose around her neck.

No, it wasn't fair to make Matt pay for the losers who had walked into her life and right back out again. Annie knew that. But she couldn't help it. To have Matt, only to lose him later, would destroy her. Completely. She'd never be able to survive it.

Sob. Sob. Sob.

Blubber. Blubber. Blubber.

She wouldn't blame Matt if he never spoke to her again. Who did she think she was, playing with both of their lives like that? Pretending they could bing each other's brains out night after night without one of them getting hurt?

Oh God. Oh God. Oh God.

She might not survive this, either.

Annie didn't know what was worse. Having Matt and losing him. Or never having his arms around her again.

When her cell phone rang, hope eternal sprang forward and grabbed it on the first ring. "Matt?"

"Who's Matt?"

Not what Annie needed at the moment.

"You know Matt's my boss, Mother. I'm busy."

"I gathered. Since you didn't return my call all day."

Annie bit back a groan. "What do you want, Mother?"

"I need to see you, Annie," Bev said. "Tonight. It's important, or I wouldn't have been trying to reach you all day. Come over. I'm at home."

Bev hung up without waiting for Annie's answer.

Annie walked up to the house she'd grown up in and rang the doorbell for the first time in her life. She'd learned her lesson about walking in without any warning on her last visit home. She had no intention of making that mistake again.

When Bev opened the door and Annie stepped inside, the first thing she noticed were the suitcases stacked to the right of the front door. It was on the tip of her tongue to ask what was going on. And she would have asked that question — if her mother hadn't taken one look at her and asked instead, "What's wrong? You've been crying."

Annie couldn't explain it, but the concerned look on her mother's face took her right back to her childhood. She threw her arms around her mother's neck and sobbed against Bev's shoulder.

"My whole life sucks," Annie blubbered as her mother patted her back supportively.

Bev allowed her to cry a few minutes before she took Annie's hand. "Let's go make you some hot herbal tea and you can tell me all about it."

As distraught as she was, Annie almost laughed as she followed her mother to the kitchen. Hot herbal tea had always been Bev's cure for everything. She was amazed Bev had never organized a hot herbal tea crusade as the answer to achieving world peace.

"So?" Bev said thirty minutes later, as they sat across the kitchen table from each other, sipping their tea. "Do you love Matt?"

Annie was surprised at how quickly she said, "Yes." She did love Matt. She loved Matt completely. His good points. His bad points. Everything in between.

Bev shrugged. "Then what's the problem?"

Good point. Annie sighed and said, "Fear, mainly. That it won't work out between us. That he'll regret giving up his freedom. That I'll never survive losing him."

"Freedom's just another word for nothing left to lose," Bev said.

"'*Bobby McGee*?'" Annie wailed. "We're talking

about my life, and you're quoting lines from a song you played nonstop when I was a kid?"

Bev only smiled, a melancholy look on her face as she stared into her teacup. "Your father loved that song." She looked up at Annie. "I know I've never liked to talk about your father, but I've thought about him a lot since I met Umberto."

Annie forced herself to ask, "Why? Does Umberto remind you of him?"

Bev shook her head. "No. It's being in love again that reminds me of your father."

"But Mother —" Annie protested.

Bev held her hand up. "I know what you're going to say. You're going to say I haven't known Umberto long enough to be in love with him. That he's too young for me. Maybe you're right. But I'm not going to let fear keep me from taking this chance. If it doesn't work out between us, then it doesn't. At least I won't have any regrets. I'll know I tried."

Bev stood up and walked over to put her cup into the kitchen sink. When she turned back around, she said, "That's why I needed to see you tonight. Umberto and I are going to Mexico for a couple of weeks. We have an early flight in the morning, so I'm going to his apartment tonight. I wanted to see you before we left."

Annie sat there for a moment. "And you want me to check on things here at the house while you're gone?"

Bev said, "Yes. But that's not all. When we get back from Mexico, I'm moving in with Umberto. Downtown. He owns the building where he has his shop. It makes more sense for us to live in the apartment above the flower shop. He needs to be close to his plants."

"You're selling the house?" Annie's stomach rolled

over. The thought of Bev selling the house broke her heart. It was home. Where her roots were. This house held her fondest memories. She'd hoped to see her own children playing in the backyard someday, making memories of their own.

"I'm giving the house to you, Annie."

Annie blinked. "Are you serious?"

Bev nodded. "It will be yours one day anyway. Why not give it to you now while you can enjoy it?"

Annie got up from the table and gave Bev a long hug. "I love you, Mother. I hope you know that."

Bev smiled when Annie let her go. "There's plenty of room in this old house for Matt, too, you know."

Annie didn't comment.

She had the house in the suburbs now.

But did she have the guts to go after the guy?

She remained sitting at her grandmother's kitchen table long after Bev hurried on her way to her beloved Umberto's. Annie still couldn't believe it. Her mother? Going off on trips? Talking freely about being in love? Moving in with a younger guy — who sang opera to his plants?

She still had her own misgivings about the bizarre relationship, but she'd never seen her mother so happy. And that made Annie happy.

Bev's new life sure beat the merry-go-round she'd been trapped on for the last few weeks. The brass ring was waiting for her — life was just spinning so fast Annie couldn't reach out and grab it.

When another tear slid down her cheek, she reached into her purse, searching for a tissue. What she came out with instead was a handful of lottery tickets.

Helena!

Between Matt and her mother both shocking her senseless, she'd forgotten all about her promise to Rico.

She reached into her purse again, this time for her cell phone. The fact that it was midnight didn't keep her from punching the button for Collin's number.

She could tell he'd been asleep when he said a barely understandable, "'Lo."

"Wake up, Collin," Annie told him. "We need to talk."

"Who is this?"

"You know who this is," Annie said. "Get up and walk around until your head clears. I need your full attention."

As Annie filled Collin in on her conversation with Rico and the plans she wanted Collin to arrange, she amused herself with the scratch-off tickets she'd spread out on the kitchen table. One after another, she took her fingernail and scratched away the hidden boxes. *What a rip-off*, she thought — until her fingernail made a swipe over the last ticket.

"Hot damn!" Annie yelled, cutting off Collin's question about where he should arrange for Rico and Helena to meet. "You aren't going to believe this, Collin. Helena just won five thousand dollars."

She heard Collin sigh. "Are you drinking tequila tonight, Annie?"

He should have been the one to play the role of Joe Video, Matt decided, after the Oscar-worthy performance he'd delivered on Friday. Annie wasn't a bad actress herself. She'd been as pleasant as a sweet Georgia peach from the moment they'd arrived for the last day of filming.

Smile. Smile. Smile.

Nod. Nod. Nod.

At least, they should be finished filming by noon, right on schedule. Matt didn't know what was responsible for the sudden change in Rico's attitude, and he didn't care. All he cared about was putting an end to his involvement in the video game that had changed his life forever. Annie's fab concept had made his promotion possible, sure. But it didn't make up for his badly stomped-on heart.

After he endured J.B.'s celebratory party, he intended to get as far away from Annie as possible. Hide out and lick his wounds. Heal a little.

He watched her from across the idiotic bedroom show-room where he was standing. She and Gretchen were talking with the women who had won the right to watch Annie's phony-ass video game star during the last segment of filming.

Every time he looked at her, it was a sucker punch straight to his stomach. Matt shook his head. At least they wouldn't be working side by side after today. They'd occasionally pass in the hall. Face each other in a meeting now and then. He could handle that. If Annie needed help screening the new employees she'd be hiring for the creative department, or with reports or whatever, he'd send Collin to help her. That's why executives had executive assistants — to free themselves from life's unpleasant little chores.

"Look happy. The day's almost a wrap," the very executive assistant he'd been thinking about said when he walked up beside Matt.

Matt looked down at his watch. "You're right. The day is almost a wrap. Where have you been? You left right after you got here this morning?"

"Running errands," Collin said with a smug smirk.

Matt glanced at the envelope Collin was practically shoving under his nose. "What's that?"

Collin put the envelope behind his back, as if he hadn't meant for Matt to see it. Then he leaned over and whispered, "Can you keep a secret?"

"I'm not even going to answer that question, coming from you," Matt said.

Collin lifted his nose in the air. "Then I'm not going to tell you that inside this envelope is a key to a premier suite at the Georgian Terrace Hotel downtown. A key Annie asked me to give to Rico. Right after the luncheon."

Right jab. Left jab. Another below-the-belt punch.

Annie was the windshield.

He was the bug.

SPLAT!

"Excellent job. All of you," J.B. Duncan said, shaking hands with Matt, Collin, and then Annie.

He put his arm around Matt's shoulder. "I told Matt earlier I wanted the three of you to take next week off. Your portion of Joe Video is completed. So enjoy your time off and relax before you come back to work and start your new positions."

Annie glanced over at Matt. He wouldn't even look in her direction. Was he thinking the same thing she was thinking? That if she hadn't blown it, they could have spent next week together? Annie sighed. If she hadn't made such a mess of things, maybe her mother and Umberto wouldn't be the only ones heading off to tropical shores with sandy beaches.

Of course, she'd blown it only if she left things the way they were. Which Annie didn't intend to do. She'd made that decision last night. They'd just been so busy all day, she hadn't had the opportunity to beg Matt for a second chance until he agreed to give her one.

What's wrong with now?

J.B. had just told everyone good-bye and left. Collin was hurrying over to give Rico the key to the hotel where he'd find Helena waiting for him. And Matt was standing all by himself, pretending to ignore her, less than two feet away.

Do it!

"Matt," she said, moving closer. "Can we talk a minute?"

He refused to look at her. Annie followed his gaze. He was looking across the patio at Collin and Rico. He finally turned his head with a pissed look on his face. "Is it a work-related talk?"

"You know it isn't," Annie said.

"If it isn't work-related, Annie, we don't have anything to talk about," he said. "My idle chitchat days are over."

He sauntered away, heading for the patio doors. Annie started after him, until Rico called her name and waved, signaling for Annie to wait.

Damn.

Annie felt like crying. She'd hurt Matt deeper than she'd thought. "I'm sorry" wasn't going to cut it.

I'll have to show Matt I'm serious.

She put on a false smile when Rico brought her hand to his lips and kissed it, the same way he'd done the first day he'd shown up at Paragon.

"You are my dream *woman*," Rico said happily. "For finding my Helena. To repay you one day, Annie, this will be my biggest wish."

Annie leaned forward and hugged him. "Just send me an invitation to the wedding, Rico. That's all the payment I need."

"That," Rico said, "I will do." He shook hands with Collin, blew Annie a final kiss, and hurried away.

"I just love happy endings," Collin said, staring wistfully after Rico. But he frowned and mumbled something overtly foul when he saw Claire Winslow heading their way.

"Did Rico leave?" she demanded, purposely ignoring Collin and looking directly at Annie. "He was supposed to wait for me."

Annie looked at Collin. "Didn't Rico say he had to hurry to the airport?"

"Airport?" Claire shrieked.

Collin rolled his eyes. "Wouldn't you be hurrying to the airport if Quentin Tarantino wanted you in Hollywood first thing in the morning?"

Claire turned and ran.

Collin and Annie burst out laughing.

"Chaos, panic, and disorder," Collin said cheerfully. "Our work here is done."

Annie linked her arm through Collin's. "Let's get out of here." But as they left the patio, she said, "Catch me up. Did you caution Helena when you took her to the hotel that it might be wise to keep where she'd been a secret? At least for now?"

"I did," Collin said.

"And did you give Helena the envelope and tell her not to open it. To give it to Rico when he arrived?"

"I did."

"And did you get Helena out of her spandex and turn

her into a supermodel during your shopping spree yesterday?"

Collin didn't answer. He opened Groveman's front entrance door and pushed Annie through ahead of him.

Annie laughed. "I told you you'd never get Helena out of that spandex."

"I just couldn't do it," Collin said as they headed across the parking lot. "Helena is one of the most unique individuals I've ever met. Turning her into a ho-hum version of everyone else would be the equivalent of turning Cher into a faceless backup singer. I just couldn't do it. We bought every piece of spandex we could find."

"Why, lovey," Annie said. "What incredible insight."

Collin smiled. "See? I'm not always as shallow and materialistic as I appear."

"*Plus* you just love happy endings," Annie said when they stopped beside her car.

"I *adore* happy endings," Collin agreed.

"I hope you mean that, Collin," Annie said. "I have a lot to tell you. You might not be happy about some of it, but I need your help. I'm running out of time."

Collin's deep blue eyes kept growing wider and wider as Annie told him what had been going on right under his unsuspecting nose.

He didn't smile until Annie told him what she wanted him to help her do about it.

CHAPTER 18

Rico's hand was shaking badly. It was his third attempt to get the flimsy plastic key to work in the hotel room's lock. He finally gave up and rapped softly on the hotel room door.

"Helena. It is me, Rico. Please. Open the door."

What he was facing, he did not know. All Collin had told him was that Helena had agreed to see him. There, in the hotel. Away, Collin had said, from everyone else so she could talk to him in private.

Fear told Rico it was too late. That Helena would honor her uncle's wishes and marry this other man. Hope told Rico he could change her mind.

Helena opened the door and he stepped inside. The opulence of the premier suite in one of Atlanta's most luxurious hotels was wasted on him. He had eyes only for Helena. And his love for her was bursting at the seams in his tight-fitting jeans.

"You will not marry this other man, Helena," he said with the authority of a man in love, not some pretty dream boy. "You are meant to be mine. The subject is finished."

Not the right thing to say, he decided when Helena turned away from him and walked across the room to sit on the side of a king-size bed. A bed that Rico would not let go to waste if he had any say in the matter.

"I do not want a big star for a husband," she said, her lips in a full pout. She tossed her dark hair over a bare shoulder that made his mouth go dry just looking at her exposed tanned skin.

Rico walked in her direction. "And you will not have a big star for a husband." He made it a point to say this much softer. "That is my promise. I am through with the acting."

He sat down on the bed beside her, leaned forward, and delivered a series of small kisses across her bare shoulder and up her neck, just the way she liked. He felt her shiver with desire for him, but still she pushed him away.

"I do not believe you," she said, but Rico could see the pulse point beating wildly at the base of her throat.

She reached out and took an envelope from the table beside the bed and handed it to him. "This is from Annie. Another big acting contract for you, maybe. I was told to give it to you. Not to open it."

Rico handed the envelope back to her. "I am through with the acting." He pointed to the waste can by the bed. "Throw whatever Annie sent me there, in the trash."

She stared at the envelope for a moment, then looked back at him. "But what if it is important?"

"You are the only important thing to me," Rico said.

When the expression in her dark eyes softened, he knew he *had* said the right thing this time. He expected her to toss the envelope into the trash. Instead, she sliced the flap open with her long red fingernail, and peered into the envelope.

Then Helena threw her head back and laughed like a woman gone loco.

"What?" Rico demanded.

She was holding up what? A lottery ticket? Rico frowned when she jumped up from the bed and began dancing around the room, waving the ticket around and around above her head. Still more laughing. Still more dancing. Rico did not find any of it funny.

"Give the ticket to me," he said, holding out his hand. "You know I hate the gambling. I will throw the ticket in the trash myself."

Helena danced over to him with a playful gleam in her eye. She pushed him backwards onto the bed and landed on top of him. "No. We will not throw away the ticket. It is a gift from Annie. We will keep it."

Rico started to object, but Helena slid her hand down to grasp what was begging for her attention. His thoughts turned to more urgent matters. When she bent down and kissed him, the taste of her sweet, full lips overpowered his reasoning.

"Please," she whispered. "We will keep the money for our honeymoon? Sí?"

She unzipped his pants, and Rico gasped, "Sí."

When she slid seductively down the full length of his body, Rico closed his eyes, knowing he would never be able to say no to his beautiful Helena again.

Of that, he was certain.

Matt walked into his apartment, thinking that the last thing he needed was next week off. He tossed his keys on the stupid rattan table by the door that would soon be history, and slammed his front door with a bang. Removing his coat and tie, he headed across the room and slumped down on the sofa.

He'd planned to spend next week burying himself in his new Annie-free life and settling himself into his new roomy executive vice president office. Now, counting both weekends, he had nine long days stretching out before him with nowhere he really wanted to go, and nothing he really wanted to do.

He'd first considered going down to see his folks. But the thought of being surrounded by his brothers, telling him what a great single life he had while they were all gazing fondly at their children playing in his parents' yard, would have only depressed him more.

Damn Annie.

She had his mind so screwed up he didn't even want to go home and see his family.

Matt got up from the sofa and headed into the kitchen for a beer. He popped the top, took a long gulp, wiped his mouth with the back of his hand, and headed back to the sofa to do some more sulking.

Maybe, he decided, he could round up a few buddies and head down to the gulf. He brought the bottle to his lips again. Fresh salt air. A week's worth of deep-sea fishing. Lots of beer and nothing but all-male camaraderie. It would sure beat sitting around feeling sorry for himself and agonizing over what Annie and her new bing buddy were doing.

Don't go there.

He couldn't. If he let himself think about what was going on at the Georgian Terrace Hotel, he would storm down there and make a complete ass of himself.

Or worse.

What he was going to do was change clothes —

His telephone rang, cutting off Matt's train of thought. He leaned over the side of the sofa, picked up his portable phone, and looked at the caller ID. The phone rang twice more before he finally gave in and answered it.

"Where have you been?" Collin wailed. "I've been calling you for hours. Why aren't you answering your cell?"

Matt wasn't answering his cell phone because it happened to be in several pieces. In the back of his Jeep. Where he'd thrown it after checking it every five seconds, thinking Annie might call after he wouldn't talk to her, and she didn't. Where he'd been was downtown, driving back and forth in front of the Georgian Terrace Hotel for the last five hours, where he finally talked himself out of possibly getting arrested for disorderly conduct and disturbing the peace.

But Matt said, "I had things to do, Collin. Got a problem with that?"

"No. But I've got a problem," Collin said. "Stay where you are. I'm walking into your building now. I'll be up in a minute."

When Matt opened the door, the first thing Collin did was shove a golden furball into his arms. Matt laughed and held the little guy out to take a good look at him. "Well, what do you know," he said. "You finally got yourself a real dog."

"He's not mine," Collin was quick to tell him. "And that's my problem. You know I'm a temporary foster parent for lost animals, right?"

Matt nodded, ruffling the dog's soft fur.

"Well, the good news is the animal shelter called me earlier to say they found this pup's owner. And the bad news is, Lars is on standby and he just got called in. I'm taking Lars to the airport now. I need you to drop the dog off for me at the owner's house."

Matt was puzzled. "Why can't you just drop the dog off after you take Lars to the airport?"

Collin gasped. "It's still in the nineties outside, Matt. You can't leave a helpless puppy locked in a hot car. Not even for a minute. Do you know that in this kind of heat the inside temperature of a car can reach —"

"Okay, okay," Matt said. "I'll drop the dog off for you." *What the hell?* He didn't have anything better to do.

"Here's the address." Collin handed over a slip of paper. "The owner is expecting you."

Matt shifted the pup to one arm and took the address.

"Better run. Lars is waiting." Collin grinned. "You can't leave a big, gorgeous, blond pilot locked in a hot car, either, you know."

"Don't push it, Collin," Matt warned.

After Collin disappeared, Matt closed the door.

"You ready to go home, little guy?"

But as he headed into the bedroom to change clothes, Matt got that sucker-punch feeling in his stomach again.

Golden retriever.

Dammit, did everything on the planet have to remind him of Annie?

It was eight o'clock Friday evening when Matt drove into the subdivision. Druid Hills was only a short distance away from the hustle and bustle of the city, but Matt felt like he was driving through his small hometown. The houses were all big and homey, testimony to the slower pace here. The rose bushes in the yards had been put there for people to stop and savor the smell, not just for show.

Matt pushed the button on his car door panel, letting his window slide down so he could inhale the sweet scent of the freshly cut lawns. This had always been his favorite time of day when he was a kid. Just before dark, when the promise of a pleasant evening chased away the misery of a long, hot Georgia day.

This was the time when fireflies came out to play with the kids. The time when parents sat on their porches, their stomachs full after a good meal, their exchanged looks filled with other promises for later, after the kids were all put to bed.

Who are you?

Isn't that what Annie had asked him?

Matt was beginning to wonder the same thing himself. If he got any more melodramatic, he was going to be a contender for Collin's drama queen role. He had to get his emotions back under control and stop giving in to all the ushy-mushy lovesick bullshit. Get his edge back. He was Haz-Matt, dammit. Not *Hazbeen*-Matt.

He drove farther down the street, checking the numbers on the mailboxes as he went. He finally found the right address. But when he pulled into the driveway, he slipped right off his edge and landed in another giant pile of ushy-mushy.

A damn minivan was parked in the driveway.

He sat there for a moment, looking at the old colonial-style brick house and stroking the pup who was asleep and had curled into a ball on his lap. He couldn't help but wonder if the woman of this house had a dream guy. She had the damn minivan and the golden retriever, didn't she?

Matt opened his door, scooped the pup into the crook of his arm, and got out of the Jeep with a deep sigh. All he needed now to really push him over the edge, were three or four excited little kids running to answer the door when he rang the frickin' bell.

Annie let out a relieved sigh when Matt finally got out of the Jeep. She'd been watching him, peeking out from behind the drapes of the front parlor window. She scrunched her hair one last time and sprinted for the front door.

Nervous didn't even touch what she was feeling. Every emotion she had was ready to explode. And the questions running through her mind were making her crazier than her wild-ass scheme to get Matt back. Would he be angry with her and leave? Or would he stay with her forever?

The doorbell told Annie she was about to find out.

She braced herself and opened the door.

Matt almost screamed like a girl.

He was that shocked to find Annie standing in the doorway.

She leaned casually against the doorjamb, as if he were some neighbor stopping by for a visit. "I checked my mail, Matt," she said nonchalantly. "The ear wasn't there."

So you think because I said the L-word I'm a pushover now.

Matt was through playing games. "I decided I couldn't part with the ear, Annie. But I doubt you'll miss it. You seem to have everything you need already. The dog, the house, even the minivan."

She glanced at the driveway. "Well, not technically,

Matt. You see, the minivan's only a rental. And the house won't officially be mine for another few weeks."

"I'm sure you'll work it all out," Matt said and handed over the dog.

Annie handed the dog back to him.

"The dog belongs to you, Matt. If you'll have us."

And the tears in her eyes pushed Matt right over.

Matt leaned forward and kissed her gently at first. Then he kissed Annie with a white-hot craving that told her happily-ever-after wasn't just a myth. It was one of those once-in-a-lifetime perfect moments, when the world tilts on its axis, time stands still, and nothing else matters.

Unless.

You're snapped back to reality with a loud horn blast and someone yelling, "Get a room, already."

She and Matt both groaned when they saw who it was.

"I take that back. About the room," Collin said as he hurried up the cobblestone path in their direction. "I already have a room reserved for you guys. At the Excalibur in fabulous Las Vegas. Lars is at the airport now, leasing a private jet. What's the point of dating a pilot if he can't fly you and your two best friends anywhere you want to go?"

Annie looked at Matt.

Matt looked at Annie.

"We're not going to Las Vegas, Collin," Matt said.

"Oh yes. Both of you *are* going to Vegas. We have the time off. And I have all the money we need." He grinned. "They have a marvelous medieval wedding chapel at the Excalibur. The bride and groom can even dress in medieval wedding attire. Annie can dress like a real princess. You can dress in a suit of shining armor. To die for or what?"

"Or what," Matt said. "Or not," he added quickly when Annie sent him a look.

Collin reached out and took the puppy. "I came to get Bing. He can stay with the sitter and Elton John." He looked at Matt. "Don't you think Annie picked a great name for Elton John's new friend? Bing — as in Crosby. Get it?"

Matt looked at Annie.

Annie grinned and put a finger to her lips.

Collin looked down at his watch. "It's only eight-thirty. Both of you go home. Get packed. And meet me at Hangar Two at eleven. Not one minute later."

He hurried toward his Mercedes with the dog. Before he got in, he yelled, "Don't disappoint me! Las Vegas is the only place outlandish enough to let me be the best man and the maid of honor at the same time."

Matt looked helplessly at Annie when Collin roared away. "What are we going to do?"

Annie took his hand and pulled him inside the house. "You know Collin when he gets like this. I guess we're going to Las Vegas." She closed the door and pulled him against her.

Matt nuzzled her neck. "Vegas could be fun, I guess. The Excalibur isn't the only place with a wedding chapel."

Annie pushed him back. "Tell me you're not serious. About a Vegas wedding, I mean."

Matt grinned. "Not a dream guy kind of thing to do?"

"Not *my* dream guy kind of thing to do," Annie said.

"Got it. You want the big wedding, too. To go along

with the house, the dog, the kids, the minivan, and this great guy who loves you."

"At last," Annie said with sigh. "My dream guy."

Matt laughed when she threw her arms around his neck.

Annie's kiss told Matt he'd never regret any of it.

About the Author

Candy Halliday would win a gold medal if the Olympic committee recognized multi-tasking as a sport. In addition to being a wife, mother, and grandmother, Candy works a day job and pens her romantic comedies by night. Her books have been published in six different countries around the world. Candy lives in the Piedmont of North Carolina with her husband, a schnauzer named Millie, and an impossible cat named Flash. Never too busy to hear from readers, she can be reached via e-mail at her homepage www.candyhalliday.com.

More

Candy Halliday!

❧

Please turn this page

for a preview of

Mr. Destiny

coming soon from

Warner Books.

CHAPTER 1

K ate Anderson flashed hot all over as she watched the mounted patrol officer gallop up the path in her direction. The summer heat wave assaulting New York City had nothing to do with it.

What was it about a man in uniform that had the ability to arouse primal instincts in a woman?

Here she was, trying to be Miss Art Gallery Manager Efficiency, capably overseeing the annual "Art in Central Park" outdoor exhibit. Yet what was she doing? She was actually imagining the handsome officer *naked*.

But not *only* naked.

Naked and sitting astride the chestnut gelding with an enormous who's-your-daddy erection.

Pre-wedding jitters, Kate assured herself. That, and her pesky subconscious trying to challenge her theory that size didn't matter.

Size didn't matter. Not to Kate. Not if you were a well-mannered prominent corporate attorney with a no-nonsense outlook on life that would finally bring focus and clarity to her life. She'd known after her first date with Harold Trent Wellington that he was the type of man she needed to keep her grounded.

Harold was handsome. He demanded order in his life.

They shared the same interests: opera, art, the finer things in life. Maybe he was a neat-freak and a tad bit anal. Maybe they had a nonexistent sex life, but they were working through Harold's feelings of inadequacy with a reputable couples therapist. The main thing was that Harold had been a calming and positive influence over her since they'd been together. Proof being, overseeing today's outdoor art exhibit; a responsibility her previously attention-deficit-impaired-self wouldn't have been able to handle in her pre-Harold days.

So size didn't matter at all.

Kate simply wouldn't allow size to matter.

She blinked twice, willing his naked image to go away. It didn't. He was still nude, rippling muscles everywhere calling out and begging to be touched. *The total opposite of Harold*, she thought briefly, whose only interest had been in passing the bar, not in pumping one.

And the significance of the imaginary colossal boner?

No. She wasn't going to go there. Not without further therapy.

He was still heading straight in her direction. Kate squeezed her eyes shut, then opened them, praying her silly fantasizing had passed. *But yikes!* Now he was staring back at her just as intently.

Oh God.

Had he read her mind?

Of course not. That was impossible. There was no way he could have known what she'd been thinking.

Still, the look on his face was more than just perplexed. He looked shocked. As if he couldn't quite believe what he was seeing.

She sent a nervous look around her. The crowd of people milling in and around the exhibit couldn't have been more orderly. There were a few couples, several small groups, some lone art admirers. Many of them regular customers, showing their support for Anderson Gallery of Fine Arts. Everyone was even speaking in hushed tones, as if the exhibit were being held inside at her grandmother's prestigious art gallery in Soho, one of the most notable art galleries in the city.

No, nothing was amiss with the crowd.

Nor would he find anything wrong with her paperwork, if that was the reason for the concerned look on the officer's face. She had her permit and everything else in order right there on her clipboard.

But wait.

Was he looking at her?

Or was he staring at the painting beside her?

Kate glanced at the large oil painting sitting on an easel to her right. She had never cared for the artist who called himself "Apocalypse." His paintings were usually dark and violent. But there was nothing offensive about this painting. Who could possibly be offended by a painting of the Madonna and Child?

She squared her shoulders when the officer pulled on the reins, bringing his mount to a stop a short distance away from her. He slid one leg easily over the back of the horse. The second his shiny black boots hit the ground, he became fully clothed again. He walked up and stopped in front of her, the name on his badge announcing he was Officer Anthony Petrocelli.

An Italian on a stallion, Kate thought.

No wonder her libido had kicked into overdrive the minute she saw him.

Kate followed his gaze to the painting. "From your expression, I can't tell if you like this painting, or if it disturbs you. And that's a first for me. I can usually read people pretty well."

His sexy grin caught her off guard.

Kate tensed.

She was *not* going to let her gaze drift any lower than his chin, even if he held his gun to her head.

He didn't reach for his revolver. Instead, he unsnapped his chin strap and took off his helmet. *Mercy.* He was all male and even more handsome than she'd imagined. Sexy brown eyes. Chiseled features. Olive skin. Just a hint of a five-o'clock shadow running along his strong angular jaw.

He ran a hand through his short black hair and hit her with another grin. "I don't know how to tell you this," he said, "but you and I were destined to be together."

What?

That had to be the corniest pick-up line ever.

The fantasizing was over.

He could have been stark naked with a willy the size of Texas, and she wouldn't have been interested in Officer Anthony Petrocelli after that idiotic statement.

"I'm not trying to pick you up," he said quickly. "If you'll let me explain, I think you'll understand why I had to stop and talk to you."

"Not interested," Kate told him.

His challenging look called her a liar. "A total stranger walks up to you and tells you the two of you are destined to be together. And you aren't even the least bit interested in why a guy would be willing to make a complete fool of himself with a statement like that?"

"Not in the least," Kate assured him.

"I'm interested."

They both turned to find the smiling face of Alexis

Graham, one of Kate's best friends. Alex also happened to be her temporary roommate at the moment thanks to the current squabble Alex was having with her husband. Dressed for success in her "important executive" power suit, her short dark hair was heavily moussed and slicked back dramatically. She would have looked manly had it not been for her dynamite all-woman figure.

"Oh, come on, Kate," she said. "Let the officer tell us his story." She thrust her hand out. "Alex Graham, best friend." She looked at Kate. "This is Kate Anderson."

"Are you the artist, Kate?" he asked.

Alex answered for her. "No. Kate's grandmother owns the gallery hosting this exhibit. Kate is the manager of Anderson Gallery of Fine Arts."

"Alex," Kate broke in. Her supposedly best friend was giving this guy way too much information.

Alex waved away Kate's protest and smiled at him.

He smiled back. "It's ironic that you should bring up the subject of grandmothers." He turned his attention back to Kate. "My grandmother is the reason I'm standing here now."

Kate still wasn't impressed.

She hoped her expression told him so.

He pointed to his name tag. "Petrocelli. Think big meddlesome Italian family. That would be mine. Think an adorable but eccentric grandmother from the old country. That also would be mine. A grandmother who reads tea leaves for every male member of the family on his sixteenth birthday so she can make a marriage prediction."

"Fascinating," Alex said.

He laughed. "Ridiculous is what it is. But twenty years ago when my grandmother read my tea leaves, she predicted I wouldn't marry until I was thirty-six years old. That I would marry a beautiful woman with blonde hair and green eyes. And . . ."

"Ridiculous is an understatement," Kate said and Alex shushed her.

"And," he repeated, "she said I would meet this woman in Central Park, standing beside the Blessed Virgin Mary."

Alex gasped.

All three of them automatically looked at the painting sitting on the easel directly beside Kate.

"Unlike the rest of my crazy family," he said with a wide grin, "I've never had a superstitious bone in my body. Tony, I told myself, that's insane, buddy. A blonde with green eyes? Maybe. But the Virgin Mary hanging out in Central Park? What are the odds of that happening?"

"Until today," Alex spoke up. "When you came riding through Central Park and saw Kate standing beside the Blessed Virgin."

He grinned again. "You got it. And since I just turned thirty-six a few weeks ago and I'm still not married, I'm not going to lie and say the *Twilight Zone* music didn't kick in for a second."

"Who could blame you?" Alex said, punching Kate with her elbow, signaling for Kate to agree.

Kate didn't comment.

She didn't like the way he was staring at her now. Searching her face. As if he were beginning to think maybe his grandmother wasn't so crazy after all.

"Wrong blonde," Kate said flatly. She held up her right hand, knowing the sizeable bling bling would snap him back to reality fast enough. "I'm already engaged. My wedding's only a few weeks away."

Alex nodded, sadly, Kate noticed, confirming everything she'd just said.

"Well, there you go," he said and shrugged. "So much for destiny. Right?"

"And such a pity," Alex said.

This time Kate punched Alex.

He snapped on his helmet. "Well, thank both of you lovely ladies for listening."

Alex sighed wistfully.

He looked directly at Kate. "And thank you, Kate, for finally putting my grandmother's prediction to rest."

Kate's nod was cordial. Almost.

He gave them a friendly salute, turned, and walked back to his horse. After sliding a boot into the stirrup, he pulled himself effortlessly up on the back of his horse, rode off down the path, and never looked back.

Alex immediately sent Kate a perturbed look. "I can't believe you. How could you just let him ride off like that without saying a single word?"

"And I can't believe you would expect me to do anything else," Kate said in her own defense. "I'm not interested in some cop with a story about his crazy tea-leaf-reading grandmother. Or about the woman's mystic marriage prediction. I know you don't like Harold, but I *am* going to marry him, Alex. You'd better get used to it."

Alex snorted. "Oh, who do you think you're kidding? I saw the way you were ogling the guy before he even stopped to talk to you. Why do you think you didn't even realize I was here?"

Kate flushed. "I wasn't doing any such thing."

"You were all but drooling, Kate. There's no reason to

feel guilty about it. Not with your hopeless celibacy situation. But what bothers me, is that I've never once seen you look at Harold the way I saw you look at the man who could very well be your Mr. Destiny."

Again, Kate blushed at the truth. "I'd be worrying about my own celibacy situation, if I were you." *There.* She could give back as good as Alex could send.

Alex sent her a sympathetic look. "At least I know my situation is only because I'm being too stubborn to go home right now."

"Don't lecture me, Alex."

"Don't mess with destiny, Kate."

Alex's warning made her shiver.

She'd had her own premonition moments earlier as she'd watched him ride away. Something told Kate she hadn't seen the last of Officer Anthony Petrocelli.

THE EDITOR'S DIARY

Dear Reader,

From an unexpected belly laugh to the perfect pair of shoes, life is full of happy accidents. But the best one is the romance you never saw coming and the one you can't live without. Just ask Danny and Annie in our two Warner Forever titles this February.

New York Times bestselling author Iris Johansen raves Annie Solomon's previous book is "a nail biter through and through." Postpone that manicure you've been planning—her latest, BLIND CURVE, is even better! Undercover cop Danny Sinofsky never needed anyone or anything. But when he suddenly goes blind in the middle of a bust, Danny couldn't feel more helpless. Now, refusing to believe his sight is permanently gone, Danny must work with mobility instructor Martha Crowe. Determined to get through Danny's wall of anger, Martha keeps one secret from him—she was the plain girl in high school who had a crush on him. But when Martha witnesses an attack on his life, they are thrown into a safe house where this man without sight starts to see the real beauty inside this courageous woman. With a relentless assassin trailing them, they must act as one, using Danny's razor-sharp instincts and Martha's eyes, if they want to survive.

The man in your life always says exactly the right thing. He never leaves the toilet seat up. And he always surrenders the remote control without a thought. Sounds like the perfect guy, right? He sure is—because Annie Long from Candy Halliday's DREAM GUY created him. Meet Joe Video, the most lucrative product the DVD and video game company Annie works at has ever been part of. Fresh out of her most recent disaster of a relationship, Annie couldn't help but wonder why we can't create the perfect man? So, with the help of Rico, a devastatingly gorgeous actor hired to play Joe Video in the DVD, Annie sees her creation come to life. The only problem— she has trouble resisting his charms. But is Joe Video really as "perfect" as he seems? Because Matt, her co-creator and an unforgettable romantic mistake, is proving himself to be more perfect than Joe Video ever could be.

To find out more about Warner Forever, these February titles, and the authors, visit us at www.warnerforever.com.

With warmest wishes,

Karen Kosztolnyik

Karen Kosztolnyik, Senior Editor

P.S. Watch for these exciting new novels next month: Wendy Markham pens the poignant tale of a widow trying to raise two children, a man who's certain there's more to life, and the heavenly matchmaker with a plan in HELLO, IT'S ME; and Susan Crandall delivers the enthralling story of a woman who's unexpectedly left a child under dubious circumstances and a man with a lot at stake who's determined to unravel her every secret in PROMISES TO KEEP.

**If you or someone you know
wants to improve their reading skills,
call the Literacy Help Line.**

WORDS ARE YOUR WHEELS
1-800-929-4458

LaVergne, TN USA
27 August 2009
156149LV00004B/2/P